THE BOOK
OF JOEL

ASHLEY STONE

Fulton Books, Inc.
Meadville, PA

Published by Fulton Books 2021

ISBN 978-1-63985-248-2 (paperback)
ISBN 978-1-63985-249-9 (digital)

Printed in the United States of America

PROLOGUE

I promised them.

I led them here. They were safe, and I put them in danger.

If I stood up and fought, I could live, but then I was choosing their fate. I lay there, claws ripping into my body, teeth in my neck. I watched the ones I love float away as I laid down my life.

"I'm a good shepherd," I whispered to myself as I closed my eyes.

CHAPTER 1

THE BOOK OF RACHEL

My name is Rachel, and I was a part of the old world. I had spent my childhood in a normal town full of normal people. My town was small, a place where children ran safely through the paved streets and where families had barbecues and invited neighbors. Everyone in town knew one another. You couldn't leave your house without having at least five unplanned conversations. I liked this town growing up. I couldn't have imagined living anywhere else as a child.

We had schools and we all dreamed of what we would be when we grew up. The possibilities were endless. In those days, everyone tried to get into the very best universities. We had been told that education was the ticket to success. People no longer wanted to work in a trade—something many came to regret. I wanted to be a dancer in the NYC ballet, a far cry from my childhood in Ohio. I never got that experience.

Back then, we had the internet, and everyone had a cellphone. We used to text each other, watch videos, even take pictures of ourselves doing things and put those things on the internet too. Though it seems ridiculous to me now, we used to take pictures of ourselves and put them on social media sites, and we based our self-worth over how many people liked the picture. It was so easy to communicate back then. We took it for granted and used it for the wrong reasons. Instead of using the phones to check in on people we loved and have rich conversations, we used them to brag and to gossip.

I met Christopher when we were children, running around the town without a care. He told me I was pretty every day of our lives until my eighteenth birthday when he proposed. He had baked me a cake, and on top of it were the words "Will you marry me?" and the most beautiful ring on top. Of course, I said yes; he was the man of my dreams. We were the same age, but he always seemed older than me, wiser. Christopher had been one of the few people who chose to go into a trade instead of planning for college. As soon as we entered high school, he was already an apprentice at the sawmill. My parents weren't happy about this. They wanted me to marry a doctor or a lawyer. They had no idea how important Christopher's skills would be in the new world.

I remember when the outbreak started. We hardly noticed it at first. Then came videos of people attacking others. We accused the videos of being fake or doctored in some way. We thought the images had been changed, just like in the movies. There were other stories that said people were acting this way for publicity or to go viral. *Viral.* That word is different now. It used to mean you had a popular video or you made a popular post on your social media. Now viral meant the plague. It meant the infection that caused people to be subhuman. To become monsters. I don't think we really realized it was a major problem until the disappearances started. By the time the disappearances started, the phones no longer worked. The internet was gone. The government had shut it down in order to prevent any more hysteria. Fliers were hung all over town. Every telephone pole was covered in missing persons posters for women, men, children, even pets. They were never found. Eventually, there were witnesses who saw people dragged off into the forest. People started to watch the streets and noticed that some people only lived in the dark places. It was known that you must stay in the light at all times.

The disease seemed to be much slower moving in the beginning than it is now. Before, it took weeks to change and become flesh hungry. I remember spending time with Christopher, going on dates, and riding in his car at night and seeing them lurking around town. People claimed they were homeless people, but Chris knew something was wrong. He told me that we couldn't go out at night anymore. He told me he thought these people weren't people anymore. He was the first in town to start building a security system.

He told others, but nobody listened. When others did start building security systems, they relied on the electricity to power them. They hired companies to install motion detectors. Christopher told people they were making a mistake and that the electricity would be the first thing to go. He studied books about building castles and how they protected them. He turned our house into an impenetrable fortress.

Some people actually believed this was a hoax despite having evidence to the contrary. My parents were part of that group. They never stopped doing the things they wanted to do. Even with people disappearing, they believed in a set of alternative facts. I tried to warn them. Christopher offered to create a security system for them. We even offered to let them stay with us. They declined all offers. They told us that we should live our lives. They warned us not to let the government control us. They said we were sheep for believing in this virus. This ultimately led to their disappearances. I still miss them. I loved them even though I didn't understand how they could be this naive. They were right about one thing: we were sheep now but not in the way they thought. The forests had grown up around our town, and we were locked into it. Like sheep in a meadow, picked off one by one.

Some people thought Christopher was crazy. They said he was taking things too far. They argued that our security system was bringing down the value of their houses by making the town seem unsafe. Instead of arguing with them, Chris offered to help, but they all refused.

Christopher was right, it seemed just as he had hammered his last nail, the lights went out and they never came back on. We spent our nights holding each other, hiding under blankets for warmth. Our meals consisted of military MREs that Chris had purchased online in bulk when he suspected this. At the time, the neighbors made fun of Christopher when large boxes of meals arrived on our porch from Amazon. They joked that Chris made a mistake marrying a girl who couldn't cook. He knew better. He stored those meals away, knowing full well that we would need them.

By the time everyone realized the infected had become monsters, it was too late. When the lights went out, so did the televisions, the news, and any security systems that relied on electricity. We were trapped and unprepared. Visitors who escaped their own towns told us that other towns had disappeared into forests. Because towns were now separated, you had to only rely on those within your town. If you tried to walk to another town, you would most likely be attacked. People still tried. We had people enter our town, some infected, some not. We heard that the military was disbanded because the disease had spread through them, and that we no longer had a government. This wasn't just here but nationwide. We learned that they couldn't enter sunlight and died in water. We weren't sure why. Everyone moved near the water; we were lucky to have a fresh water source across town. The men in our town spent their days cutting back the forest so that the sun could continue to offer us refuge during the day.

I was lucky to be with my best friend. Christopher and I truly enjoyed each other's company. We used to lie down and tell each other stories. When one of us would stop, the other had to continue. By the end of the night, we had laughed as hard as two people could. I was so thankful for him…for that time. I loved the man who had worked so hard to keep me safe. I dreamed of the old world. I longed for the ability to have a normal life. To have my parents. To have a family. Chris would have been a good father. This world wasn't fair. It was cruel. The old world wasn't perfect. People were selfish, this is true, but you could still choose. You could still be a good person if you wanted to be. In this world, it didn't matter if you were a good person. Those things didn't care about your soul. They took everyone.

Sometimes Christopher would teach me to fight. He taught me how to use a sword and how to shoot a bow and arrow. He took me fishing so that I could learn. We used to spend hours outside target practicing. Then we would head to the lake to fish. If I did it wrong, Chris would correct me. I appreciated his feedback. My parents were amazing, but even if I had been terrible at something, they would have lied to me. At this point, our neighbors were all gone. There were very few families who lived through this.

In the beginning, thousands of the infected would run through the streets at night, tearing into people's houses, dragging people into the forest. The screams rang through the streets. I used to close my eyes and bury my face into Christopher's chest. He would sing to me as he held me. Quietly. Those things are drawn to sound. I felt sorry for people who had crying babies. It made me shudder when I thought of it. Now there are less of the infected coming into the town at night. They still come. Every night. The scratches we hear on the side of our house are occasional instead of constant. Chris thinks either they moved on or they don't live a long time once they're infected. They can't get in our house. Christopher made sure of that. I was thankful for our home. For my husband.

Christopher constantly told me that if something happened, I would need to know how to do things. I would need to know how to repair the house and how to find food. I didn't even like to think about things like that. I didn't want to live in a world where Christopher didn't exist. Our souls were so intertwined I couldn't imagine being able to breathe without him, but in this world, sometimes things like that don't matter. He used to tell me that bad things happen to good people every day. There are no favorites, he would say.

I remember the day it happened. It was July twenty-fifth, our anniversary. He took me out on a boat. It was a boat that had belonged to my parents. On the side of the boat, it said *Tom and Rosie*, which were my parents' names. I felt closer to them when I was in this boat on the river. I know this was their favorite place to be. It was a beautiful day. The sun shined so bright. The water was still. Our boat created small ripples as Christopher rowed. The reflection of the trees danced on the surface of the water. The trees. The forest. I used to find such beauty there. Now the forest was filled with terror. I placed my hand in the water, breaking apart the reflection of the trees.

The infected can't touch water, so this was the safest place we could be. It was amazing to me that the waters were still a place of enjoyment even during these terrible times. The infected had taken over the forests and all the dark places, but the water was still the light. We moved through the water as he sang to me. I loved his voice. I had packed his favorite meal that day. Well, it was just about our only meal these days. Fish and berries. We floated on the boat, enjoying a picnic. Christopher had brought a bottle of wine he had been saving—a real treat for our special day.

We said every year we wouldn't exchange gifts, but we always did. I gave Christopher a necklace with a key on it. I wore a necklace with a heart. "The key to my heart," the card I made him read. He gave me flowers. He gave me flowers every year, and every year I scolded him for being dangerous. The only flowers in town were tucked away in the forest. He told me he only ever went when the light was its brightest.

We started to head back; it was important we hit land before darkness, but this night, the darkness was violently fast. We hit land just as the sun was hitting the land and we ran. It was miles back home, but we just ran as fast as we could. I could see our home in the distance, but it was too late. The infected were shadow-jumping through the town, and their eyes were locked on us. Christopher ran away from me, screaming and clapping his hands. He led them from me and told me to run, and I listened. I ran all the way home, and as I turned around, expecting to see him, he wasn't there. That night, I sobbed for hours, waiting for him. I considered just leaving the house and letting them have me too.

In the middle of the night, a knock rang out on the door.

"Rachel! Open the door!" I heard someone scream.

I looked through the hole in the door, and there he stood. As I opened the door to let him in, the first thing I saw was blood and bite marks all over his arms and neck. There were also scratches down his back. I latched the door back into place and went to get the medical kit. I don't think I breathed for a whole minute after seeing him. I was trying to bandage him up, knowing that I was bandaging a dead person. I was bandaging up the only thing this cruel world had let me have.

"How did you get away?" I asked him. "It's dark out there."

I tried to change the subject. I knew in my heart that he was already dead. A heavy weight covered my heart.

"I had to get back to you. I fought my way out. They were chasing me, and someone else was in the street. They went after him instead," he said, tears streaming down his face. "I had to say goodbye."

I was not afraid of him yet. He was still Christopher for now. I knew he wouldn't put me in danger, infected or not. As I cleaned him up, I cried. I cried for our love, for our future, and he just stared in my eyes. He wasn't scared. He was worried about me. That's my Christopher, always worried about others.

"It's my fault," he said. "I should have docked earlier."

"It's not your fault," I told him, wiping my tears away with my sleeve. "It's this world's fault."

That night, we made love for the last time. We both cried. It was such a bittersweet memory. So painful. So pure. Then he kissed me and he held me in his arms, rocking me. He told me to be safe and that he had faith that things would be all right and not to mourn him. He told me to survive.

Then he said goodbye. He told me he was going to the water. This is what the brave do. Once they are infected, they go into the water, knowing the water will kill them and they will not feed on others. I did not run to him as he walked away. I knew this was what had to be. That was not my Christopher anymore. That was a monster.

We had always been very careful not to have children. Neither of us wanted to feel the overwhelming sadness the loss of a child brings, and this world was no place for children. This world was cruel and cold. Six weeks later, I couldn't stop throwing up. My stomach was already protruding. I knew. There was no other reason for it. I was going to have a baby. Instead of being upset, I realized I had a reason to live. A reason to take care of myself. I read every baby book I could get my hands on. I tried to make sure I ate enough, drank enough water, got enough sleep. I read about childbirth, knowing I would deliver alone. I had hoped that this would be okay. I wasn't sure, though. After all, bad things happen to good people every day.

My labor with Joel was quick. I did breathing exercises. I walked around the house during my labor and squatted with the pain. I was thankful I gave birth during the daytime, so I didn't have to be silent. He came out crying, strong, beautiful. I considered naming him Christopher, but I remembered that Christopher didn't like sharing a name with his father. I remembered years before, when the virus hadn't happened yet, Chris and I had been sitting in his car, talking about names. I asked him if we had a baby, what name he would give it. He told me he always liked the name Joel. I decided I liked it too.

When Joel was born, I knew he was different. He is special, my son. I realize every mother thinks that, but Joel really was different. When Joel was three years old, we were attacked by a group of the infected, and he was bitten on the arm while I ran away. His arm had drifted into a shadow for just a moment, and one of them grabbed him. I waited for weeks, months, years for the changes to begin, knowing in my mind what I would have to do. I told myself I would take him to the water and I would jump in with him; I would sacrifice my own life as well. It would be a much more peaceful death than what would happen otherwise. I waited and watched, and he never changed. He healed from the bite, and new skin formed. He was still the strong, happy little boy he always was. I tried to read books about viruses. I tried to figure out why Joel healed, what made him different. I don't know what I expected to find. There was no information about things like this. Books weren't being written anymore. The only thing I have come up with is that because Joel was conceived after his father was infected, he is immune. I don't believe he is even fully human. I don't tell him that.

There were other situations that occurred. Joel was bitten a total of three times by the time he was ten years of age. Each time, he would come to me, and I would hold him in my arms for days, waiting for the infection to spread, waiting for him to become infected. The change never happened. I would watch as his bites healed and new skin formed.

I remember the day he drowned. He went into the water to swim. He got his leg stuck on an old fishing net and was stuck under the water. By the time I swam out and found him, he was completely unconscious, and his heart had stopped. I had to do CPR on the side of the water and bring him back. In a way, I'm glad it happened. It showed him he wasn't immortal. I always told Joel that even though he healed from the bites, I didn't think if they ripped him apart he would heal.

And so the days went on. Joel was strong and healthy. I spent hours every day helping him learn skills just as Christopher had taught me. I taught him how to build things. I taught him how to use tools and to repair the house. I didn't waste my time teaching Joel how to use weapons. He didn't need them. He didn't even need a fishing pole. He would wade out into the water and grab the fish with his hands. He was so strong he could lift a tree trunk himself. He was always faster and stronger than the other children. As an adult, he could do the work of ten men by himself. He was also extremely intelligent. He spent his teenage years reading books and learning about the way things were. I was thankful to have books. I always kept every book I ever read. We had a large library. When my parents were gone, I went to their house and got their encyclopedias.

Joel didn't sleep like I did. He only slept a few hours a day. He usually spent the evenings working out plans on paper of how we could be a normal world again. He had so many ideas. He reminded me so much of Christopher. He was creative and kind. He felt that he could somehow fix things. I remember being that young, thinking you can change the world. Joel was so optimistic, so hopeful. His sense of humor was incredible. He could make me laugh even after everything that had happened. He didn't think he was funny. Maybe he wasn't funny. Maybe I just laughed because he is my son.

Joel was handsome. His looks were almost surreal compared to others his age. His skin was amber, and his eyes were icy blue. The blue of Joel's eyes belonged in another world. If anything about Joel said that he was not human, it was his eyes. I believe the infected part of him caused his eyes to be that color. His arms were the size of a grown man, and his chest was broad. Before the outbreak, he could have been a model. His face could have been seen on magazines or television.

The girls in town were really starting to like him. There weren't many of them, but the ones who walked around during the day would pass Joel while he was working about twenty times, hoping to get his attention. He never looked up from what he was doing. He wasn't interested in love. He said that he wasn't ready for that type of thing and he needed to learn more about the world first. Maybe he just hadn't met the right one yet. I wanted Joel to find someone. I wouldn't live forever and I didn't want to leave him here alone.

Joel spent his days helping people in the town rebuild their homes. His goal was always to keep them safe. He had done such a good job protecting the homes in town that the infected couldn't get in. There were less of those things roaming around at night. Our town was safer because of the work Joel had done. He spent his days working on houses and cutting back the canopy of trees that threatened the town. He fished and provided food for those who couldn't go out to fish. His heart was pure.

This place seemed more peaceful now. I could hear the crickets, something I had not heard since I was a girl. In town, we had meetings, and at these meetings, Joel spoke to us. I was amazed at his age that he is as wise as he is. He never got angry when people argue or have different views. He used these meetings to help delegate tasks. First, he took on the task himself, and then at the meeting, he found others who could take the task from him. He told me that everyone has a purpose. A certain set of skills that are unique. He had made sure every person in our town was important. He even helped one of our elders get a sewing machine so that she could make clothes. The people in town traded her food for clothing. She took such pride in that job. I knew something was happening when Joel delegated every task he was responsible for during the day. I wondered what my boy, my beautiful boy, was up to.

Joel waited until he got home from the meeting that day to tell me. He told me he could hear people in the distance screaming for help all night long. He said he couldn't sleep. He didn't know where these people were or if this was all in his head, but he couldn't just let it go. He needed to try and help them. He sat down and told me his plan. He had it all figured out. He showed me a map that he had used to figure out how long it would take him and where he would stop to rest. He seemed to have this whole journey planned out. I held onto every word. I debated telling him what I needed to.

I looked into his beautiful eyes, this boy I had raised. I told him the same words Christopher told me. I told him to be safe and that I had faith everything would be all right. I told him to survive and not to mourn me as I showed him the bites on my arm... I had gone into the forest to pick daisies. It was July twenty-fifth, my anniversary. I had been missing Christopher. Then I told him something else that Christopher had not told me. I told him not just to survive but also to save others. Then I kissed his head. The rest is his story. This is where mine ends.

CHAPTER 2

THE BOOK OF PURPOSE

I watched my mother walk away in the direction of the water. I couldn't see her face, but I knew she was crying by the shaking of her shoulders. With every step she took, I had to fight the urge to run after her. I knew if I did, I was only delaying the inevitable. My mother was infected. There was nothing I could do. Although I had told her I wouldn't, I did mourn her. I screamed and I broke things. How could I not mourn the woman who created me, who loved me? The woman who protected me and held me through each and every trial that this world gave me. I gave myself a few moments to break down, then I collected the things I would need. My mother wouldn't want me to give up. I knew that to be true. She believed in me more than anyone in this world. I grabbed a backpack from the closet, my father's backpack. I packed three canteens, a tarp, an extra pair of boots, socks, a change of clothes in a plastic bag, dried fish, berries, and bread. Just enough. I ripped the page of the encyclopedia that contained my map and folded it up. I put it inside the front zipper part of the backpack. I placed the backpack by the door. I would leave in the early morning light.

The next morning, I walked to town where a young woman and her children lived and I gave her the keys to our house. I explained the safety features of the house. I told her it was hers now, then I walked into the forest, leaving behind the memory of my life, of my mother. When I first entered the forest, I had a moment of self-doubt. What if I couldn't do this? What if I failed? I thought about this for a few moments, then I realized that if I went back to town, I was going back to nothing. My mother was gone. She was all that I had. I was alone in this world.

I moved west. Maps are helpful, but they don't fully prepare you for a journey. The map only tells you how to navigate; it doesn't show you the landscape. It doesn't show you where the sun is shining and where the shadows fall. I realized I didn't even need to pack it. It was in my head. I knew the way. I had imagined this journey for a long time. I had planned for this. I had to do this. I had to make the screams stop. I needed some way to connect the people who had been divided by the forests. I walked along the floor of the forest, paying extra attention to the canopy above. I thought about my life. About my mother.

My mother was the most graceful, beautiful, and talented person I have ever known. I'm not just saying that because she was my mother. In her younger days, she was a dancer. She was always dancing around the house on the tips of her toes. She told me my father used to play the piano while she danced. I would have loved to have seen this. I wished I could have met my father. My father accidentally prepared us for his absence well. He had built the house to be impenetrable. My mother told me that when I was born, she was afraid my crying would attract the infected to our house and they would find a way in. She told me I came out crying and then I never cried again. She said I would stare at everything and everyone. I didn't sleep, but I let her sleep. When she would open her eyes to check on me, I was next to her, staring at her, completely silent. She said she was worried about me. She also told me that my staring was creepy. We always laughed about that. I wiped a tear from my eye.

I fished and gathered for our meals. I took on this trade as soon as I could. I took our boat out from the age of seven to get fish. My mother stood by the shore and waited for me each time, hands on her hips. I still remember her yelling at me to come inside. I had to go in hours before the other kids in town. She always told me that if I heard the birds chirping, it was time to hide. She told me that the birds used to be awake during the day and that you could hear them chirping in the early morning light. That's not how the world works anymore. The birds became nocturnal to avoid the infected eating them. The animals in the forests were the first to go. I had never seen any animal. My mother said she believes that's why it took us a while to figure out what was happening in the beginning. The infected were feeding on the animals in the dark. They started to come into the towns only when they had eaten all the animals. I had read about all of these animals who were gone. I was certain if I found one, I would know what it was. I knew that in this area of Ohio, where we lived, I would find squirrels, rabbits, and deer in this forest.

My mother was always overprotective even though she knew I was immune to the infected. I was bitten not just the three times as a child. My mother would have died much sooner had she seen all the marks that had healed. To be honest, it was strange that the older I got, the more immune I was. It took only minutes for the bites to disappear now. I studied science books each night, trying to find a medical reason for this, and the only thing I could come up with was that because I was born half infected, I was immune. My mother hated when I referred to myself as half infected. She would argue with me and tell me I was just immune. It didn't mean I was like them. I knew she was only saying it because she loved me. I told her once that maybe I was immune because I had a purpose in this life that I must fulfill. She told me that I needed to take care of myself and not put myself in unnecessary danger. I know deep down she was afraid of losing me. She had lost both her parents and my father and she couldn't take any more pain.

I was not and had never been like the other children my age. My mom had been telling me this my whole life, but even if she had hidden this from me, I would have known. My senses were more intact. I could see farther, hear better, and run faster than the others. When I was a kid, we would race across the town and I never lost. I actually had to try to slow down to make it look like it was a fair race. My mother always told me not to tell anyone that I was immune. She was afraid if people in town found out, they might make me leave, thinking I could infect others. The only person in town who knew I was immune was Lois.

Lois was the seamstress in our town. Once, when I needed a pair of pants for my mother, I offered to pay her in fish. She told me she didn't need any fish. She asked for a secret instead. I told her I didn't have any. Her response was that my eyes said otherwise. My mother always said my eyes were too blue to be human. I told Lois my secret that day, and she gave me my mother's pants and threw in a pair of socks. When I told her to make sure she didn't tell, she made a joke that she had already forgotten. After that, Lois gave me everything I asked for as long as I would sit and tell her about the journey I planned. Those were some of my favorite memories, sitting with Lois as she pushed the pedal on her sewing machine with her foot in a continuous motion and wove fabric together in many different patterns. I would ask her if things sounded like a good idea, and she would just nod her head and smile at me. Sometimes I wasn't even sure she was listening. I think we both just liked having company.

I walked down a beaten trail that wove in and around different objects in the forest. The light shined down through the canopy of the oak trees that towered over my head. With every breeze that blew, I had to adjust my steps to make sure I stayed in the light.

As I stepped over a log, a shadow overcame me, and one of them leapt out of the forest. I quickly ducked, and it missed. The light came back. I took a deep breath. I could hear them. My ears weren't human. I could hear them breathing always. Snarling, growling. They hid and waited. They followed their prey, hopping over one another in the darkness, trying to get in the best position for an attack. They could be killed. I thought that was something that many didn't know. I know. You have to hit them in the head with enough force. If you hit anywhere else on their body, you will only temporarily slow them down. They're so fast that most people don't have the opportunity to try. They don't attack individually. They attack in a pack and they fight over the person. This makes it almost impossible for any victim to get away.

I told my mother I could hear screams in the night because I can. I was not even sure how far these people were, but I heard them all around us, screaming, crying, calling out for help. I didn't hear them much during the day. It seemed as I lay down at night and close my eyes that the screams invaded my mind. I wanted to help them. I've heard these screams my whole life. When I was little, I thought they were the screams of local people who were attacked. I didn't real-ize that these were different. It took me a while to figure out how to control my enhanced senses. I always felt that the human part of me was fighting the part that wasn't. I could also sense when people were near. I couldn't tell how many there were, but I knew when humans were near. I sometimes wondered if I could sense both the infected and humans because I was part of both. I shuddered. I didn't want to be part of the infected.

When the infection began, the people hid it. They knew they were ill and they didn't want the others to know. They were afraid of death. My father was brave. He took his own life before he would be driven to feed on others. Most people were too afraid to do this. These were the most dangerous, the ones who had only been infected for a few days. They walked among us. Their crimes existed in the shadows during the day. They looked like people and would talk their victims into submission. After a few days, they couldn't be among people anymore because they started to change. Their hair started to fall out, and their skin turned to a pale green. They smelled like death, and their backs started to hunch over. They became ani-mals, killers. They no longer resembled the human they started out as. We didn't know their life span. I didn't know my own life span. They lived in the forests. These forests that had grown had separated us from other towns, other places. It was through these forests I must move.

It was hot outside. Very hot. It rained less in the new world. When it did rain, it seemed to rain for days, then not again for weeks. It seemed to me from the stories I was told from elders that the rains changed along the same time the virus came. I also heard there were earthquakes. When it did rain, we always made sure to collect it. Water is important. Water is life. I had built each family in town a rain barrel to collect the rains that had a large funnel at the top. My father had created the one we used at our house, so I modeled my design after his. As I moved through the forest, I rubbed my hand against a plant, and it broke. So dry. Dead trees hung onto the living, how fitting, I thought.

I'd never minded being alone. My mom used to tell me I needed friends, and I told her I would make friends to please her. I never had a need to make friends. The boys my age were all so different from me. The only thing they thought about was girls, and I was just not ready for all that. There was so much more I wanted to do. Maybe it was because I had spent my life watching the pain in my mother's eyes, but I really had no desire to find a girl. I had spent most of my time with my mom; she needed me. My mom always told me that if she had to lose my dad all over again, she would have done it all the same. She was stronger than I am. I never wanted to lose anyone again.

I realized I had been standing in the same spot in the forest, thinking and looking around. I had to go. I had to move. I saw an opening ahead in the forest that led to a clearing, and I closed my eyes to see if I felt anyone near. I didn't. If there was a town ahead, it was empty. Of that I was sure. I continued to walk toward the opening where the sun shined bright. As I walked out of the forest, I came across an open field without any trees. Nothing. No houses. Only tall grass. I realized this would be a good time to eat something while I was in full light. I opened my backpack and pulled out some of the dried fish and a handful of berries. I ate as I walked. I drank a full canteen of water and placed it back in my backpack. The field only led to another forest. I walked along the line of the forest, trying to find the best point to enter. I saw a creek up ahead where the canopy was open above and decided this would be my safest route. I climbed into the creek and walked through the water. The creek seemed to be heading west. If it changed course, I would need to find a different way.

As I walked, I could hear them in the shadows, leaping from one dark spot to the next. The creek was well lit. I was thankful for that. I stepped on rocks when I came to them. My feet were almost fully soaked inside my boots. I realized this was the longest I'd gone without someone talking to me. I was used to my mother talking. My mother. I hadn't thought about her for a while. My mother used to talk just to break the silence. She hated quiet.

The forest was almost beautiful if you didn't know what was hiding in it. The creek flowing over the rocks created a peaceful ambience. The light danced across the trees. I could hear them breathing, snarling. They were hungry. If most of the existing towns were like mine, they'd gotten good at protecting themselves. I couldn't imagine how many meals they had out here. The animals disappeared from the forest before I was born. Other than an occasional injured bird, I couldn't imagine what else they would eat. I wondered how long they could go without food.

The only time people entered the forest was to scavenge for nuts or berries. Always in the light. Even during those times, there were situations where the person never came back. I'd seen them enter into dim light. Trees bent, winds blew, the sun shifted. In those moments, a once-lit area would be momentarily shrouded in darkness. That was all they needed, a moment. They were fast. They needed mere seconds to kill. One leap, one bite, and the person was dragged into the darkness, or they escaped and they either went in the water or succumbed to living as a monster. However you looked at it, getting bitten was a death sentence.

The creek took a hard right, and I realized I was going to be headed in the wrong direction. I decided that I would leave the creek and follow the lighted path that went west. There was a clear line in the canopy that let enough light through for me. I began walking down the path, then I decided to run. Running could be dangerous. When we ran, we didn't pay attention to as much. We aren't as in tune. But I'm faster than them, I knew that. I had that going for me. As I ran they ran in the shadows. I looked over and could see the bushes moving next to me. They don't stop. They keep going until they get what they want. I was still running when I heard it. A bird chirping. Just one. My sign. Time to find a place to stay for the night. I would need to find water. I stopped in an especially sunny part of the forest and kneeled down to feel the earth. I squeezed the dirt in my hands, it was wet. I felt around the area to know which way to move. About 100 yards away I found a freshwater pond.

The pond was not in a well lit part of the forest, but it was water and it didn't matter if it was dark, they can't go into water. I stood in a lit area of the forest wondering how I would get to the pond and more importantly, what I would do once I got there. I could float all night if I had to. It wasn't ideal. I didn't need much sleep, but I did need some. I squinted to see the far end of the pond. I realized that there was a beaver dam at the end. I knew what that was from the books I had read. If I ran to the pond and jumped in, I could safely swim to that dam. I could probably even lay my clothes out to dry. More birds. More chirping. I decided I had to run and make that jump before I lost the sunlight. I took a deep breath, closed my eyes for a moment, and then sprinted toward the dark pond.

Snarling, growling, jumping. One of them almost hit me from the right side, and I threw it over my head. Another leapt and missed me by a hair. I jumped into the air and landed in the pond. They stood at the dark edge, snarling. I laughed when I landed in the pond. I had expected to jump in and be completely submerged. Instead, I was standing in water to my knees. The pond had mostly dried up. It didn't matter. They wouldn't even enter a puddle. Or the rain. I walked to the dam at the end of the pond. I broke the dam on the sides that connected to land so nothing could climb on.

I sat down and opened my backpack. I took the tarp out and laid it across the dam. I took my clothes off and laid them next to me to dry. I placed my boots next to my clothes. I rang out my socks and laid them out. My socks. I thought of Lois. I missed her. I hoped she would be okay. I ate some more of my dried fish and a few more berries. I drank another canteen of water. I would need supplies soon. I lay down on top of the dam and stretched out. It was hot even though it was getting dark. As I lay there, I looked around, trying to ignore the growls of the infected. I tried to see in the dark where I would go to begin my journey when the sun came up. I could see the openings in the canopies of the trees. I closed my eyes and drifted off to the snarling of the infected and the screams of the living. I wondered if this was a punishment. A personal hell. I decided it was a gift instead. I convinced myself of that. I couldn't imagine this being a mistake right now. Not here. Not lying on this dam on this tarp with those things waiting for me. I had to think of this as being for a purpose, for a reason. I needed to believe that.

I think I had the worst night of sleep of my life. I didn't need much sleep and I'd had some bad nights, but this was definitely the worst. I didn't know why I expected anything different. I had only ever slept in my secure home. Sleeping in a pond on a dam with the infected growling all night was the opposite of what I was used to.

The sun coming up was the most beautiful sight after a night filled with fear. I put my clothes back on. I decided to save my dry outfit for when I really needed it. I could see the path I would take after leaving the pond. There was a lighted trail through the forest. It looked like it used to be some type of dirt road. The canopy of trees was open above the dirt road. It looked safe. I left the pond, making sure to only stay in the lighted parts, and I jogged toward the road. Once there, in the full light, I made sure my shoes were tied. I took a drink of water from my canteen and placed it back. I put my backpack on and snapped it in front of my chest to keep it secure. I started to move.

The road was long. I couldn't see the end of it even when I squinted. As I was walking, I came across an old tractor that was broken down on the side of the road. It seemed like it used to be red, although now it was completely rusted. Grass was growing through it. A tree had sprouted out of its engine. I wondered if this was some type of farming road. The road was made of dirt and rocks. The grass had grown through in patches, but there was still a decent path to follow.

I followed the road as long as I could before I had to continue into the forest. For a moment, I wished that there was a road that just went all the way to the west that was covered in light. I continued through the forest and I could see another opening up ahead. This area of the forest wasn't nearly as dense. I was certain as I approached the opening that I was going to walk out into another open field. As I walked into the open area, I stood staring, in complete disbelief. I was standing at the edge of a town. I looked around for signs of life. I saw none.

"Hello," I called out, walking down a desolate street. "Hello, is there anyone who can hear me?"

Silence.

I walked from the east side of town all the way to the west. I sensed nobody here. It didn't take me long to figure out what happened. The windows were broken out of most of the homes. There were places where entire walls were ripped off. This town was smaller than mine. I walked past a grocery store that had been boarded up. Signs half-hung on the outside advertising the deals of the week. It was smaller than the market in our town that had been boarded up. Small market for a small town.

I stood in the middle of the street and closed my eyes. No one. There was no one here. The town ended not long after it began. If I stood on one end of town and squinted, I could see the other end.

I kept walking toward the forest on the west side of the town. I was turning down the road leading away from town to continue on my way when I saw it.

There lined up on the road leaving town were the cars of the people from this town. They had tried to leave but were engulfed in darkness. I saw a doll on the ground next to an open car door and I dropped to my knees. The windows had been knocked out of the cars. The paint was scratched. Doors had been flung open. These cars were from the beginning, the cars were completely rusted out, and grass grew around them as well as through them. I closed my eyes. I heard the screaming.

I walked along the line of cars and counted. Twenty-one. Twenty-one cars filled with families trying to escape. Trying to get to another town for help. Tears fell from my eyes as I realized the terror these people must have gone through. I imagined mothers and fathers trying to protect their children from those things, knowing that they couldn't. They must have made the decision to leave as a community. Seeing their town, I understood why. I wondered how many more towns I would find like this. Would I find anyone alive? Were the screams I heard from the living? Or were they from the dead?

Anger started to replace the feelings of remorse inside me. I looked toward the forests. I could hear them breathing. Hungry.

I clenched my fists. I walked away differently than how I had arrived. I walked away with purpose. I would find people. I would save them. I would connect the towns.

I turned around to the cars and stared at them for a moment. "I couldn't save you, but I won't let them win." I looked at the forest. "You won't win. I promise."

I continued down the road.

CHAPTER 3

THE BOOK OF ERIC

There had been others who had tried to move through the forest before the trees had grown up when it was just grass separating the towns. I had been told stories from my mother about those who drove vehicles through the grasses, never to be seen again. Maybe they made it to another town or maybe they didn't. At this point, I was almost certain they didn't. That must hurt. To have that kind of faith in something and have it crumble. Just like those cars I found lined up. They were ready to start a new life, and then that didn't happen. What made me think my journey would end differently? Bad things happen to good people every day. I wasn't sure I was good.

I had studied enough books to know the terrain I was facing. I would try to help as many people as I could, if I was able to find anyone at all. I closed my eyes. Nobody. I sensed nobody in this forest. There was nothing living here other than those things hiding in the shadows, and I wasn't even sure they were living.

"I hate you, you know that, right?" I told them.

I had to break the silence.

"You took everything from me!" I shouted.

Snarls.

"You're subhuman. You don't belong in this world or any other. You're also cowards. You aren't like my parents. When you were bitten, you chose to feed on people. That was your choice."

I paused, looking through the grass.

I heard growling. They understood nothing. Or maybe they just didn't care.

"Monsters," I whispered to myself.

It was the hottest, sunniest summer day I had ever known. I thanked the skies for their cloudless glory as I walked, paying extra attention not to walk in the shaded areas. A breeze. I stopped for a moment to let the wind hit my neck. So hot. I kept my eyes on the blowing trees and shifting sun as I took my canteen out and took a drink. Seconds. That was all they needed to attack. I kept moving west. I was walking on a trail. I wasn't sure how a trail existed other than the possibility the infected had created it running at night.

As I walked, I wondered what life would have been like in the old world. The world my parents had grown up in sounded like an amazing place. My mother had told me stories about universities where kids my age would go to learn. I couldn't imagine a place with that many books. It wasn't all good. She told me people would fight about things like money. We no longer had money. We lived in a world of bartering now. What would a piece of paper be worth now? I had used my skills to support us. I would build people security systems with latches and traps in exchange for food and clothing. The elders told me that before money, bartering was the way that people survived. They said that we had gone backward in time. In the old world, you could go to a store and buy anything you needed. That is a hard concept for me to wrap my head around. I once installed a security system on someone's windows for a new cooking pot. I would catch fish and trade them for socks. Shoes were especially rare. Most of us walked around barefoot. Some people made their own shoes using old tires and pieces of clothing. I did have a few pairs of boots that belonged to my father. I only wore those boots in winter and then now.

I continued to walk west and I could tell it was close to the evening by the birds circling overhead. I knew I needed to hunker down for the night. I was coming up on a river and I knew there would be at least one area that would have a dam. I had slept on a dam the night before. It wasn't ideal, but it was safe. The infected hated water. I really couldn't understand how they didn't need water. I read in a book that all living things need water. Did that mean they weren't living? I didn't know.

I was correct in my theory and I found a dam that had water covering all around it. I waded into the water, carrying my boots tied around my neck. The water here was waist deep. I climbed onto the dam and laid my clothes out to dry. I was tired. Exhausted. I hadn't been this tired in a long time, if ever. I laid the tarp out over the dam and used my pack as a pillow. It would be a damp sleep but safe. I was still in the midwest. Nothing in these waters would be a danger while I slept. The danger was beyond the water, hiding in the brush. I've healed from bites, but I wonder if I was torn apart like some people are if I could survive. I didn't think so. I was not immortal.

I didn't sleep like humans. My senses were too in tune with what was going on around me. I was half asleep. My mind slept, but my body was slightly awake. I think this might be the infected part of me. I could hear them lurking all around me. They stood at the water's edge, plotting.

"Oh, I hear you," I said to the infected. "I just don't play your games. See, I'm not actually scared of you. You should be afraid of me. You can sit there all night."

I knew I was safe. They would never risk getting wet. The water was a deterrent. I believed it was like rabies. They didn't like water because their throat would spasm and they'd die. I could be wrong. I had studied every encyclopedia that existed, and this was the only thing I could come up with. It amazed me they could exist in a world that was covered with this much water.

The majority of the people who used to live in my town became them. After seeing that other town, I wondered if that was what happened everywhere. They were the dominant force now, and we people were few. I was just surprised at how few we had become. I thought on my journey I would have found at least one person so far.

I was told in the beginning that thousands would descend on one town, destroying everyone within it. I hadn't seen that in my lifetime, but my mother had. I closed my eyes and drifted off to sleep to the snarls and growls of the infected, the cries for help.

The morning is a glorious occurrence. The shining sun told us we had been given another day. The infected were gone. I felt them lurking in the shadows, hiding in the trees. The sun burned them almost instantaneously. This was how people were bitten and not eaten. This was how they became infected. They were attacked in the shadows and ran into the light. The infected was either burned by the sun or stayed in the shadows. The person ran away only to face another death. I packed up and decided to follow the river until I couldn't anymore. It would take me north a ways, but if my map was correct, the river system was connected and I could follow it back west. The good thing about a river is that if you have to, you can just jump in. The walk today was the easiest I had so far. It seemed too easy.

It had been days since I had spoken to another person. It seemed surreal to just exist in silence. I had always considered myself to be a quiet person, but this was too quiet. The only noise I could hear was the movement of the river and the breathing of the infected. Up ahead, I could see a spot where the canopy completely covered my path, and I would have to enter the river to safely move through. I took my boots off and put them into my backpack. I put my backpack on top of my head and climbed into the river. The river was deep here. I had to swim it. The current was moving in the direction I needed to go. For that, I was thankful. The swim was easy. I swam beyond the darkness and pulled myself out into the light.

I sat on the riverbank for a moment and looked down the river. I could see the river flowing downhill and winding around. The path along the side of the river was completely bathed in light. I opened my bag and took out my canteen. I sat sipping water and reflecting on my journey so far. I wondered what would happen if I found no one. Where would I stop? Where would this end?

I closed my eyes. "Nobody," I whispered to myself.

My fear. I worried I wouldn't find a single person. I watched the point where the river curved and knew that I was close to Lake Erie. So far, I hadn't found one person alive. I had hoped at this point I would have found someone. Now sitting here on this riverbank, I wasn't sure. I wondered if I had made a mistake. Even if I had, nobody would know other than Lois. Even then, she wouldn't ever hear about it. I thought about my mother telling me I needed to protect myself, not put myself in danger. I looked down at the water, watching it flow below my feet.

My mother was gone. She was never coming back. Clinging on to her memory wouldn't help me. I decided I had no choice but to go on. I continued down the river's edge.

I am not afraid, I would tell myself this every day. I felt that I had been given a gift that others need. I wondered sometimes if there were more like me. I wondered if there were others who were born to parents who had been bitten. I wasn't even sure how many humans were left. This war had been twenty years long. I only know there were people out there because I could hear their screams, but what if the screams were cries for help from the past? What if that was what I was hearing? What if my town was the last one left? Maybe I should have stayed there. Maybe I should have followed my mother's advice to make friends. To find a wife. Maybe I should have stayed so the human race stood a chance. I walked on in silence. Silence. Every day now was complete silence. An omen that constantly reminded me of my mother who was never silent. This was my life now. The only sounds I heard now were the noises of monsters in the shadows who wanted to eat me. Great. Great, I thought. I had placed myself in the exact situation that my mother warned me not to. I could live out here, but what kind of life would this be? I knew one thing—it would be a lonely one. I closed my eyes. I imagined being at home and my mother dancing around, telling me about the old world. An encyclopedia in my hands.

In my pack, I had bread left. I had eaten everything else. In books, I'd seen pictures of bread that looked fluffy and soft. That wasn't the bread we made in my town. Our bread was made by grinding down oats into flour and mixing that with water and salt. It was thin and dry, but it lasted a long time. I would need to fish at some point. I had only enough rations to make it through today.

Fishing wasn't a difficult activity for me. Because of my increased senses, I did not need a fishing pole. I stood in the water and grabbed the fish when they swam by. When I was a child, I tried to use a pole and I was terrible. I actually got angry once and used the pole to stab the fish instead. I scared the boys I was fishing with. I realized then that I didn't need the pole. I started fishing by myself to avoid the others making fun of me. I used to care so much about what others thought. Now I didn't care. I was thankful it was easy for me. Fish was the main source of food we had now. Not only have I been able to feed myself and my family with this skill, but I have also been able to catch extra and feed others in town who were not able to fish.

I walked the river until it came to a huge lake. I closed my eyes and imagined my map.

"The Great Lakes," I whispered to myself.

I had to find a place on this lake to stay for the night. I stood, standing on the bank, looking over the water. A bird chirped in the distance. I walked around the side of the lake to get a better look. I was not immortal. I had to constantly remind myself of that. Even though I healed from the bites, I could still die. I drowned once. I was gone a few minutes before I came back. It was at that moment I realized I was not a superhero. I needed to make sure I took care of myself. I wondered what else could kill me. No matter what, I was driven to move. There had to be a reason I was like this.

I stood on the side of the lake.

I closed my eyes, connecting with nature. Someone was near.

My eyes shot open. I felt someone. Someone human.

I could hear the infected snarling in the brush just beyond the light, but this...this was louder. A human. I didn't know where and I didn't know how many, but at that moment, I had hope. I wasn't even sure how far the person was. I wasn't alone. Somewhere out there, a person existed.

I made my way through the brush. I waded in and stood in the shallows, listening to the movement of the water. I rubbed my hands over the surface of the water, waiting for a fish. As I connected with the water, I could hear snarls, growls, breathing...a man's voice. My eyes shot open again. I heard a man. I looked around, frantically searching for this person. I squinted my eyes.

In the distance, I could see a man standing on a boat. The boat looked like it had a shanty on top of it. The walls were makeshift from pieces of other things. I saw that he had used fruit crates and old aluminum shingles for roofing. He was using large bottles that said

"Crystal Water" on them for the flotation part of his raft. Looking at this boat, I wondered how it floated, but more importantly, I wondered what this man was doing out here in the middle of nowhere.

"Hey!" I shouted. "Hey!" I ran deeper into the water.

"Hello!" the man bellowed in my direction as he started to row toward me.

"Hello, my name is Joel. I come from the east," I told him.

"Are ya bitten?" he questioned.

"No... I'm not...," I replied and I could tell my pausing while saying my response made him leery of believing me, so I followed it up with, "Actually, I can't be infected. I'm immune."

I knew that my mother had told me not to tell anyone about this part of my life, but I just had to tell him. This man out here in the middle of nowhere had no reason to harm me. It would bring him nothing but loneliness.

"How is that?" he asked.

I could tell from the look on his face he was interested.

"Come here and I'll explain, or I could just swim out to you. You know, if I had been bitten, I won't make it out to your boat. If you want, I will stay in the water while I talk to you," I explained.

"Okay, come on then. My name is Eric, by the way," he said.

I swam out to the boat, which took very little effort, and I floated next to it. I was aware the sun was going down, but if this guy wouldn't let me on his boat, I would just spend the night floating around. I felt sure this man would listen, though.

"My name is Joel. I was conceived after my father had been bitten. My mother was human. I am a half-infected, half-human hybrid. I am strong and fast like the infected, but I am kind and caring like a human. I eat food, drink water, and I feel love and compassion. I also sense the presence of the infected, and I heal quickly from their bites. I am immune to the disease."

"Well, that was a lot of information," he said, turning his head sideway.

When I finished, I expected him not to believe me. He looked to be in his sixties. His white beard made him look like the Santa Claus in the books I had read. He was wearing frayed clothes and looked like he lived a hard life. He looked down at me, put his hand on his head and rubbed his temple, and then shocked me with his response.

"Right on…want to ride with me? You said you can sense them, right?" he stared inquisitively.

"Yes, I know when they are near," I responded.

"You hungry?" he asked. "I want to see you eat this before I'll let you on here," he said as he leaned over and dropped a few berries in my hand.

It was known that the infected could not eat fruits or vegetables, and I knew this was a final test. Obviously, this man did not live to be this old by being naïve. I ate the fruit and climbed on his boat.

"Where are you headed?" Eric asked.

"I'm headed out west. I know it probably sounds really strange for me to tell you that, but I can hear people screaming. They need help, and I want to help them. I feel like this is my purpose," I told him.

"Don't take this the wrong way, kid, but nothing you say from here on out will be as weird as telling me you're immune," he said.

"This world needs help. This is not the world it was meant to be. It can't be this cruel," I said to him.

Eric stood up and walked into the part of his boat that looked like a little house and emerged with a pile of old pictures. He showed me his family and told me he was from Illinois. He grew up on a farm, and when the outbreak happened, he lost his wife, his children, and everyone he loved. He went north to the Great Lakes, which is where we were. He had spent the last twenty years sailing around the Great Lakes and going up and down the rivers that connected them.

"My wife was the best mother in the world. She was a teacher, you know. She loved to read. Great cook. She quit teaching after she had our fourth child, our first daughter. She couldn't leave her. She told me she would have twenty children to have one daughter. My sons were strong-willed, daring, wild." Eric laughed. He wiped a tear. "My little girl was different. She was loving and calm. Beautiful like her mother. She melted my heart with every smile."

Eric looked out across the lake. He picked up a jar and took a drink out of it. "That's why I drink moonshine, you know...to numb myself...to forget."

"I'm sorry, Eric," I said to him.

His face was tormented as he gathered the strength to finish his story.

"I wasn't home when they came," Eric said. "I wasn't home to protect them." Eric looked straight into my eyes. "They weren't killed by the infected, Joel. They were killed by men. Human men. Men came into my house and they robbed us, and instead of leaving my family, they killed them. My wife, my children..." Eric sobbed into his hands. "I was out fishing. That's where I was. I felt that since I worked all day I deserved a break. I had a good catch that day. I couldn't wait to show the boys..." Eric looked up at the stars. "Are you a religious man, Joel?" He looked into my eyes.

"I believe so, though I'm not sure what religion I am," I said.

"Well, I am. Faith is the only thing that keeps me going, Joel. I hope that someday in the next life I see them again. It's all I have left in this world. Everything else was ripped away from me. Part of me died the day my family died. I am not the same. I never will be."

Eric took another swig. He wiped his eyes. "Okay, enough of this. I got myself all worked up." Eric looked at me. "I haven't seen anyone in years. The lakes are huge. I don't leave this boat," he said.

"Do you know where this disease came from?" I asked.

This was something I had wanted to know for as long as I could remember. Nobody knew where the virus had started.

"We did this to ourselves," Eric explained. "We were so worried about bacteria and germs. It seemed that every product on the market was bragging about being antibacterial. People were so afraid of illness they were killing all the bacteria, both good and bad. We became a fear-driven society, and by killing the good bacteria, we actually created a series of superbugs. These superbugs were immune to our antibiotics. Nothing killed them. One day, this virus showed up. It worked its way into the brains of victims, like it hijacked the person's body completely. Maybe if we hadn't been so worried about getting sick, our immune systems would have been prepared to fight this. It was a plague. A plague that is our fault. It happened world-wide. Nowhere was safe."

"How do you know so much?" I asked him.

He looked at me and smiled and he reached his hand up to his forehead as if to salute me.

"Lieutenant General Eric Anderson, United States Marine Corps. I know everything. I saw it all go down. The military training prepared me for these extreme conditions. I was part of the naval part of the marines. I spent all my military life on boats. This is what I was trained to do and what I know how to do. It's what I was good at. So I went back to it when I needed to. You are the first human I have seen in three years…well, you're kind of human."

"You said three years? What people did you see three years ago?" I asked him.

"There is a settlement on the other side of Lake Huron, or at least there used to be. We're on Lake Erie right here," he said, taking out a map. "The settlement is here." He pointed.

"There used to be more of those things out west than here, less water out there. There are also less trees in certain areas, and when there are less trees, there are less infected, but don't forget about caves. They love caves," he said, looking around.

The sun was going down, and I could tell he was starting to get nervous.

"I feel them watching me. Always." He shuddered.

"I hear them. They are out there, but we are safe now. They aren't close," I told him.

"I like having you around, kid," Eric said as he slapped my back. "You can sleep in here if you like." He pointed to the house atop his boat.

"Thanks, but I'll stay here and take point," I said, smiling.

"All righty then, soldier. Can I call you soldier?" he asked.

I nodded in approval.

I had lied to Eric. There were a lot of infected this night. They were close. Very close. I wondered how long these things had been waiting for Eric to dock. They lined the shore. I could hear their breathing and snarls. I wondered what they lived on out here. Eric hadn't seen anyone in three years. They must be able to live a long time without eating.

Eric had thrown in the anchor so the boat wouldn't drift to the side. His anchor consisted of four milk jugs filled with sand. As I lay at the front of the boat, I stared up at the stars. I thought about Eric's story. So much tragedy. I had tragedy, too, but not at his level. I closed my eyes and fell asleep to the sounds I did every night— the growling snarls of the infected and the distant screams of people needing help. Nothing in my life told me this would work out the way I planned, but somehow I still had faith that it would.

CHAPTER 4

THE BOOK OF HEINRICH

The next day, it rained. It rained for three days. I sat on the boat with Eric, and we played chess. The pieces were made out of old nails and pieces of tin. He beat me every time and loudly cackled afterward. He drank moonshine from an old coffee mug that read *World's Best Mom.*

"What happened to your jar?" I asked him.

"It's making my moonshine." He pointed over to jars inside of a crate. "They need to ferment until they get good."

"What's in them?" I asked.

"The best moonshine uses grain, but I can't grow that on my boat. I use corn. Different taste, same effect." Eric pointed inside his boat shanty to the back corner. Corn grew to the ceiling. "I grew up in the middle of a cornfield. I know corn," he said. "I use my stove to make it. Then I let it ferment until it's ready. I use an old shirt as a filter. And here I am, living the life." He smiled at me and took a swig.

Eric's stove was actually just a pile of sticks burning in a shallow barrel. He had an old oven rack over it.

"You find treasures out here on the water. Everything I have was from here. When I came here, I just had an old rowboat. I lived on that while I built this boat. This doesn't look like much, but it's sturdy. I've lived through some crazy storms on this thing. Sure, it breaks and I have to fix it, but it gives me something to do. It's home." Eric patted the side of his boat.

As the rain stopped, we started to make our way to the other side of the lake where there were people living. The boat mostly drifted, but he had a sheet he rigged to a pole in the middle to "catch the wind," as he called it. It took us two days to get to the other side of the lake.

A realization hit me during the rain while we sat and played chess. I realized that during the rain, I couldn't sense any of the infected around us. They must hide somewhere when it rained. I wanted to ask Eric to continue my journey with me. Not only did I need him but I also enjoyed his company and I trusted him. I told Eric my plan and asked if he would come along, and he told me he would think about it.

I peered over the water. They looked like huts lining the sides of the water. I was shocked by their vulnerable shelters…how unprepared they were. I wondered how many had been taken. I saw them before Eric did.

"Right there are the people I was telling you about," he said, pointing toward them. I had not seen a person yet, just the structures. As we started to get closer, I could make out the people. They were sitting on the sand on the side of the water. Some of them were making baskets, some were cleaning fish. They were people, just like my people back home, except they all looked alike. Most of them were tanned from being outside. They all had the same shade of blond hair. This seemed like a family.

"They all look alike," Eric said to me. "It's creepy."

I laughed.

Eric and I anchored the boat. He said he wanted to see what he could barter. The people ran from us when they saw us. Men ran from the forest with their arrows drawn.

"Get in the water," one man said, his arrow aimed right at my head.

Eric and I sat on the side of the boat and lifted ourselves into the water. We swam around to appease them and then climbed out soaking wet to prove we were not bitten.

"Hello, I'm Joel from the east, and this is Lieutenant General Eric Anderson from Illinois."

I reached out my hand to shake hands with them, and they seemed confused by this gesture.

"Come with us. You must talk to Heinrich if you want to stay here," they said and walked toward the hut in the middle. I abided even though I knew I would not be staying here.

I went inside the small house and was surprised by how kept the entire house was. There was not much inside. There were some low-lying tables that were being used for food, and it seemed some type of ceremony. There sitting at the table with his eyes closed was the oldest man I had ever seen in my existence. He looked to be one hundred years old. He opened his eyes and looked at me and smiled.

"And here you are," he said. "I expected you."

He stood up and lit a stick and stuck it into another bowl. The fragrance that came from the bowl smelled like flowers, and he bounced around the hut, adding different types of things to it. He then dipped his fingers into the bowl and took the black dust, and he used his thumb to draw a cross on my forehead. He looked at me and smiled and said, "Dolce angelo della misericordia."

I knew the translation from my studies. He had called me the sweet angel of mercy.

"Hello, I am Father Siloam."

"I am Joel, son—" I was interrupted by the man.

"Son of Christopher and you came from the east," he said, smiling matter-of-factly. "I told you I knew you were coming."

"I was told I needed to speak to Heinrich," I said to him, confused.

"Only if you are staying here, which you are not. Heinrich is in charge of housing," Father Siloam said to me.

Then he stood up and asked me to walk with him. I followed him through the door of the hut as he started to speak about the old times.

"In the old days, I was a priest. I knew something bad was coming. I felt it every day of my life. I told people, but nobody believed me. I knew I had been right in my intuition when people started changing, disappearing."

Eric was near the boat. He had old fishing poles in his hand. He was trying to talk some of the people into trading them. I saw him acting out how they work. He pretended to catch a big fish. I laughed to myself.

"You got a good sidekick in that one." Father Siloam pointed toward Eric. "Rough around the edges but strong. You know, diamonds get stronger under pressure, even diamonds in the rough." He smiled at me. I didn't know what he meant by that.

He sat down on the shore and asked me to sit with him. I abided.

"Why do you think they can't go into the water?" he asked.

"I think the virus is like rabies, it makes their throat close," I said.

"Interesting," he said.

"What do you think?" I asked him.

"Demons can't swim, water is sacred," he told me.

He took my hand in his and began to trace the lines up and down my hand as he mumbled to himself. Then he stopped and looked me in the eyes.

"From the time I was a boy, I knew what I would become. For me, it was a calling I felt I was born to do. Being out here in nature, I have really been able to live and appreciate creation. I knew you were coming. I dreamed of you. In my dream, God spoke to me. He told me to give you a message." He put my hand down and closed his eyes and said something that shocked me and sent chills through me.

"You carry the key to saving us."

"How?" I asked. "I know I'm strong and immune, but how do I save people? What is the key?"

"Follow your heart," the priest said. He winked at me, stood up, and walked away.

When I saw the huts on the shore of the lake, I had assumed this was where these people lived. I learned that I was very wrong. These huts served as fishing quarters for the men during the day and a port where trade could happen. Eric and I had been guided into the forest by guards so that we could meet the rest of the people and see how these people had adapted to survive. I was surprised at how light the forest was, and then I realized that the canopy of trees above me had their leaves removed in order to create a lighted path that people could safely pass on.

"Look up," one man said to me.

As I raised my head and looked up, I could see houses in every tree. There were bridges created from one house to another. I could see people walking around inside their bustling tree city.

"They climb, though, how do you keep them from climbing up there?" I asked the men.

Both men laughed a little, and that was when I saw it. About halfway up the tree, they had built large round stoppers so that the tree could not be climbed.

"Then how do you all get up there?" I asked.

Just then, a rope was thrown from the top of the tree.

"We climb up the old-fashioned way," the second man said, smiling.

Both the men climbed so quickly. When I tried, it took me a little longer. I reminded myself to work on my climbing skills.

"I'll meet you back at the boat. I ain't doin' this," Eric said and walked the lighted path back to the beach.

"Welcome," a woman said to me as I climbed onto the first bridge. "Would you like something to eat?"

"Sure, that would be really nice," I said and followed her into one of the tree houses.

Inside the tree house, there were beds made of pine needles and blankets made of cloth. There was a small wood stove that she was using to cook something inside of a pot.

"Fish stew. It will give you strength. We don't get many visitors here. It is always special when one comes along."

"How long have you all lived here?" I asked.

"We have been here since the beginning. We started out on the beach, but it wasn't safe, so we figured out a way to live in the trees. Some of us are not allowed on the ground. I live each day in the trees. I am one of the elders, so my stories are important. Children under the age of sixteen are not allowed to walk on the ground. They stay here for their youth in the safety of these trees," she said, stirring the soup.

She grabbed a wooden carved bowl and filled the bowl with the hot soup.

"Are you all from the same place? You look alike," I asked her.

"We are all related," she said to me, smiling. "It's quite unfortunate for the children, really. They'll have to leave in order to marry. My own son will have to leave to marry. The only women close to his age are his sisters. I truly wish more people would come."

I hadn't realized how hungry I was as I lifted the soup and began to drink it fast. I barely tasted it on the way down.

"What is the plan? Will you expand?" I asked.

"These trees are very old, and they won't last forever. The weight of our houses bearing down on them will make them break. My son is an engineer. He built most of these houses. He says that we can rebuild, but it will take time. Most of the good timber is inside the darkness, and even that timber is dry."

"Hello," a man said as he entered the home.

I lifted my head when I heard his voice. Before me stood a young man in his twenties; his shoulders were broad, and his muscles were protruding. He had the light hair and the light eyes that were typical of these people. He held his blistered hand out to shake my own. When I shook his hand, I was amazed at the strength behind it.

"My name is Heinrich. I see you met my mother." He walked across the room and kissed his mother on the forehead, and I felt a twinge of pain inside.

"Come take a walk with me," he said. "You're young, how young are you?" His forehead was creased as he studied my face.

"I'm eighteen, I'll be nineteen in four months," I said.

"You're different, aren't you? I can tell there is something different about you. I just can't put my finger on it," he said.

I studied his face for a moment. Eric wasn't here to give me advice. I wondered if I could trust him. Looking into his eyes, I decided I could.

"My father was infected when I was conceived. I was born immune," I said.

"Wow," Heinrich said, his mouth gaping open. "That is incredible. You're a miracle."

"I don't know if I would call myself that," I responded.

"Look at this place," he said. "This isn't going to hold for very much longer, you know. I don't know what we are going to do. This forest is completely infested with those things. If we move to the ground, it will be the end of us. It has been so dry here. We really needed that rain the other day. Our crops are being destroyed. The trees are brittle, and I believe at some point they may start to break."

"Burn it," I said as if the thought had just burst into my mind. "Burn the forest down."

Heinrich looked around and thought about it for a minute. He crouched to the floor and felt the tree that the bridge was connected to.

"You know, I think that might work. I don't know, though, what about oxygen? Isn't it important we keep every tree?" Heinrich asked.

"We won't need oxygen anymore when we are all dead," I said, staring at him. "These trees separate the towns. They are home to those things. We can never rebuild while these forests isolate us. We will never recover. There aren't many of us left. There will still be enough trees for oxygen."

"Joel," he said, "I actually agree with you. With so few people, we could stand to lose a forest to survive. The forests are mostly dead, anyways. Come, we have to tell the council your idea."

He grabbed a rope and swung down to the ground. I followed after him. We walked to the beach and went inside one of the huts. Father Siloam was at the head of the table. The two men who had led me to the trees were there as well. I knelt at the table with Eric on one side and Heinrich on the other and explained my plan to the seven men in the council.

"We have to burn the trees down," I explained to the council. "They have isolated us by corralling us inside these meadows like sheep they can pick from. They have taken over our towns and killed and fed off our children. They hide in the shadows of the forest. In the darkness. Fire will save us. It is through fire that we must end them. If we burn all the forests, we will be able to freely walk during the daytime. We still have the night to worry about, but if they have nowhere to hide, then they will be too far to find us in the night.

This is the only way we can survive. The forests are dying, and they are dry. I will travel and burn along the way. We will build enough boats for you and your people to float on until the fires end, to sleep in. You will live on the land in the day and on the water at night. You will build a floating town. Water will be your sanctuary."

I waited for Father Siloam's response.

Father Siloam looked down and then around the room and nodded his head.

"Go then, make your preparations," he said to me. "We will start burning in three days. We will have that amount of time to build the boats. Heinrich, you are in charge of the building of the boats. When we start the burning, you will stay for two days. After those two days, Heinrich will accompany you west. He is our best engineer and will be able to help you along your way."

Heinrich looked worried. "Who will care for my mother?"

"I will." A man around the same age stood up. "I would be honored. My mother passed away when I was born. I lived my life without a mother. I will fish for her and protect her as if she were my own mother."

Heinrich nodded approvingly.

"I will be honored to follow you, Joel." Heinrich knelt in front of me.

Heinrich learned everything he knew in life from his father. His father shared the name of Heinrich. He told me his mother and father had moved here from Germany. His father was an engineer and worked building amazing bridges and buildings. His father had died when Heinrich was little. He had fallen from one of the trees and never got up. Heinrich learned from him how to build houses and bridges and how to protect the homes.

Unlike me, Heinrich remembered life before the infected ruled our world. He was six when the virus came. He had a happy childhood filled with video games and TV shows. He told me he played with electronic devices all the time. All the kids did. I had read about these games in my inventions book back home. Home, I had not thought about that place in a very long time.

Heinrich helped me find wood, and we began building the boats that the people would spend their nights on. There were fifty-three people in the village. Nineteen of them were children. I was amazed at how he used math to calculate how many rafts would be needed, how much food and water. He used a stick to draw numbers in the sand. These numbers meant nothing to me, but to him, they seemed his language. After talking to himself for some time, he seemed to have it all figured out.

"We will need one boat for every five people. We will need to build at least eleven boats, but I would like to build one extra in case something happens. We will build twelve boats. The boats will be flat rafts, and we will need to make a covering over part of them for sleeping quarters," Heinrich explained.

He told me to follow him to the forest to find some wood, and I followed. When we got into the woods, he told me to look for fallen trees that we could use.

"The dead ones that fall down float better," he said.

With our strengths combined, it did not take long for us to drag eight large trees from the forest onto the beach.

"What now?" I asked. "Do you have tools?"

"Yeah, of course, I have tools. How else would I have built all those homes?" Heinrich responded.

He went into one of the huts and came out with a bucket of saws, hammers, wooden pegs, and other tools. He showed me how to saw each of the trees into logs and then showed me how to split them with an ax. He explained to me that it was important to make the pieces of wood uniform in size. After we had axed and sawed the wood into pieces, he grabbed some twine out of his bucket and showed me how to make knots on the wood.

"There, that should work," he said.

We heard laughing and turned around to see Eric laughing at us, amused at himself.

"That will never float," Eric said. "You got too much weight on there to make it float. You need air."

He pointed out to his boat.

"You see them things underneath my boat. The clear things. They are filled with air. You need something that has air in it. Do you have anything here like that?" Eric asked.

"I've got some plastic barrels up in the trees we use for water. We have two in each home, so that should be enough. We just need to find something else to put the water in," Heinrich said.

"You did a good job with those houses in the trees, but the water is my expertise. Let's get them barrels down here, and I'll show you how to strap them onto the raft." Eric walked over to help us.

Heinrich and I went into the trees and gathered all the barrels. We also gathered all the plastic bottles we could find and any other item we thought would float.

We sat on the beach for hours, meticulously tying each of the bottles onto our raft. When we were finished, Heinrich and Eric helped me pull the raft to the water, and Eric volunteered to test it. We put the raft onto the water, and it floated.

We spent the next two days making rafts. We were even able to recruit a few other builders to help us with the splitting of the wood and tying of the logs. By day three, we were all set to go along with the plans that Father Siloam had made.

We stood on the beach as people came from the houses in the forest. Women came—some young, some very old. Some people carried babies or held hands of children. Strong men carried elderly people who couldn't walk. They made their way to the beach, and we began grouping the people into "boat crews."

It was much more involved than I thought it would be. We had to try and keep families together and at the same time we had to make sure there were enough adults on each boat to safely protect the children.

We were able to individually load each raft and launch them and move onto the next one. The goal was to float to the middle and then tie the rafts to one another so that none drifted away. These would be anchored in the middle by the largest of the rafts. This would be the raft of the council and Father Siloam.

The last to board a boat was Heinrich's mother. I watched her speaking to him in another language, and she held his arms and said,

"Be strong, my son." He kissed her on her forehead and then led her to the raft and said goodbye. The last words he said to her was his promise that they would meet again.

Eric, Heinrich, and I went to the forest. We called out to make sure nobody was inside. I watched as Eric splashed his alcohol all over the forest floor. He then took two sticks and rubbed them on a rock. After he started to get smoke, he took some dry pieces of the forest floor, and they smoldered inside the small flame. He took his shirt off and put it inside the fire. The shirt immediately went up in flames. He threw the shirt onto the alcohol-soaked forest floor, and a roar erupted.

"Wow, I wasn't expecting that," he said and turned to me. "I mean, I knew the forest was dry but not that dry. I thought we would have to try to light it a few times. I'm a little sad I wasted my moonshine."

I watched as Father Siloam chanted words I had never heard. The forest fire spread so quickly I was thankful we had gotten out of there when we did. That' was when we heard them, screaming from the forest. People gasped, children held their eyes, and Father Siloam chanted even louder as we watched them running from the forest and leaping into the water to their deaths. The plan had worked.

I heard people cheering, and Father Siloam turned and put his hand in the air to silence them.

"Do not forget that these were once people. They were some-body's mother or father, sister or brother, or even their child. We must remember this, we must pray for them. We must pray for their souls." He then instructed everyone to remain silent as he chanted in Latin.

After a few hours, the screaming became more distant. The fire had spread as far as our eyes could see. This was due to the dryness of the forests. I was suddenly overwhelmingly thankful for this fresh water we sat on. In this fiery furnace, we had a water and food source right underneath us.

We kept our word to spend two days here in the water, floating off the smoldering shore. I overheard Heinrich giving instructions to Father Siloam. He kneeled in front of him. Father Siloam said a prayer and then placed his hand on Heinrich's head. Heinrich nodded to his people, to his mother, to the man who stepped up to care for her. Then he turned to me and nodded to me last.

"You decide if you're coming with us yet?" I asked Eric.

"Yes, I did," Eric said, staring at the people we just met. "I am coming with you. Mostly because I feel less judged drinking moonshine with you." He smiled and winked at me. "Plus I think you need me out there, kid."

I gave him a hug. He pulled back and then slapped me on the shoulder. We loaded up Eric's boat. We decided to stick with the original ship we started on. We pushed the boat off the shore.

I turned to address our departure with the group we were leaving.

"We will burn our way to the west, and when we come back through, we will meet again. If you choose to leave, be safe. Stick together." We started to float away. "Thank you, my brothers and sisters."

Father Siloam lifted his hand to say goodbye to us, and we all stood, drifting farther away until they were tiny specks, and then we were alone again.

CHAPTER 5

THE BOOK OF DUTY

We sat on the boat in silence, floating away from Father Siloam and from everything Heinrich had ever known. He sat next to me with his legs crossed, almost stoic. I could tell he was hiding his emotions. The water rippled away from our boat as we drifted. Eric's makeshift sail flapped in the wind. I could tell it wasn't really helping us along.

"To new beginnings." Eric raised his jar of moonshine in the air. Neither of us responded.

"Okay then. To new beginnings." Eric toasted another jar of moonshine in his other hand.

"You okay?" I asked Heinrich. I put my hand on his shoulder.

"I will be," he replied.

He scooted toward the edge of the boat and put his legs in the water. I did the same. Heinrich was leaning back on his hands, looking at the sky.

"You know, my dad was a carpenter. I don't think I told you that," I told Heinrich.

"No, you didn't," Heinrich responded.

"Yeah, he made our house to be able to withstand any attack. Then he taught my mom how to build, then my mom taught me," I told him. "That's what I was doing before I went west. I was making sure everyone in town was safe, but what I did wasn't even close to what you built. You're a true builder."

"Thank you," he said. "I didn't know you had building experience," he added. "That's good to know."

"Your mom is really nice," I said to him. I was trying to get him to have an actual conversation and get his mind off leaving home.

"I'm sorry about your parents, Joel," Heinrich said. "When I start to feel sorry for myself, I think about you. I know I don't have any room to feel that way. I still have my mother."

"I can understand that," I said to him quietly. "I think about Eric and what he's been through when I start to feel sorry for myself."

"I guess in this world everyone carries around their own unique trauma," Heinrich said.

"Some carry around a lot," I told Heinrich. I looked back at Eric, who was playing a game of solitaire while he drank his moonshine.

"You know, I never wanted to be a builder," he told me.

"Really? What did you want to be?" I asked him.

"I wanted to be…happy," he said.

"You aren't happy?" I said in response.

Heinrich didn't answer immediately, and I regretted asking him that question.

Heinrich pointed across the water.

"You see that opening over there, Joel?" he asked.

"Yes," I said. "I see it."

"Well, there used to be another settlement right there when I was sixteen years old," Heinrich said

There in the distance was an open field next to the water. The trees had been cleared. Only grass grew there. I could see the remnants of old structures that may have previously been housing.

"One day, they decided to sail east. I wanted to go. I wanted to see what was out there, and I didn't," Heinrich said.

"Why didn't you?" I asked.

"Because I had a duty to my mother. I promised my father that if anything ever happened to him, I would take care of my mother and the others," he told me. "I was also the only other trained engineer we had."

"They were lucky to have you," I said, looking at him.

"I didn't want to be a builder, but it was something I was good at. Sometimes our duty has more to do with everyone else and less to do with ourselves," he said. "Sometimes we have to sacrifice the things we want for the things others need."

"You sacrificed because you're a good person," I told him. "That's why you came with us."

"That's one reason I came with you," he said. "I would be lying if I told you it was the only reason…and I don't lie." Heinrich stared toward the open area where the settlement used to be.

"What's the other reason?" I asked him.

"I want to find someone, Joel," he said to me. "I want to find a wife. I want to have children. I want to build a home so safe that I can have that." He was staring at me now.

I looked away. I wasn't sure we would find that for him, but I hoped we would.

"That's why I wanted to leave at sixteen. Growing up around people you're related to is great, but I wanted to meet people I wasn't related to," Heinrich said.

"I can understand that," I told him.

"I can be quiet at times, Joel. Please don't think it means I don't want to be on this journey. This is all I've ever wanted," he said. "In a way, I feel like it's my turn."

I put my hand on his shoulder.

"What about you, Joel? Any love interests back home?" he asked.

I laughed. "Not at all. I don't think I'm ready for all that. You know, I think watching my mother mourn my father may have made me not want to go through that. You know?"

"I still remember when my dad fell. I was with him. I had been working with him. By the time I got down to him, he was gone. My mother was screaming." He shook his head. "I'll never forget her scream."

"But even with having gone through that, you still want to get married?" I asked him.

"Of course. Just because that happened to my dad doesn't mean it will happen to me. I think we have the amazing opportunity to learn from the mistakes of others. For example, that day my dad fell, I had told him to tie off onto the tree he was building on. He had told me to tie off and even helped me, but when I told him to tie off, he laughed. He said he didn't need to. Now, because I went through that, I learned that I must always tie off when I'm working no matter how confident I might be. Does that make sense?" he asked me.

"Yes, it does," I said.

I thought about my parents' deaths and what I could learn from them. I realized that both of their deaths were by errors in judgment. My father had died because he docked the boat too late. He thought he had enough sunlight to get home. My mother died because she thought the area she was picking flowers in was safe enough. I had the ability to not repeat those mistakes.

"Heinrich, thanks for that. Seriously. I had never thought about it that way." I reached out and shook his hand. "I'm glad you're here."

"Absolutely," he said, shaking my hand in return.

"So now that you've given up your duty, do you feel different?" I asked him.

"Oh, Joel, I haven't given up my duty," he said to me. "Our duty is never done. It's a lifelong promise we make to this world."

"What is my duty?" I asked, questioning him.

"I don't know, Joel, that's for you to figure out," he said.

I sat next to him. Neither of us spoke. We watched the fires of his village rise up into the trees and the black smoke billow off his home. We floated away as Heinrich's hard work turned to ash.

"Anybody hungry?" Eric asked. "I've got some fish steaks ready to go on the stove."

"Fish steaks? What's a fish steak?" Heinrich asked.

"It's like regular fish, but I say the word *steak* after it to trick myself," Eric said, laughing.

We both laughed.

"You guys seem to be having a super deep, secret conversation over there, but I think I heard the word *duty* being thrown around," Eric said.

I laughed at Eric.

"Okay, yes, Eric, we were. What's your duty?" I asked.

"I don't know now. It's weird. When you fail at your duty, you don't really know what your purpose is anymore." Heinrich and I both looked at Eric. I could tell we both felt sorry for him.

"Maybe you need a new duty," I suggested.

"Oh yeah," Eric said. "What do you have in mind?"

"Hmmm…maybe fish steak maker?" I laughed.

"Oh, I could do that," he said as he tossed one of the fish in the air, and it landed back on the stove.

"See, you're a natural," Heinrich said, smiling.

"You know, I never even liked fish," Eric said, chuckling. "I loved going fishing and catching them, but I didn't really enjoy eating them…still don't."

"It's the only thing I've ever eaten," I responded.

"I like crab, though. Crab is really good," he said, turning the fish again.

"I've never had it," Heinrich responded.

"Well, it's best with some butter for dipping, but you guys will never know the joy of that," Eric said, taking the fish off the stove and placing them on a few old plates.

"What's butter?" I asked.

"Do you know what a cow is?" Eric asked.

"Yes, I know what a cow is," I told him. "Milk comes from them, right?"

"Yes, exactly," Eric responded. "Butter comes from milk."

"Oh." I realized there were things I hadn't learned in my books.

"I remember cows," Heinrich said.

"I remember them too. I remember hamburgers and steaks and meatloaf," Eric said. "You know, my doctor told me a long time ago I should eat more fish." He laughed. "I bet he would be so proud of my diet now."

"Why?" I asked.

"Why what?" Eric asked me.

"Why did he tell you to eat more fish?" I asked.

"Joel, this is going to be hard for you to wrap your brain around. In the old world, food tasted so good that people had a hard time losing weight," he said.

"Why would anyone want to lose weight?" I was confused by all of this new information.

"Joel, I used to be three times as big as I am," he said. "That's how delicious cows were."

We all laughed.

"I thought I learned everything in books," I told him.

"I don't think they wrote a lot of books about how good food was, Joel," he said, laughing.

"I remember school lunch," Heinrich said.

"School lunch, huh." Eric laughed. "Was it a good school lunch or a bad one?"

"It was good," Heinrich responded. "I was only in kindergarten. I was five years old."

"What did they give you?" Eric was intrigued.

"They gave us chicken nuggets. I miss chicken nuggets...and macaroni and cheese." Heinrich seemed excited about his memory.

"Another gift from the cow. Cheese," Eric said.

"I liked school," Heinrich said. "I remember recess. That was fun."

"Recess was the best part of school," Eric said.

I sat quietly. I had no idea what they were talking about. Eric must have sensed my confusion because he offered an explanation.

"Joel, recess was your break during school. You had to sit in a chair all day and not talk and do your work, then at recess, you got to run outside and play."

"Oh. That sounds fun," I told them. "I think my whole childhood was recess."

They both laughed.

"Do you think there will ever be school again?" Heinrich asked us.

"I really don't know," Eric said. "I don't even know how many children there are still left who would attend."

We all got quiet. In those happy moments where everyone was sharing stories, it was easy to forget exactly how bad this world had become.

Eric made our plates and served us. He came and sat on the side of the boat with Heinrich and me. We all let our legs float in the warm water as we ate. My plate had a picture of a butterfly on it.

"Where did you get these plates?" I asked Eric.

"I found them along the rivers. I collect things I think would be useful," he said, taking a bite of his fish steak.

Heinrich had gotten quiet again.

"Does it hurt watching the things you built burn?" I asked him.

"No," Heinrich said. "It's like somebody set me free."

CHAPTER 6

THE BOOK OF JORDAN

Eric explained to me that we needed to move from Lake Huron to Lake Michigan. He held a map in his hands. We would take the Strait of Mackinac. He explained to us that once we reached the west side of the Michigan, we would need to find a different waterway. He said he had seen plenty of waterways that weren't mapped in the years he had been out here on his boat. The map was just a rough guide now. He wasn't even sure we would find Lake Michigan. He had joked and said maybe there would just be an empty lake.

We had been drifting for two days now. Sometimes Eric raised his sail and attempted to catch some wind, but the weather had been dry and mild. We spent our days lying around in silence. Sometimes I would ask Heinrich questions, and he would give me one-word answers. Eric drank. Heinrich seemed distant. I could tell he was homesick. I'm sure I would feel the same if my mother was still living. I sat right next to Heinrich, and we took turns skipping rocks across the water.

For the two days of drifting, I did not have to burn one forest because the fire had spread so quickly. It was an amazing sight to see, so many burned trees. My mother had always told me that we didn't take care of the old world and that we made Earth sick. She said the hot weather and the lack of rain were our faults. She believed Earth would eventually heal itself with less of us humans. The dryness of the trees and the underlying grasses made the fire catch easier.

They followed us now, the infected. The ones who had escaped the fires moved alongside us on the same route, hiding in the not-yet-burning trees.

We spent three days total floating to Lake Michigan. I could see where the lake ended and the strait began because of the change in the flow of the water.

"Brace yourself," Eric said as he used his makeshift oar to guide our raft to the mouth of the Illinois River.

When we entered the strait, the raft moved faster than we had on the lake. I was amazed at how torrential this water was, and I wondered if Eric's boat would fall apart on us. Almost as quickly as I had worried, I realized the water was calming and the raft had steadied itself. Heinrich loosened the death grip he had on my arm.

"Sorry, Joel, I guess I got a little rattled," he said.

"No, don't worry about it." I laughed. "I thought we were going to be swimming there for a minute."

"The mouth of a strait is always the worst because of all the different tows. Should be steady sailing now," Eric said.

"You probably need to burn again soon. I don't think the fire will spread this far," Heinrich said.

I thought for a minute as I looked around the forest.

"I'll go into the forest in the daylight tomorrow. I'll hack my way through and see if I can find any people before we burn. I don't want to burn people," I said as I looked at both of their shocked faces.

"Joel, I don't think that's safe," Heinrich said, concerned.

"I'm immune, remember?" I told them.

"Are you immune to being eaten or ripped apart?" Heinrich said.

"No, but I'm strong. It would take a whole bunch of them to take me down," I said.

"I'm going to make an assumption that there are a whole bunch in there," Heinrich said, pointing at the forest.

Heinrich was correct in his assumption. There was a bunch of them in there. More than before. The ones who had lived in the forests we burned had joined with the ones who previously inhabited these forests. They were now doubled in size.

Eric walked across the raft and put his hand on my shoulder, and then he pointed to the forest.

"There are streams and creeks leading all through here. We just need to find a stream you can walk down. If there are people in there, they will be living on the water. If you walk along the water and call for people, they'll hear you. I doubt you find anyone in there, though. These forests are dense. These forests are infested with those things. Trust me, I'm from this area," Eric said, eyeing the forest.

Eric was right. I could hear them everywhere. These forests had to go. We let the river take us until we saw a small dammed-up stream attached to the river.

"Let's dock here tonight and wait until the morning for you to go in," Eric said.

He picked up his sand-filled milk-jug anchors and dropped them into the murky water. I fished and Heinrich began to make a little fire in Eric's stove. I used my toes to dig into the riverbed and find a real treat for dinner. Oysters were always a nice change from regular fish. When I was finished fishing, I had made a haul. I had four fish and a whole pile of fresh-water oysters.

We ate in silence. I think that was the worst part about traveling with men. There wasn't anyone talking. It was so boring it became painful. In silence, my mind wandered to the past. I spent most days thinking about my mother. I wondered if she would believe in what I was doing. I decided she would because her last words to me were to save others, and that is what I was doing.

I thought of my town and of all the people there I had helped. I decided I would walk back to them when I was finished. I needed to burn the forests surrounding my town. I needed to burn the place where my mother and father were bitten in their honor. Even though my town was safer than the one I had found, it didn't mean there would be no more victims. Shadows can be unpredictable, and so can people.

I didn't sleep at all. My mind raced with the possibilities that going into the forest would bring. I heard the screaming clearly that night. The cries for help. I wondered if I would be successful in this journey, and if I was, if the screaming would stop. I hoped it would.

I wondered how many of the infected were packing together in the forest. Hundreds. Thousands. I wasn't sure. The most I had ever fought off at the same time was nine. I once was ambushed at dusk and had to fight off that many. I would have been killed without my strength and immunity. I remember I thought I was going to die that night. One thing that the infected were weak at was teamwork. They were selfish. While attacking a human, they would often turn on each other. That helped me fight them off. I used their weakness against them. Still, even though I had fought off nine, I didn't want to do that again. I would have to be as safe as possible.

I looked at Eric and Heinrich for a moment. I thought about how they had become like family.

"Hey, Eric, when I go into the forest, I want to make sure you both stay here on the boat. No matter what," I said.

"I wasn't planning on going with you," he said with his eyebrows raised. "I'm no superhero." He chuckled.

"What if you don't come back?" Heinrich asked. He looked concerned.

"Then you go on without me and burn to the west," I told them. "Follow through with our plans without me if you have to. Save others along the way."

"Why don't you just set them woods on fire? Nobody lives there," Eric said, shaking his head.

"I can't. I have to try to save people. I have to," I told him matter-of-factly.

Just as I could feel the infected around me, I could also feel people around me. I realized that Eric and Heinrich would not understand this, so I kept it to myself. I felt people nearby. I also felt many of the infected in the forest, but I wasn't sure how many. The next morning, as the sun was rising, I prepared myself for my journey. I packed only the necessities, knowing that Heinrich and Eric would need these things more than myself.

I used a sack with a drawstring to pack a sleeping tarp, a canteen, and a few pieces of fruit. I was walking on fresh water, so that was one worry I did not have to think about.

"Do not follow me in there," I said. "You understand this. You will be killed," I told them.

"You got it, soldier," Eric said, slurring his words. He was already drunk.

"I'll try not to," Heinrich said to me. "Just please come back, don't leave me with him."

We all laughed.

"Hey now, I'm fun. Let's play cards. It passes the time." He went into the tent to get them.

"If you feel like you must go in there, then you must," Heinrich said. He slapped my shoulder and told me, "Good luck."

"Give me two days' time," I said to them.

They both nodded.

I climbed into the water and swam to the stream. I had planned on needing at least two days to walk the streams and make sure there were no people here. I climbed over the dam and stood in the shallows of a narrow stream. I was happy to find that the sun was shining through the canopy of trees and I smiled as I took my shirt off and basked in the warmth. It was nice to be off the boat.

"Hello!" I shouted. "Can anyone hear me? I won't hurt you!" I shouted.

I heard nothing in return besides the gnashing of teeth in the darkness and the sounds of growling and hissing. Humans would not be able to hear this, but my hearing was better tuned to their sounds. I knew I needed to find a bigger body of water to sleep on at night. I also considered climbing a tree and rigging it the way that Heinrich had shown me. If I found a tree inside the water, this would be ideal.

"Hello!" I said again.

I heard nothing but I felt people nearby. Not Heinrich and Eric. Others.

The stream ended and came to a fork with two creeks flowing away from it. I decided to take the better lighted path, though the other path had more water flowing. I knew that if I did not find more water at the end, I could always run along the creek back to where I stood now. A single bird flew above me. They weren't usually out at this time. I wondered if the fire had stirred them up. How wonderful it must be to live in the sky. The safest place to be in the entire world was flying above the chaos.

I realized I chose the right path as the stream narrowed and then almost disappeared before giving way to a beautiful scene. Up ahead, I could see a lake with a waterfall. Sunlight danced across the blue water. Flowers grew here. I had not seen flowers in a while. Lily pads covered the edges of the water, and fish circled around. This lake was a miracle, the most beautiful thing I had seen in a long time. The creek became deeper. The water was at my knees, then my thighs, then my chest until I was swimming. I swam into the lake and toward the waterfall. I knew I could sleep on the rocks behind the falling water and be safe.

That was when I saw her.

There are moments in life that we never forget. Some of these vivid moments are horrible things that happen, like when I lost my mom or saw the infected attacking for the first time. It seemed I had too many of these bad memories. Then there are good moments that you will never forget. I would never in my entire life forget the first time I saw real beauty. It was in the forest under a waterfall. I sucked my breath in and let it stay there.

She was standing under the waterfall wearing only a pair of shorts, bathing. I felt embarrassed staring, but I just couldn't look away. Her hair was dark like the night, falling all the way down her back. Her skin was the color of copper. Her back muscles tightened as she smoothed her dainty hands over her hair. Her legs were long, but she wasn't tall like my mother. She was smaller framed. As I stood in the light staring at her, our eyes met.

I exhaled loudly. Her eyes were dark, almost black.

She crouched down, growled at me, and then leapt through the waterfall, disappearing behind it.

I laughed.

"I won't hurt you. I'm sorry I stared at you. It's just I have not seen anyone as pretty as you before, and I was stunned. Please accept my apology?"

Pathetic. I thought I was pathetic. That sounded ridiculous. I had just met this girl, who was obviously scared, and the only thing

I could say in that moment was that she was the prettiest girl I had ever seen. I considered just letting myself drown.

I was swimming through the water now toward the waterfall.

"Look, I'm not infected." I picked up the water and drank it.

I realized I seemed desperate, and this made me swim back a little.

"See, not infected," I said, twirling around playfully.

I couldn't be positive but I thought I saw this beautiful girl smile. I climbed onto the rocks and stood in front of the falling water, looking through to her.

"Look, I know I probably seem like the worst type of person right now. I'm sorry I stared at you. You surprised me."

I looked down.

"I'm not a creep, I promise."

I looked through the veil of water that separated us. I stared into her dark eyes, and she stared back. We stood like that for a moment. Saying nothing. I thought my heart was going to explode in my chest.

Then she reached her hand through the water, grabbed my neck, and pulled me through. I really didn't care where Eric was; in this moment, there was just me and her.

"Stop staring at me and say something. I asked your name?" the girl said.

"I am Joel, son of Christopher, and I came from the east. What is your name?"

She was trying not to laugh as she said, "I am Jordan, daughter of no one. I come from this waterfall."

"What do you mean daughter of no one?"

"Well, my parents died when I was little, I don't remember them. They left me with my uncle." She shuddered. "He was horrible to me. He was a really bad man."

She looked down and covered her body.

"Turn around," she said.

I turned around, and she said, "Okay, I'm done."

When I turned back around, she had dressed herself in a dingy torn T-shirt.

"How long have you been living here?" I asked, looking around at her makeshift home behind the water in the cave.

"About a year. Those things can't dig through rock, you know. I hear them behind the wall, but they can't get through."

"What do you mean you hear them behind the rocks?" I asked.

"They live in the ground, you know. That's where they hide in the rain. They built caves under there. I hear them digging. I have heard them digging for a year."

That made sense. That's why I couldn't feel them in the rain.

"How do you eat?" I asked.

"Excuse me?" Jordan said, standing up. "You think because I'm a girl I can't fish?"

Then she did a backflip, grabbed a knife, and had me pinned against a wall before I could even respond.

"Okay," I laughed. "I'm sorry, obviously I underestimated you completely."

"I was a gymnast, you know, when I was younger. Well, I mean I learned from my mom before she passed away."

"I thought you said you don't remember your parents," I asked, confused.

"I really don't like to," she said.

I knew what she meant, and so I let it be. Losing your parents is painful.

"Can you teach me how to flip like that?" I asked. "Can you spot me?" I smirked at her.

She punched my arm, catching my joke on her size compared to mine. She really looked completely delicate. I couldn't believe this was the same girl that had me pinned to a wall a few minutes before.

"So what are you doing out here? How did you get out here… and how have you not been bitten?" she asked accusingly.

"I am going west. I walked here and I have been bitten hundreds of times," I said, eyes locked on hers. I turned my head away. For some reason, the acceptance from this beautiful girl was so important to me.

She backed away from me, terrified. "What are you?"

"My father was bitten before I was conceived. I am a half-infected, half-human hybrid," I said to her. "I know it's crazy to hear that…it's crazy for me to say it too. I kept that secret from people my whole life."

"So you've been bitten and, like, you just don't turn into one?" she questioned.

"I don't turn into one, and my skin completely heals. I don't even have scars," I told her.

"You're lying, right?" She laughed and punched my arm.

I didn't laugh. I could tell that my expression was enough to convince her.

She thought about it for a minute.

"Do you think you're the only one like that? Do you think there are others?" she asked.

"I'm not sure. I never found anyone or heard of anyone yet on my travels. In fact, I've only found two of you on your own and one village of people so far on my journey."

She sat on the floor of the cave and crossed her legs, then she put her hands on the ground, and the next thing I knew, she was standing on her head.

"I get really bored in here by myself," she said. "You should try this. When all the blood rushes to your head, you get really dizzy."

"How old are you?" I asked curiously.

"How old do I look?" she said playfully, batting her eyes.

"Twelve?" I said. Again, she punched my arm. I had expected it.

"I'm eighteen," she said, twirling around on her feet, "almost nineteen." When she twirled, she reminded me of my mother.

"My mother was a dancer. I spent my childhood watching her dance like that. I'm almost nineteen, too, in four months."

She looked pained as she stared at me.

"Is she dead?" she asked.

"Yes, she was bitten. She dove in the water. My father, too, before I was born," I told her.

"I'm sorry," she said. "Hey!" she shouted almost too loudly. "I have something to show you. Come sit down with me."

I sat down and she showed me her treasures. She showed me a locket that had a picture of her parents when she opened it. She showed me a jewelry box with a little ballerina inside that twirled around and played a song when it was wound. She also showed me where she kept her food and where she slept.

We sat and talked for hours. I had never met anyone so full of life before her. She was excited to hear about my travels and my town. She laughed at my jokes, and we teased each other. It was like we had been friends for years.

"Have you seen anyone else out here?" I asked her.

"One time," she said, looking around the cave. "One time, these men came through. They were talking about things they had done. Terrible things. They were bad men. They were talking about staying the night behind the waterfall. I can fight…but I knew I couldn't fight all of them off."

"What did you do?" I asked her, leaning forward.

"I waited until they were close enough, and I started growling like the infected." She laughed. "I'd heard them enough that I had basically mastered their sounds. The men got scared and ran off."

"Do you know where they went?" I asked her.

"They ran down the creek that leads here. I never saw them again." She pointed down the path I had come from.

"Will you come with me? To the west?" I asked.

I took her hand in mine. If she said no, I was afraid I might stay in this waterfall with her forever.

"Yeah, I'll come," she said, smiling. "I have to protect you, you know."

She winked at me.

"I have to burn this," I told her, pointing to the forest.

"But…it's beautiful. Why?" she asked.

"I know, and someday it will be beautiful again, but I have to burn the forests to connect the towns so that people can move across the land safely. Otherwise, I'm afraid in a few years there won't be any more people."

I looked at her, hoping for approval.

"I trust you," she said, smiling.

We looked through the water and, seeing it was still daylight, decided we could make it back to Eric and the boat. Jordan talked the whole way back to the boat. It was nice to have something to fill the silence that had overtaken my life. I had not had a conversation like this since my mother passed.

The walk seemed to go quickly as though no time had passed. I stuck to the trails, and just like she was my shadow, Jordan moved with me when the trails edged toward darkness. Her movements were different from mine. My movements were bigger, but her movements were more graceful. Jordan told me about dreams that she had about being rescued. She said she always felt like someone was coming for her and someone would save her.

"It's the only thing that got me through this with my sanity," she said, smiling at me. "When I was little, my mother used to read me a story about a princess who was locked in a tower. Then one day, a prince came and rescued her. I guess you're kind of like a prince." She smiled at me.

"Then that would make you the princess." I smiled back.

"What if I'm the dragon who tried to fight the prince?" she said, laughing.

"Not a chance." I laughed too.

We made our way to a stream and sat by it, and I handed her a canteen. The water was clearer, and I could see it bustling with fish.

"You want to see what I can do?" I asked.

I proceeded to reach down and grab two fish. Instead of being impressed by my skills, she poked her lips out and gave me a look like she wasn't impressed.

"You want to see what I can do?" she asked.

She stood up, grabbed a big rock, walked down the stream, and stood in the shallow part. She held the rock up over the water and dropped it. She then discarded the rock and came back with three dead fish.

"I killed them, too…now we just need a fire," she said.

I put the fish in my pack and told her we would share with Eric and Heinrich when we got back to the boat. I could see the shore up ahead and I started to feel excited to introduce her to both of them.

When we had exited the forest, I started a fire. I added in dry bits from the forest floor until the flame had caught. It spread slower than the last time I had lit. I watched the flame spread first across the forest floor, and then it started to climb a dead tree. When we saw the fire was spreading, we made our way to the water.

"There in the water, do you see it?" I asked.

"That is your boat?" She laughed. "I can't believe it floats. Are we swimming out there?"

"Yeah, and I'll race you," I said as we ran to the water.

I was amazed at how fast Jordan was. For being human, she could really keep up well. We hit the water and raced. I let her beat me to the raft as I shouted out to Eric she was safe and with me.

"Well, look at what he found in the forest," Eric said, nudging Heinrich.

"I was getting nervous. I considered going in after you," Heinrich said.

I laughed. "I told you to give me two days, it hasn't even been one. Is Eric really that bad to be alone with?"

Heinrich gave me a look.

"Did you get it lit?" he asked.

"Yeah, let's spend a day here to make sure the fire spreads," I responded.

We watched as the smoke rose to the sky. I saw tears in Jordan's eyes as she kissed her hand and bid a farewell to her home.

"Jordan, you never told me where you're from," I said to her.

"It doesn't matter," she said, watching the smoke rise.

"Why not?" I asked her.

"Because it no longer exists. I was the only survivor. Those things killed everyone." She held the locket in her hands.

"Did those things kill your uncle too? The one who you said was a bad man?" I asked.

I immediately regretted asking her when she didn't answer.

"No, they didn't." She paused. "I did."

CHAPTER 7

THE BOOK OF JUSTICE

We floated in silence while we watched the smoke fade into the night sky. I sat with Jordan, our legs in the water. Eric and Heinrich played chess behind us. I heard Eric complaining that Heinrich took too long to make a move. The truth was that Eric was so good at chess he couldn't wait to make the other person realize their move was a mistake.

"Fire is kind of beautiful," Jordan said. "It's kind of scary, too, but also beautiful, especially at night."

She leaned over and splashed me with water. We both laughed.

Jordan hummed in the darkness. Her voice was beautiful even without words. I stared at her in the dark. She was truly the only woman I had ever noticed. She stared at the stars and traced her hands in the water.

"Do you think they can hear us?" she said quietly to me.

"Who?" I asked.

"Our parents," she said, staring at the stars.

"I think they can. I like to believe that," I said to her.

"My parents weren't brave like yours. They didn't go into the water." She looked down. "They tried to hold on as long as they could to take care of me. Then one day, they became people I didn't recognize anymore. I had no choice but to leave. The only place to go was with my uncle," Jordan said, looking away from me.

A tear fell down her cheek.

"That doesn't mean they weren't brave, Jordan," I said, looking at her.

"How so?" She didn't look at me.

"They loved you. Maybe they thought they could fight it." I gently cupped Jordan's chin in my hand so she was looking at me. "Maybe you were just too hard to leave behind."

We were interrupted by an argument breaking out between Eric and Heinrich over their game of chess.

"You always want to play, and the game lasts five minutes," Heinrich said.

"Well, don't make bad moves," Eric replied, laughing. He took a swig from his moonshine jar. "Anyone want a drink?" he asked. "Illinois's finest."

"I'll have one." Jordan popped up and walked to Eric.

She took a swig and then immediately spit it into the water.

"Yeeccccchhhh. Eric, that's so gross." She dry-heaved a few times before recovering and then walked back and sat next to me.

I laughed. She was funny. I wasn't brave enough to drink anything Eric created or carried around with him.

"Put that candle out, man, save it," Heinrich said. "We should get some sleep."

Eric obliged. We lay down on the boat and moved toward the center as not to throw the boat off its axis. The last thing we wanted was to tumble into the water in a deep sleep.

"The fire is kind of nice," Eric said. "It's like having a nightlight." He laughed. "You youngins don't remember those, do you? You weren't allowed to be afraid of the dark."

"We weren't allowed to be afraid of anything," Jordan said under her breath.

I turned over to tell her something, and she had already fallen asleep. I didn't think Jordan could be any more beautiful than the way she was during the day, but asleep, she was even more beautiful.

"You can be the princess," I whispered to her.

Jordan snored. I watched her. Hearing her snoring made me smile. I was already a light sleeper, but hearing her snore kept me up longer. I didn't mind it, though. I found it comforting in a way I hadn't felt for a long time. Listening to her snore made me drift off to sleep deeper than I had during the journey.

*****

"Hey, wake up!" A foot kicked the boat.

I opened my eyes and sprang up, ready to defend us. I had messed up. I was usually on alert when asleep.

"Whoa, brother, calm down," a man said.

His hair was tucked behind his ears, a pipe hung from his mouth. "You landed in our camp. We just want to make sure you're trustworthy." He grinned.

At this point, we were all on alert. Jordan stood behind me. Eric and Heinrich stood on the other side of the boat. We all stared straight at these strangers.

"My name is Lyle," the man said, extending his hand.

The moment I reached to shake Lyle's hand became slow motion when my brain connected to a familiar sound. The sound of a bow pulling taunt and then releasing an arrow permeated my consciousness, and in that moment, I jumped left to intercept. I caught the arrow right before it pierced Eric's heart.

"What is this?" I yelled angrily at Lyle.

"Hey! Whoever shot that will have to deal with me," Lyle said, turning toward his men.

I sized up his camp. There were about fourteen men I could see, including the shooter, who nervously ran from the bushes toward us.

"I'm sorry!" the man shouted. "I made a mistake."

"Yeah. Don't make it again," Lyle scolded. The man sulked away.

"Sorry about that. That's no way to welcome new company," Lyle said, again extending his hand. "I apologize, we're just on edge after encountering so many bad men."

"It's okay," I said. "I understand. Let us just dock and let me speak to my people, and then we can talk."

Lyle left the boat and went to speak to his men. I turned to Eric, Heinrich, and Jordan, who were all staring at me with wide eyes.

"You realize they just tried to kill me, right?" Eric questioned.

"It was a mistake. Lyle said that they met a lot of bad men," I said, trying to convince them.

"What if they are the bad men?" Heinrich questioned.

"No, they're not. They didn't shoot a second arrow, right? They would have shot a second if they were bad," I said, trying to ease their worry.

I could see they weren't feeling as accepting as I was.

"Maybe they didn't shoot a second one because you caught the first one? Did you think about that, Joel? Do you think it's possible that they're up there discussing how you caught that? Maybe you've been living in your superhero world a little too long. What you just did is impossible, and they're scared of it. I bet they're discussing a way to kill you so they can pick us off. You should also think about Jordan. I haven't seen one lady yet. I did see how Lyle looked at her, though, and I don't like it. I say we keep moving. We just push off, and you catch the arrows they shoot as we float away," Eric mumbled to himself as he finished talking.

"Let's just give them a chance," I said. "They're human. There aren't many of us left. Let's just get off the boat, get to know them. If I'm wrong, we will leave, I promise."

I looked at Jordan first and squeezed her hand. She nodded in approval, as did Heinrich.

"Okay, man, I'll do your bidding. I'll get off this boat. I'll try, but if one more arrow comes near me, I'll leave you all here." Eric grudgingly threw the anchor in the water. He took a big swig of moonshine and stepped off the boat.

"How long were we asleep?" I asked the others.

"Based on the moon, I would say we were out about two hours," Eric said.

The men's camp was well kept. They had a tent area, plenty of food and water, and a weapons arsenal. Their tents consisted of old clothing and bedsheets that had been stitched together and were tied onto poles. I was surprised they chose to sleep on the ground, and I wondered how that had worked out in their favor. I realized after looking around the camp that the tents were on a dry island that existed inside the tide waters. Their camp was slightly elevated. I wasn't sure if they had built it this way or this is just how this piece of land was. I watched how the men interacted, trying to gauge this group. It seemed that Lyle was the top of the chain here. They needed his approval for even the smallest of tasks. I realized that there were really two options in this situation. Either Lyle offered the men fear or he offered them hope. There was no in between.

In total, there were sixteen men of all ages. They lit a fire and shared food. We spoke of the infected, the water, the bad men they had encountered. I waited for the question I knew was coming.

"Where are you guys from?" I asked.

Nothing but stares.

"You're new here," Lyle said, smiling. "We don't hold on to the past. It's too painful, you know." He took a drag of his pipe and blew it into the night sky. "We aren't who we were in the old world. We evolved for this new world." He smiled again.

I watched his smiles. I tried to gauge his sincerity. It was hard. I wanted to believe him. This journey might have caused me to be more accepting than I should be. I was aware of that, but I was also nervous because of the arrow. I hadn't told Eric at that moment. They said they made a mistake; maybe they did.

"Hey, uh, how'd you catch that arrow like that?" Lyle asked.

I watched the other men lean forward. I don't know why I seemed surprised by their curiosity. I looked at Eric, who sat across from me. He shook his head no at me. When Lyle looked over, Eric acted as if he had been looking in the sky at the birds. I realized in that moment that Eric still didn't trust these men.

"You know, I think I need to use the restroom," Eric said. "Where would I go to do that?"

Lyle pointed to an opening in the forest that was still within the tide.

"Okay, thank you." Eric bowed, eyeing me. "Please don't shoot me in the back when I walk away, okay, sir?" He curtsied.

Two of Lyle's men got up.

"They'll go with you for protection." Lyle smiled. I still couldn't read him.

"No need, I have to go too." Heinrich stood up and followed Eric.

They walked away toward the forest. I took Jordan's hand in mine.

"You good?" I asked her.

"I'm okay," she said, flashing a false smile.

She wasn't okay. She was scared.

Just then, Eric and Heinrich came back from the forest. They looked as if something concerned them. I could see Eric, red in the face, fuming. He kicked over a lantern that was sitting on the sand. He walked right up and faced Lyle.

"Want to tell me why there is a whole pile of human bones back there?" he asked, hands clenched. He spit right at Lyle's feet.

The men stood up in defense. Lyle held his hand up.

"Stay down. Stay down!" he shouted. "I can explain. We've had camp here for fifteen years. We've met a lot of bad people out here. Some came and tried to rob us. Some came and tried to kill us. We've done what we had to in order to survive. We aren't monsters. There are monsters in this world both infected and not, and we are not them. I promise." He smiled at me. A fake smile. I saw it. For the first time, I understood.

"It's getting late. Let's get some shut-eye. The tide already closed in our tents, so we are safe on this dry patch. Tomorrow we can work all this out." Again, he smiled.

Fake. Fake smile. How had it taken me so long to read him?

The tide had supposedly come in, creating an island for Lyle and his men for fifteen years. I was surprised they put so much faith in nature. I had seen the village Heinrich's family had built in twenty years. This camp looked like they had just arrived.

We went to the tent that Lyle had assigned to us and settled in. None of us lay down. We were all on alert, but Eric was the most nervous of us.

"You guys don't even remember the old world. You never saw a movie, none of you. Well, maybe Heinrich when he was, like, three. Anyways, they used to make horror films about murderers. Someone who was trusting would fall asleep, and then a murderer would break in and gut them. This is a horror movie, guys. There isn't enough moonshine in the world to make me sleep right now." Eric sat up and peeked out of our tent. "They aren't moving. What are they doing? They're planning something." He bit his nails as he watched them.

The tide water created a moat about a foot deep. I hadn't forgotten what Eric had said about the pile of bones, and I wanted to see it for myself before deciding how I felt about these new people. Earlier he had told me that the bones weren't within the tide. They were just beyond. Eric hadn't gotten a good look at the pile because he didn't want to cross the tide waters. He could only tell they were human.

"I need to go to the bathroom," I said, looking at Eric and Heinrich.

"Liar, liar, pants on fire," Eric said, taking another drink of moonshine. "You want to see the bones. Go ahead, see if I'm lying."

I left the tent and headed toward the forest. There were small amounts of light coming from the campfires of the men. I could see the men sitting inside their tents, awake. I saw one sharpening a knife. I wondered to myself what he would need thar for.

"Where are you headed?" Lyle poked his head out of a tent.

"Just need to use the bathroom," I said with the same false smile on my face he had given me.

"Well, be careful. Those things are out there when you cross the tide," Lyle said, pointing.

"Okay, buddy, thanks for the warning," I said, and this time my smile was genuine. I lit a stick off a fire for a torch. What Lyle didn't know was that I couldn't hear any of the infected near us. I knew I was safe.

I carried my makeshift torch toward the forest where I had seen Eric and Heinrich enter earlier. The tide rushed in front of my feet, and I took a deep breath as I stepped over it into the forest. I was as quiet as possible. I didn't sense the infected here, but I didn't want to attract them either. I tiptoed deeper away from camp.

I wasn't far into the forest when I discovered the pile of bones. I thought about what Lyle had told me about being camped here for fifteen years and the bad men they met. I thought about how, in my own town during the initial stages of the virus, seemingly good people robbed others. These times can make people truly desperate. I understood Lyle and his men had to defend themselves. There are monsters in this world that aren't infected. Lyle was right.

That was when I saw it. There lying among the bones was a tiny skull. I walked over to it, picked it up, and held my torch to it, and in that moment, I realized this was the skull of a baby. As I looked among the pile, I saw many small skulls.

I fell backward with the baby's skull in my hand.

"They killed children," I whispered to myself. I stood up, staring at this innocent child's remains. I thought about Lyle, about the fake smile, about the arrow. I stood up and ran toward camp. I leaped over the tide.

"You killed children!" I shouted as I ran from the forest toward Lyle's tent.

I ran to Lyle's tent and I ripped it from the stakes. In my hand, I held the baby's skull I found in the pile.

"Explain," I said to him.

My eyes were locked on him, and he started to search from side to side.

"Don't bother plotting," I said to him.

He smiled at me, shaking his head.

"Let me guess. You think you're just going to sail around this world and find men like me and get rid of us, right? Is that what you think? Did you think you would come stay with me and we would rename this place Smiley Island?" He laughed. His men laughed. "That's not how this world works anymore. The world got tough, and we got tougher." He stepped toward my face.

"You think that's tough?" I asked. "Killing innocent people?"

I leaned into his face.

One of Lyle's men attempted to run at my side, and I threw him. Another tried to run from my back, and I threw him too. An arrow aimed at my head was caught. Another arrow aimed at my heart was caught.

I grabbed Lyle's shirt.

"You're not tough, Lyle. People who are really strong don't do things like you." I glared at him.

"What are you?" he muttered to me, taking a step back.

"I'm part of them, those monsters who roam the forest. But you...you Lyle, you're a different type of monster. You're a murderer. You killed babies and children. You killed families. You are a wolf, Lyle."

I could hear the infected nearing. They had heard the altercation.

"Joel, what's going on?" Jordan called out to me.

"They killed babies, Jordan...and children. They're not good men. They're evil," I told her.

Tears fell from my eyes. Tears fell into the tide waters that protected Lyle and his men. I looked down as my tears mixed with the waters that kept these monsters safe.

Lyle sneered. "Boys, we've got a crier." He laughed, and the others did too. "Weak," he said.

I looked at Lyle. I wanted to rip his head off. I could have, but then that would make me like him.

"Eric, get the boat, we are leaving!" I shouted.

"No!" Eric shouted. "We don't leave them, Joel. We can't. If we do, what is the point in connecting the towns? Is it so families can be led to this?"

I stood there staring at Lyle, rage in my heart. I didn't know the answer. I had never harmed a soul in my life. I took a few steps back. I closed my eyes for a moment. I heard cries for help, screams. The same ones I heard each night.

I felt the tide waters begin to recede. I realized that nature had already made its decision.

"Eric, get the boat," I said.

"Joel, I told you we can't leave them here to hurt others," Eric said.

I turned to Eric and nodded. "Get the boat," I said to him. He ran off to get the boat with Heinrich and Jordan at his heels.

I walked toward Lyle and grabbed his shirt, pulling him toward me.

"You are the type of monster who thinks that this world is an excuse for your behavior. You think that because things got difficult, you're allowed to live by a set of rules that only you dictate. That's not how the old world worked, Lyle, and isn't how this world works either."

I picked Lyle up by the front of his shirt and stared into his cold eyes; I felt the last of the tide recede. I heard the breath and snarls of the infected. I let go of Lyle's shirt and walked backward, keeping an eye on his men.

"What are you doing?" Lyle said, confused.

"You're right, Lyle. There are monsters. Some are living and some are infected. I am no judge. It seems that nature holds the scales of guilt. Nature is the one who will serve your justice. Lyle, I will tell you this. Eventually, the bad things we do come back for us. It seems this world, not me, has determined your fate." I stepped backward onto the boat.

"What are you talking about?" Lyle said, scowling.

"The ground is dry. The tide is gone," I told him.

I pushed the boat off the shore as the screams of Lyle and his men pierced the air.

"Believe me, next time I have a feeling about someone," Eric said, shaking his head.

"I will. I promise I will," I said as I took Jordan's hand.

CHAPTER 8

THE BOOK OF ANTHONY, DANIEL, AND JAMES

We traveled across Lake Michigan toward the Illinois Waterway, which connects it to the Mississippi River. Eric told us old stories of the Mississippi River. We listened intently to the tales we had never heard before. The old world was such an exciting place to live in. This world was also exciting but not in a good way.

I had set fire again to the forest near Lyle's camp. The forest was extremely dry. Jordan and I sat with our legs in the water as we drifted, watching the smoke rise. Eric was singing, and Heinrich was lying next to us with a shirt over his face. I wasn't sure whether Heinrich was sleeping or trying to drown out Eric's voice.

"Do you think those are the same bad guys that came to the waterfall?" I asked Jordan.

"No, I don't think so. I remember their faces well. I didn't see those men there. Trust me, if I had even thought for a second that they might be those same guys, I would have told you we needed to leave immediately," Jordan said.

"I can't believe how naive I was to believe that they might be good. Looking back on everything that happened, I should have been able to read the signs better," I said, looking at the water. I didn't want to make eye contact with Jordan.

"Stop it." Jordan took my hand in hers. "Joel, you're different than us. When you see people, you try to see the good in them. It's my favorite thing about you."

I took her hand and kissed it.

"My birthday is coming up," Jordan said. "I'll be nineteen, I'm getting so old." She laughed.

"Hey, I'm the same age!" I said to her.

"She's older, though." Eric laughed.

"How old are you, Eric? Three hundred?" She shared a laugh with Heinrich and me.

"Want to play a game?" Jordan asked us.

"Cards?" Eric asked. "Chess?"

"It's not fun getting beat by an old man," she said under her breath.

I chuckled to myself. I knew I was the only one that heard her. She turned to face me now.

"The game is called rock, paper, scissors. I learned from some of my old friends in my town."

She then showed me the three different hand gestures. To my surprise, the game was actually fun, and even Heinrich started to play the game with us. My favorite part was when she chose rock and I chose paper and I was able to put my hand on top of hers. When I touched Jordan, sparks went through my body. She made my hair stand on end and my heart beat faster. We continued to play for the next hour or so until it was time to fish some more. The fire was still sparking into the sky. The soft roar was comforting.

"What happened to your town?" I asked Jordan. "Is it near where I found you?" I had asked her before, and she hadn't talked about it, but I felt like she would this time.

"Yeah, it was a few miles from where you found me. It's gone. It became too dark, and the trees took over our town. Those things were everywhere. I ran away from them through the water and found the waterfall," she said.

"Why didn't you just light the forest I was inside of?" Jordan asked me.

"I don't know. I felt you, I mean I felt like someone was in there. I can sense people and I don't sense anyone right now. I hear silence in there. I don't think there are any humans in there. I hear them, too, you know, the infected. I can hear them breathing and growling.

I hear them fighting and screaming," I said, looking across the water. "It never stops."

"Really?" Jordan asked. "I hear nothing."

"It's because I'm part of them," I said. I shuddered. I hated saying that. I looked at her. "They are everywhere. We won't kill them all by burning them, but we will create a path so that people are not stuck in the shadows anymore."

"I think what you're doing is the bravest thing I have ever heard of," Jordan said. The compliment made me suddenly shy, and I turned away from her in embarrassment.

She laughed and said, "Sorry I embarrassed you." Then she punched my arm.

"Want to go for a swim?" she asked me. "We could take a rope and swim behind the raft."

"Sure," I said, excited to get away from the other two.

I used one of the anchor ropes to tie onto Jordan's waist.

"What about you?" she asked me.

"I don't need that." I laughed. "Remember, superhuman strength." I pointed to my chest.

"Whatever," she said, shoving me into the water.

She sat down on the edge of the raft, and I helped lift her down into the water.

"I didn't realize how strong the current would be," she said. "Does Eric have anything I can use to float on?"

"Try this," Eric called back to us, throwing an old five-gallon water bottle in our direction.

I caught it with one hand and gave it to Jordan. She used it to throw her arms over the top and floated on her back. I held the other anchor rope as I swam. The current had slowed, and we were able to relax a little.

"How old were you when you learned to swim?" I asked her.

"Oh wow, I don't even know. I've been swimming as long as I can remember," she said in response.

"I was three," I told her. "I still remember how scared I was. The water is the only thing that has ever beat me so far."

"How?" she asked inquisitively.

"Well, when I was young, I went swimming. My mom was with me. She was so overprotective. I used to get mad at her for that. I swam to the bottom of the water and tried to see if I could find anything on the floor of the river. I tried to swim back up for air, and my foot got tangled in an old fishing net." I grabbed onto the water jug to float with Jordan and stop swimming.

"Then what happened?" Jordan asked. "Obviously you made it out."

"I didn't make it out myself. My mom swam out to find me. She swam the floor of the river until she found me. Then she swam me back to the riverbank and brought me back to life. She said my heart had stopped." I looked at Jordan.

"Your mom loved you so much, Joel," Jordan said. Her eyes were teary.

Jordan wiped her eyes and changed the subject.

"I'm done, do you want to go lay down on the deck?" she asked me.

I helped her climb back onto the raft and then pulled myself back up. We lay on the deck while Eric and Heinrich played cards. She took her hands and began to trace shapes on my skin.

"Your skin is flawless," she said. "Is that because you're immune?"

"I don't know. I guess I never really thought about it. Mom always told me that I was abnormally handsome, but she's my mom, so she has to say that." I laughed to myself.

Jordan sat up and looked down at my face and said, "No, I think your mom was telling the truth. You don't look like other boys. Your eyes are like...really blue."

"Oh, stop," I said to her. "You're perfect-looking."

"You need to stop," she said shyly, turning away from me.

"You really are perfect. I think you're the prettiest girl I have ever seen, but you're not just pretty. You're exciting and brave...and smart and clever," I said.

"You're funny," she said. "I'm not perfect. I have flaws, you just haven't seen them yet. Most of them are inside," she said, looking at me.

"What do you mean?" I asked her.

"My uncle used to do things to me, terrible things. I still have nightmares about it. That's how I learned to survive in the forest. I spent so much time running away from home and fighting him off when he drank. He was an awful person. He eventually was bitten, and the coward fed off others. He wasn't like your mom and dad, he didn't go into the water. He went into the woods. I killed him, you know. He came back to feed, and I killed him." Jordan looked at the water.

"That's not a flaw," I told her. "My father used to tell me that bad things happen to good people every day. You're a good person." I reached down and held her hand. "I'm sorry you went through that."

"I haven't let it get to me too much. I realize he was sick in the head, you know. Some people aren't normal." We both looked at Eric, who was singing an old sailor's song, completely intoxicated. We laughed.

She lay there, looking up at the clouds, and started to outline them with her finger. I watched her close one eye and draw imaginary pictures.

"I remember something my father used to say," Jordan said as she stared up at the clouds. "When you realize how perfect everything is, you will tilt your head back and laugh at the sky. He told me those were the words of a very wise man."

"Yes, that's a quote from Siddhārtha Gautama, better known as Buddha," I said to her.

"How did you know that?" she asked me, confused.

"I used to read a lot." I smiled at her.

"Nobody would think this world is perfect," she said. "It's a sad world."

"There is still perfection," I said, staring at her.

"Oh, Joel, stop. You're being ridiculous." She leaned over and shoved my arm.

The next morning, we took the boat to shore to gather supplies and burn.

"Tag, you're it!" Jordan yelled as she smacked my arm.

I chased her down and tackled her onto the sand. We laughed while I pinned her arms back and tickled her. Eric stocked up on supplies, and Heinrich started a fire to light the forest. I lay on the beach of the river, completely enthralled by this girl. She made me smile like nobody before. We ended up lying on the riverbank, staring at the clouds and telling each other what we thought they looked like.

"That looks like Eric's head," she said, and we both erupted in laughter because it did resemble the rectangle shape of his head.

"That looks like a heart," I told her, looking at her and smiling. She got embarrassed and tossed sand at me.

"Come walk with me," she said.

I obliged.

Are you venomous?" she asked.

"I have no idea," I said. "I don't think so. It's hard to say I never bit anyone before."

"Well, there is one way we can find out," she said and walked over, jumped onto me with her legs around my waist, and kissed me. Not the kind of kiss that's quick but the deep kiss where our tongues meet. It was at that moment that I knew she was for me. My body made a promise to her, and so did my soul. I thanked the skies for the waterfall, for this girl who sang to my soul.

"Hey, come check this out." Heinrich interrupted my moment.

I walked over to where he was standing and was surprised to find the remnants of human belongings. A wooden bowl, silver forks and spoons, and a few large pots, as if someone had been cooking here on the shore.

I looked at the artifacts, but they seemed older.

"I don't think these are recent," I told Heinrich.

"Me either, I just wanted a second opinion before I started the fire," he said.

He lit the fire and started the flames.

"We better get back now," Heinrich told us. I held Jordan's hand, and we swam out to the boat.

We all sat on the boat and watched the flame spread. It was a strange sight watching a fire catch and begin to burn, and then two days later, the trees have disappeared and nothing stands in the forest. I still heard them scream as they died, a little more distant than before. The forests burned, and we sat floating, playing cards.

"We will wait a day to continue," I said.

Eric also agreed that this was the best way.

The next morning, the sun shone bright. We decided to move down the water.

I sat with my back turned to Jordan while she slept. I was working on Jordan's birthday gift.

"What are you doing?" Jordan asked me, edging toward me and trying to peek at what I was doing.

"None of your business," I told her as I smiled over my surprise.

"Okay, I'll let it slide because I know this is probably for my birthday," Jordan said.

I spent day and night carving away at a piece of wood, trying to make the perfect gift.

That night, we fell asleep holding each other. It was the most peaceful sleep I had ever had. Then a deafening thud awoke us. I shot up and heard the second thud. In the darkness, I could make out rocks protruding through the shallow river bottom.

"Eric, wake up! Eric, we hit land," I screamed.

Eric stood up and squinted his eyes toward the water's edge. The sun was beginning to rise, and the sunlight cast on the rocks confirmed that we had hit land. Eric stood on the end of the boat, map in hand. His face was as white as a ghost as he turned around and looked at our terrified faces.

"The river is gone," he said.

The sun was bright enough now that we realized we were staring at miles and miles of dried-up river.

"What are we going to do? I asked. "Does anyone have any ideas?"

"We could travel in the trees?" Heinrich suggested.

"No, that fire might eventually spread, we don't want to be in there when that happens," I said.

"We could travel the way Joel did when he started. We can walk the river's edge until we find a stream or a creek and follow it west. It may not be enough water to take the boat down, but we could walk and swim it." Jordan smiled nervously.

Eric sat down and placed his hands on his boat. I heard him let out a sigh.

"I reckon that's the only way then," he said. "We've had good times, old friend."

"We will take only what we need," I told them.

We packed dried fish and fruit to eat. I placed mine and Jordan's canteens in my sack.

"Thanks," she said, smiling at me. "You're sweet."

I folded up the sleeping tarp and tucked that in the pack. Eric filled every one of his flasks with his homemade moonshine. I wondered what he would do when he ran out. When I saw him shove his jars and seeds into his pack, along with a sack of corn, I realized he had no intention of running out. Heinrich grabbed his tools and put those in a sack. He handed Jordan a folding knife.

We waited until the sun was casting full light onto the river's edge before attempting to climb away from the water. I leapt off the raft and onto the rocks on the edge of the dried-up river. I watched as Jordan gracefully leapt farther than I and then again to the edge of the river. She was the first into the grass and laughed at all of us as she did her victory dance.

"Come on, slowpokes," she called after us. "There are trees to burn."

I was the next onto the shore. I immediately put my arm around Jordan's waist. I knew this girl was stronger than most men I knew, but I still felt the overwhelming urge to protect her.

"Hey," she said, twisting out of my hold, "that is insulting. I can walk myself!"

"Okay." I laughed at her, shaking my head.

Heinrich climbed onto the edge, followed by Eric, who kept eyeing his boat.

"You know you don't have to follow us," I told him.

"Nah," Eric said, looking toward his boat. "That's the past right there. We can't live in the past." He started walking along the edge, and we followed.

It was amazing how wild the landscape was. I felt like we were the first people to walk across a new land as we walked. It was easy to forget the danger that loomed in the shadows of these forests. I still heard them breathing, waiting for night to fall.

We walked along the river's edge, mostly in silence. Jordan skipped along, holding my hand occasionally. Sometimes she would tell me a story or start to hum a song. I think Jordan hated silence. Whenever the silence started to grow, she had to break it. Then she was satisfied and could be silent a little while longer.

"What is the longest you have ever been quiet, Jordan?" I asked her.

"A year," she said proudly. "In that waterfall."

"I bet you talked to yourself," I said, laughing.

"I did," she said, laughing too.

"Stop!" Heinrich shouted. "Nobody move."

There lying in front of us was a trap. This trap was made with rope and had been recently set. It was the type of trap that would pull a victim into a tree.

Heinrich used a stick to reach down and trigger the trap. We all jumped back and gasped. I crouched to the ground and closed my eyes. My eyes shot open.

"People are near," I warned the others.

I realized I had spoken too late when an arrow shot through my satchel and pinned me to a tree.

Heinrich immediately threw his hands into the air.

"Peace, we come in peace!" he said.

We all followed suit and threw our hands into the air.

From the hill above us, we saw three men dressed in military uniforms coming down the hill, weapons in hand. They were jogging down the hill in a line.

"What are you doing here?" the first man said to us.

"We are on a journey to help others," I stated. I placed my hands out, palms up.

I saw the man hesitate, and then he motioned back to the men behind him, who still had their weapons raised.

"General Anderson, United States Marine Corps," I heard Eric say behind me.

The three men looked at one another and then did something that made me so thankful Eric was with me. They all three saluted him.

"I'm Private Anthony Blake. These fine men are Privates Daniel Colin and James Harrison. United States Army," he said.

They all reached out and shook Eric's hand. This was the first time I had seen this side of Eric. Before long, he was rubbing their heads and high-fiving them. Me and Jordan stood there hand in hand. Heinrich was already at the forest's edge assessing the trees.

"Where do you stay here?" I asked them.

"Up the hill, we made ourselves a home," Daniel told me.

"Is it on the water or in a tree?" I asked.

They all three laughed.

"No, we found a different way," James said.

They led us up the hill and through a lighted meadow. The tall weeds were blowing in the breeze. I marveled at the difference in landscape from what I was used to. There were less trees here and more grass. We followed the men across the wildflower meadow, and that's when we saw the mouth of the cave.

"Of course," Jordan said. "They can't dig through rock."

"Right." James smiled at her.

I felt a twinge of jealousy in the way he looked at Jordan. She must have felt this in me because she reached down and took my hand.

"What we do at night is to seal the cave. I have a boulder that we all three roll in front of the entrance of the cave. Those things don't even know we are in here. The rock does something to their senses. They spend the whole night walking around and looking for us, but it has been years and they still haven't found us," Anthony told us.

We went into the cave where the men placed their weapons at the entrance.

"We will stay here tonight to make sure that we have a place as the sun goes down, as long as that's okay with you," I said.

"Excellent," Anthony said.

We all sat down together in a circle.

"Where are you from?" I asked.

"I'm from Kentucky," Daniel said. "We all are. We were training near here when it all went down."

"It was crazy. One day, we were at basic training, things were tough. Even though this was going on, we were still expected to behave as if it weren't," Anthony said, looking around the room. "Then one day, the lights went out. The drill sergeant never showed up. We waited and waited. Those things started to pick us off. Then one day, we decided to make a run for it."

"That was twenty years ago." Daniel lowered his head. "We've met some bad people over the years. Never any good."

"Do you know where those bowls and cooking supplies on the beach came from?" Eric asked.

"Yes, we do. They came from bad guys," James responded.

"Those men showed up with a lady. They had taken her from somewhere. She didn't want to be with them," Anthony told us.

"Yeah, one day, she escaped and we found her. She was trying to tell us what happened when they shot an arrow straight through her head." Daniel looked me in the eyes. "Worst thing I've ever seen."

"What did you do with the men?" I asked them.

None of them spoke. James changed the subject.

"So what about you?" James asked us. "What are you doing out here?"

"We are burning the forests, connecting the towns," Jordan said, smiling at me.

I didn't bother sharing about my immunity. It wasn't the right time for that.

We sat down, and they shared some of their food with us. We feasted on fish and berries. They showed Eric their wine, and he was enthralled. I lay on the floor of the cave with Jordan's head on my chest. I stroked her dark hair and carefully tucked it behind her ear. Was it normal to love someone you just met so much? I didn't know, but one thing I did know was that this girl was made for me. I had always felt like something was missing before Jordan. She healed wounds that I never knew existed.

The morning came fast as it usually does. You would think that inside those rock walls the screams I heard at night would be muffled. Not true. Those screams were amplified during the night.

"Boys, let's get a move on breakfast," Eric said.

James, Anthony, and Daniel followed him out of the cave. I was happy that Eric had something to focus on other than the loss of his boat. I decided I would head out with them. I gave Jordan's beautiful sleeping face a kiss and then I left, following behind them. I knew she would be safe with Heinrich while I was gone.

"Hey, hold up," I said to Eric. "Mind if I come?"

"Not at all, soldier," Eric said, smiling at me.

We headed to the part of the river that wasn't dried up but was no longer a river.

"Hey, you think it's safe?" I asked Eric.

Half the wetland area was engulfed in darkness. There were puddles but also lots of dry patches.

"It's fine, brother," Anthony said to me. "I think there is enough water around, right?"

He had taken a single step forward into the darkness when it happened. One of them leapt. In that moment, time slowed down. I leapt toward Anthony, throwing the monster into the forest. Anthony tumbled into James, and they both fell into the darkness. More of them leapt. I intercepted two, throwing them into the light. I stood hunched over James and Anthony with my arms up. They growled. I growled. I picked both men up and walked slowly backward into the light. Another one lunged, and I threw the men behind me. Teeth. Teeth in my arm. Teeth in my neck. I yelled for the two men to run as I clawed the monsters off me. I threw the last one off and ran into the light to join the others.

"Have you been bit?" Eric said to them, running his arms over theirs.

"Check Joel," Anthony said. "He fought them. I watched him get bit."

Anthony had tears in his eyes.

"I'm not worried about Joel, he's immune," Eric said to them.

At that moment, all three men stared in shock as the scars covering my body began to disappear.

James looked up at me. "What are you?" he asked.

They all scooted away as if I was a monster.

"I'm half them and half you," I responded.

All three men sat staring, shocked.

"Wow, that's the thanks Joel gets for saving your butts?" Eric said.

"No, I'm thankful, man, super thankful. Thank you. I'm just shocked," Anthony said.

"Yeah, same," James responded.

Daniel stood up and walked toward me. He rubbed his hand over my healed arms.

"You guys know not to go into the darkness," Daniel said. "Why would you do that?"

"I got too confident. I wanted the general's praise," Anthony said. "We messed up. We could have died without Joel. Let's go back. Joel, I want to make you breakfast. As a thank-you for saving us."

"We don't have breakfast," James said.

"I can help with that too," I said as I walked into the dark water and grabbed four large fish. "Let's find some berries, too, for breakfast and also for Eric's new love of wine."

All four men saluted me.

CHAPTER 9

The Book of Sarah and Thomas

The next morning, we awoke rather abruptly to the smell of food cooking on the fire. I couldn't believe how deep I had slept within the confines of the cave walls. The morning sun shone down on the meadow as I walked through the opening of the cave. Wildflowers blew in the breeze. I took a breath of air. It was dry and sweet. My mother would love it here. The smell of fish and berries permeated the air. Daniel was cleaning the fish, James washed them, and Anthony was cooking.

"Today's breakfast is the river's finest bass cooked in a wild berry sauce. We will be having it all week, maybe every week for the rest of our lives," Anthony said.

We all laughed.

"You felt safe last night, didn't you, bro?" Daniel patted my back.

"Yeah, I did." I laughed.

"I could tell. You snored a little." Daniel laughed. "The night before, when I woke up in the night, you were just lying there staring at all of us. Kind of creepy." We both laughed.

"They said they know of a few more humans down the river," Eric said to me.

"We don't mess with them, and they haven't bothered us," Anthony stated.

"Do you know anything about them?" I asked.

"Just that it's a woman and a man. I see her gathering stuff at the edge of the forest sometimes," James said.

"All right, well, we need to find these people," I stated. "We appreciate you letting us stay with you. Would you all like to come with us west? We could really use your help."

The first to step forward was Daniel. He saluted me. "I would be happy to follow you, Joel."

Anthony and James looked at each other and nodded their heads in unison.

"Of course, we are with you, man. You saved our lives. We have only ever existed here, barely," Anthony said, extending his hand to shake mine. "I would say that we will protect you, but I think we all know you're the protector here."

"Thank you all," I told them.

I took a moment to shake each of their hands and listen to their stories. They each were part of the last organized military twenty years ago. All three were eighteen when they entered the army. James and I really connected. He grew up without a father. His father passed away from cancer in the old world when James was little. He had joined the military in hopes of someday taking care of his mother. Anthony told me he always knew he would be a military man. His father and his mother had both served. It was in his blood. Daniel didn't say much. He seemed guarded about his family. If I'd learned one thing from the people I'd met, it was that we should always let them wait until they were ready to talk about things.

I listened to their warfare ideas, from water guns to ultraviolet lasers. Eric drank less today. I found it amazing how these men made Eric feel needed. He seemed happier with them. It was like he found his family.

"How are you planning on helping people?" Anthony asked.

"Right now, we're burning the dry forests. These things have separated us with the trees to the point where we are trapped in our towns. I'm trying to open up the paths so that we can move to find people without going through the forests," I told them.

We spent the morning packing up what we needed from the cave. I found that the more people we had with us, the less we all had to carry. I also noticed that the more people we accepted into our group, the more enjoyable this journey had become.

We all walked to the river, through the cannulas and the echinacea. I rubbed my hands over the lavender as we walked. There was still beauty in this world. I thought about how these flowers were like a trap. They made you feel like you were safe when you weren't. Just beyond the meadow, I could hear the snarling and the growling, and they shifted as we did, jumping over one another in the darkness. Occasionally, one of them would rattle a bush, and the others would look over.

"I hate them," Jordan said, shaking her head. I took her hand. "I don't hate you," she said. "You aren't them."

We stepped down into the dried river to continue our journey to find others. The river had been dry awhile. As we walked, dust flew around us, causing everyone to occasionally cough. Every time one of us would cough, I could hear the growling intensify.

"Are there more of those things here, Joel?" Heinrich asked me.

"Yeah, I think maybe it's because the river is dried," I responded.

Jordan took her foot and flung some dirt on my leg and smiled. I tripped her on purpose and then caught her and lifted her up for a kiss.

"Quit making out," Eric said, shaking his head.

"Okay, Grandpa Eric," Jordan said.

We all laughed.

We continued to walk two by two.

"What is the one meal you miss from the old world?" I heard Anthony ask Eric, breaking the silence.

"Hmmm… I guess if I could only choose one, it would be meatloaf and mashed potatoes," he said. "I wish a cow would just walk in front of us right now carrying a bag of potatoes."

We all laughed.

"What about you?" Eric asked Anthony.

"Mine would be my mother's lasagna. Or her manicotti," he said.

Everyone went around saying their favorite meal from the old world. Heinrich told us about something called a happy meal. He said it came with a toy. It was from a restaurant.

When it became mine and Jordan's turn, everyone started laughing. So did we. We had never had anything from the old world. Fish and berries were all that Jordan and I knew.

"You know, the one thing I've always wanted to try is fluffy bread," I said to the others.

"What is fluffy bread?" Jordan asked.

"I saw it in a book one time. They had a recipe for bread, and it was so fluffy. Not like the bread we make back home," I responded.

"Fluffy bread sounds delightful," Eric said. "Maybe that cow that walks by can also be pulling some fluffy bread behind it. With butter."

We all laughed again.

As we walked along, I looked at the people around me. These were the conversations that made time pass more quickly on this journey. I was thankful for the company of the people around me.

I glanced at Jordan. She walked along, half-smiling, staring at the ground. Her birthday was tomorrow. I wondered if she would like my gift.

"What are you thinking?" I asked her.

"About life...it's funny, right? One minute, I think I'll spend all eternity alone, and then there is you." She looked up at me with her deep sparkling brown eyes. My mother always told me that the eyes are the gateway to our souls. When I looked into Jordan's eyes, I wanted to be a part of that soul. We let the others walk ahead for a moment, and I turned and rubbed my hand on her cheek. She pushed her face into my hand, and I pulled her chin up and kissed her nose. We were about to kiss when I realized the others were too far in front of us.

"Come on." I laughed, pulling her along with me.

The men don't look at Jordan the way I do. They treat her like she is part of the unit. They don't stare like Lyle and his men. I realized that good men are able to see women as an equal. It's the bad ones that see them as something different, as an object.

Anthony pointed down a slow, sloping downward hill covered in yellow grass up to our knees.

"There, do you see it?" he asked.

I was able to see it before the others. There at the bottom of the hill was a small cottage. It seemed like a house out of one of the children's books I had read before. I once read a story about a girl who escaped into the forest. She found a small cottage in the middle of the forest. This place looked just like the book I had read. I tried to figure out how they built it. From what I could see, I think they must have used some type of mold to make mud bricks. I bet they mixed in the yellow grass from this meadow to make it stick. I had read about mud bricks in a book. They used to mix in hay, but there was no hay around here. There was smoke coming out of the chimney. As we walked toward the house, I could see a large circle around the house. The circle seemed like a hole that had been dug around the cottage. When I squinted my eyes, I realized what it was.

"Ha!" I laughed. "How clever. They built a moat."

It seemed on this journey I had found people who were so creative in the ways that they had protected themselves from the outbreak. Growing along the outside of the house were vegetables and flowers. Many different beautiful pops of color caught my eyes. A woman walked out from the house and smiled at us. She looked to be in her late fifties. Her hair was brown with gray streaks throughout. Her round face was youthful and kind.

"Can I help you boys?" She smiled at us." She looked at Jordan. "Oh, and girl, of course."

"I'm Joel, I come from the east. We're on a mission to connect the towns that have been separated by the forests," I told her.

"I was wondering when someone was going to try to do something. Let me get the bridge," she said.

She walked around to the right corner of her lot and started to turn a crank. We watched a long wooden bridge slowly lower its way across the moat. "Come on in," she said.

"Aren't you nervous we aren't good people?" I asked her.

"Bad people wouldn't ask me that." She chuckled. "Also, I've seen you three soldiers around here, and you've never given us a problem. I wondered when you would come meet us."

We walked one by one over the rickety wooden gate.

"We could have just swum." I smiled at her.

"No, you couldn't have," she said. "That's not just water in there. It's electrified water." She smiled. "It keeps the infected out and any humans that might want to harm us. You would have danced if you tried to swim."

"You live here with a man, correct?" I asked.

"My brother Thomas, we are twins. Neither one of us ever married. We inherited this land when our parents passed away. We used to spend summers here as children. We were vacationing here when the outbreak began. Some men came when we were out foraging one day and robbed us and burned the house down. We had to rebuild," she said.

"What did you do for protection while the house was being built? I asked her.

"My brother is very creative. Thomas knew about their fear of water, so he built the moat in a single day. We slept in the refuge of the circle of water while we built the house."

"Smart idea," I told her. Very smart.

"The infected come every night and sit around our house in a circle. Thomas has a gun with infrared that he uses to see in the dark. He picks them off one by one. They don't die here, they run to the forest. He says he is doing them a favor, and I believe he is right. I'm Sarah, by the way." She reached her hand out and shook mine. "You sure are a looker," she said. "I bet you're the one who got the girl, right?" She smiled at Jordan.

I laughed.

Jordan was standing next to me, smiling. "Maybe it's because he isn't completely human," she said.

Sarah looked intently at her face and said, "Excuse me? What do you mean he isn't completely human?"

"Oh, I'm sorry, Joel. I shouldn't have said anything without asking you first." She looked at me, concerned.

"No, it's fine, I would have told her, anyways." I looked around the room, and it was empty. I walked to the window and saw Eric and Heinrich outside examining the electrified water with the soldiers. I looked back at Sarah, and she was staring at me. "I'm immune," I said to her.

"How?" she asked.

"My father was bitten the night I was conceived. The virus had not spread completely through his body, and somehow he passed on immunity to me," I said.

"What about your mother, was she immune?" Sarah asked.

This was the first time anyone had ever asked me about my mother's immunity. It made a great deal of sense that she would be.

"No, she wasn't. She became infected and went into the water," I said.

"Interesting," Sarah said. "I was a doctor before the outbreak started. My brother, Thomas, is a scientist. He goes out and finds the remains of the killed infected he shoots at night and takes samples for me. We have been trying to find a cure for years. I would have never thought that immunity would be passed in that way. I wonder, Joel, would you mind if I took a blood sample from you to run a test?"

"No, I wouldn't mind at all," I told her.

"Good, then come sit down and I'll get my kit," she said.

I sat down in a wooden chair, overlooking the moat and my crew. I could see Daniel outside pretending to electrocute himself in the moat. James almost threw himself into the electric current to save his friend. Daniel then fell on the ground, laughing hysterically. Anthony walked on the other side, looking at the plants with Heinrich. I could tell Heinrich was teaching him something.

"All right," Sarah said. "You will feel a tiny pinch. I watched as she filled three small vials of blood from my arm. "Thanks, Joel," she told me.

She immediately went and grabbed a microscope and a few petri dishes and started to combine my blood and other types of things. I watched as she added drops and shook things.

Jordan used her shirt to wipe the blood off my arm, and then she bent down and kissed the spot where the needle had been.

Sarah walked back, and I could see the disappointment in her face.

"Well, Joel, I am back to square one," she said. "I attempted to inject the dead virus from your body into a living cell, and it separated. In her hand, she held a bird's egg. This is the way we have grown vaccines. I learned this in medical school using the flu virus and chicken eggs. The way I can describe this to you is that your blood isn't human enough to create a vaccine. You're too much like them."

The words stung, and I hung on to them. Too much like them? Could I be like them? Maybe someday I would stop trying to be good and become like that. Would it take over my body?

"Joel, don't worry. The virus in your body isn't an active virus like theirs is. Your body has killed the virus in itself. The fast healing of your body is a medical mystery, but if human beings can turn into monsters, then anything is possible."

Just then, Thomas entered the cottage. "Hello there. I just met your friends outside. I'm Thomas, I'm very pleased to meet all of you." He reached forward and shook my hand. He took Jordan's hand and lightly kissed it. I sensed his good nature and immediately knew we would be great friends. I felt the same way about Sarah.

"I see my sister has been showing you our work." He smiled.

"Thomas, there is something I have to tell you about this boy." She smiled at him and shook her head yes.

Maybe it was some twin thing, but he immediately guessed what she was talking about. His mouth dropped open, and he looked at my face.

"He's immune, isn't he?" he shouted loud enough for Heinrich to come check on us. I motioned that it was safe for Heinrich to go back outside. "But how?" he asked her.

"His father was infected before conception," she told him.

"That actually makes perfect sense," he said. "You see, when you pass on your genetic makeup to your children, they take on certain traits from the father and certain ones from the mother, but see, in this case, your father wasn't really your father anymore, so the genetic makeup got all screwy, and here you are!" he shouted the last part. He pointed at Jordan and said, "Is she?"

"No, I'm not," Jordan said. "I tried kissing him, but it didn't make me immune."

Thomas laughed. "I thought maybe that's why you were so pretty, my dear," he told her. He turned toward me. "You don't look totally human, you know."

I laughed. "So I've heard," I responded.

"It's the eyes. I've never seen eyes that color. They're blue but too light to be human," he said, leaning into my face. "Truly magnificent," he whispered.

"You can all stay here tonight. I want to show you this place at night. You will never believe it," Sarah said. "They are everywhere."

"So what have you been doing so far to help fix this world?" Sarah asked.

"Actually, we have been burning the forests all the way here. We have been burning so that we are no longer trapped in meadows without any way of moving from town to town to see people," I replied.

"Interesting," Thomas said. "Are you going to burn us down?" he asked defensively.

"I won't if you stay here, but I'm going to ask both of you if you will come with us. I'll let you guys test on me all you want, and we could really use a medical team in cases of emergency," I pleaded. It took them about three seconds to answer.

"Yes," they both said simultaneously. "Finding a way to stop this virus is our dream. I think you might somehow be the key," Sarah said to me.

The key. There was that word again.

"What do you mean the key?" I asked her. "I feel like everyone keeps saying I'm the key."

"I mean, I think somehow you may lead us to the right path to create a vaccine," Sarah said.

"Great. How long do you need before we can leave?" I asked Sarah and Thomas.

"We will need tomorrow to gather supplies from the forest that we need for medicines and to pack up," Thomas said.

We spent the rest of the evening sitting around a woodstove and popping corn. This consisted of putting special kernels into a pan and placing a lid over the top of it. The corn would explode and fill the pot and even pop the lid off. We all rolled around laughing at the sight. Jordan and I had never seen popcorn before. It was nostalgic for the others.

"Thank you for the flashback," Eric told Sarah and Thomas. They both smiled in return.

"I used to pop corn with my family in Illinois. We were surrounded by cornfields. Such wonderful memories," Eric added.

Thomas went and looked out the window at the disappearing sunlight.

"Well, I hope you all are ready to see them like you have never seen them before," he said.

He walked across the room and grabbed a record out of a box. He placed the record onto the record player and cranked it. An upbeat jazzy saxophone player filled the cottage with lightheartedness. I knew Thomas was just doing this to make us feel at ease about what we were about to experience. Jordan's eyes were huge. I had never seen her scared this way before. The bridge had been raised already, and we were now just surrounded by electrified water. The humming of the electricity was drowned out by the music.

Thomas went and grabbed a gun and went to the window.

"Come see them," Thomas told us.

We all took turns looking through the night-vision scope on his gun. When it was my turn, I gasped. There were thousands of them as far as our eyes could see. We could hear them snarling, growling, moaning, and fighting among themselves.

"I can't believe they used to be human," Sarah said. "What a shame."

I watched as Thomas began shooting them one by one.

"What do you use for ammunition?" James asked.

Sarah grabbed an old wooden bucket of rocks. "River rocks. Thomas used several guns and built that one to be able to shoot them with rocks."

"Can I try?" Jordan asked. Thomas showed her how to aim and let her take a few shots.

"Everybody, watch out," Anthony joked.

"Hey now, cut her some slack, she got two so far," Thomas said to him.

"I might lose my aim if you say anything else," Jordan said quietly. Everyone was silent. We all took turns shooting the gun, but eventually it became apparent that we were not even going to make a dent in them.

"How will we burn if we will be walking on the land?" Eric said.

"We can walk in the trench that was the river," Thomas said. "We will be safe from the flames if we are below them."

"Sounds like a plan." I smiled at Thomas.

I was happy to have them both with us. I waited until Jordan was asleep, and I explained Jordan's birthday to them. Eric and Heinrich knew, but I wanted to make her day special, and I needed everyone's help to keep it a secret.

"This is weird," Eric said. He was lying next to me.

"What is?" I asked.

"Being here in this house. It seems perfect," he said.

"It can't be perfect as long as those things are out there," I responded.

"I know that. It just seems like such a waste to burn," he said, looking around.

"Think about if we left it. Remember when I wanted to leave Lyle and his men and you told me we couldn't just leave him because people would come through and run into him?" I asked.

"Yeah, so?" he said.

"This is similar. Do we really want to leave some place like this so that someone like Lyle can come along and squat here, waiting for innocent people to walk through?" I responded.

"I guess that's true," Eric said. "All right, I'm shutting my eyes now, Joel. We can't all function on two hours of sleep." He rolled over.

Jordan rolled toward me and draped her arm over my chest. She snored in my ear. I thought about what Eric had said about this place being a waste to burn. I thought about what would have happened if I had met Jordan first. If we had found a place like this. Would I have even pushed on through my journey? I wasn't sure. Maybe I just longed for normalcy. Tomorrow was Jordan's birthday. I wanted it to be the best birthday she's ever had. I thought about the present I made her.

I was just about to fall asleep when Thomas knelt down close to my face. He looked concerned.

"What's wrong, Thomas?" I sat up.

"Ummm… I can't sleep, something is bothering me."

"What is it?" I asked him, sitting up.

He bit his fingernail. "What if this isn't safe?" he said, visibly worried. "What if one of those things attacks Sarah?" he said.

"Thomas, I'm stronger than them," I whispered in response. "I've fought them before and won. I'll protect her and you. And the others," I told him. "I promise."

"Interesting," he responded, running off into the other room.

I knew he was surprised by my statement about my strength and was probably trying to connect my immunity with this trait. I could hear him talking to Sarah. Instead of trying to listen, I decided that I would try and sleep. Tomorrow was a big day. I kissed Jordan's forehead and fell asleep to the humming of the electrical moat and the snarls and growling of the infected.

CHAPTER 10

THE BOOK OF CHARITY

I wasn't able to sleep well; I became restless. I tiptoed over the others who were sprawled across the living room of the cottage, making sure not to wake anyone. I went to the kitchen to get a drink of water and found Sarah and Thomas sitting together across the table from each other.

"Someone sleeps as poorly as we do," Thomas said.

"Hey, Joel, come sit with us," Sarah said, smiling.

I sat with the two of them, and Sarah poured me a glass of tea.

"Well, I'm not human, that's my reason not to sleep. What's yours?" I asked them.

"Age," Thomas said. "I feel like I need less sleep the older I get." Sarah laughed.

"Maybe a combination of age and having a lot on our brains," she said. "This tea will help you relax."

Sarah had a pot of tea steaming on the table. Inside the pot were white flowers that had been steeping in the water.

"Chamomile," she said, smiling.

I took a sip. I immediately felt more at peace.

"Do you guys always stay up this late?" I asked.

"Not usually this late," Thomas said. "Only when we are leaving on a cross-country journey on foot and need to talk about what to bring."

Sarah laughed. "Oh, Thomas, don't be so dramatic." She smiled at him.

"Well, I'm off to bed," Thomas said. "Good night, Sarah, good night, Joel." He nodded.

He walked into the living room and realized there was no room, so he walked back into the kitchen and sat down at the table.

"Never mind," he said. "I'll just rest my eyes here."

He laid his head on his hands at the table. He was asleep within minutes.

I took another sip. Sarah was just smiling at me.

"What would you have been in the old world?" she asked. "I'm sure you have thought about it."

"I know what I would want to do, but I'm not sure if there is a name for it, or if it was even a real job," I told her.

"Well, tell me what you would do, and I'll try to find a name," she said.

"I would like to travel around and study people. I want to know everything about them. I would like to dig and find things that people used to use thousands of years ago so I can learn how they lived. I also want to meet many different types of people. I want to know about religions and their food. Those are the books I liked to read the most. The books about the many different types of people in the world. That's what I would have done in the old world," I told her.

"Oh, you wanted to be an anthropologist," she said, smiling. "Interesting, Joel. That's kind of what you're already doing."

She stood up and went to a box and took something out of it.

"I have something you might be interested in." She showed me a small bowl with a cylinder in it.

"What is it?" I asked.

"It's an ancient mortar and pestle," she said. "I consider it to be one of my most favorite possessions."

"What was it used for?" I asked.

"For grinding things up. Food. Medicine. There are many different uses," Sarah said, smiling at her treasure. "I always wanted to open an apothecary shop. Joel, do you know what that is?" she asked

"No, I don't. What is it?" I asked.

"It's a little shop where they sell herbs and different items that are natural forms of medicine. Of course, I still believe in modern medicine, but I like using holistic approaches too. That's what my dream would have been if the virus never came."

"What made you become a doctor?" I asked Sarah.

Sarah took her glasses off and rubbed her eyes. Then she put them back on.

"Joel, it's been a long time since anyone has asked me that. Forgive me," Sarah said.

"If you don't want to talk about it, it's okay," I said. "I was just curious. My mother told me to be a doctor, you had to go to school for a long time. I think I would have loved school."

"It's okay. I'm fine," Sarah said, smiling at me.

She stood up and went to the window, looking out. I could tell she was about to tell me something difficult. I recognized her hesitation.

Thomas slept on the table, snoring.

"When we were six years old, our mother told us she couldn't care for us anymore. She drove us to our aunt's house and dropped us off. Our mother had suffered from mental illness, Joel. Do you know what that means?" Sarah asked me.

I shook my head.

"Well, she couldn't take care of us anymore. She had also started to self-medicate with drugs and alcohol. You can't imagine this, Joel, but in the old world, it cost a lot of money to go to a doctor, especially a doctor who treated mental health. She didn't have the money. I still remember her giving us a kiss and telling us that she was sorry." Sarah wiped a tear.

"I'm sorry you went through that," I told her.

"When I was little, I always wanted to take care of others. I was already trying to parent Thomas." She smiled. "Then when my uncle got sick, I took care of him. He told me I should be a nurse, so I went to nursing school first."

"Oh, you were a nurse first," I responded.

"When Thomas decided to stay longer in school to get his doctorate in science, I stayed to get mine in medicine. I didn't want to leave him at school. But, Joel... I always liked nursing better." She winked at me.

"Why?" I asked.

"It's different. It's more patient-focused. I enjoyed making sure my patients were comfortable and happy," she explained. "My best memories of working in health care were from being a nurse."

"You're good at that. I'm comfortable here." I smiled back. "What did you do after medical school?"

"The first thing I did after medical school was to take care of women and children at a women's shelter," Sarah said.

"What is a women's shelter?" I asked her.

"It's a place where women can go and live with their children to get help. A lot of the women there were abused by their partners. They had nowhere else to go." She frowned.

"That's so sad. I never heard that story about the old world," I told her.

"It's not something people like to talk about, Joel," she said. "My mother was abused by my father too. I saw my mother in each and every one of those women and I saw myself in their children. I wanted to make sure that they had a chance to love their children and take care of them. I wanted to make sure those children had a mother because I never wanted anyone to feel the abandonment that I did." A tear fell from Sarah's eye.

"You're a wonderful person." I took Sarah's hand.

"Thank you." She smiled. "I don't think of myself that way. I just think I always did what I needed to do to make sure others were healthy and happy."

"Then what did you do?" I asked her.

"Then Thomas and I went overseas. We went to where they needed immunizations from viruses that were already eradicated here," she said.

"Where did you guys go?" I asked. Sarah's life was fascinating.

"Bangladesh," Sarah said. "Thomas studied the viruses and created new ways for people to get clean water. I gave the vaccines and cared for those who were sick," she explained.

"Why were the diseases eradicated here and not there?" I asked her. "Were we unable to get over there to help in time?"

"Joel, no, nothing like that. We were selfish. We only worried about our own people. The old world had beauty, but it was also filled with pain," she said. I could see that pain in Sarah's eyes.

"I guess I only tried to see the good in it," I told her.

"Well, you never lived in it, so that would be easy to do," she said. "You also had a good, kind mother… I mean in all honesty, Joel, you've only ever known this world, so if you're comparing the two, then it would be easy to see only the good back then."

She was right. I only ever knew that we had to live in fear. We had to hide in our homes at night and hope those things didn't get in. We had to worry about our loved ones. Constantly. Constant fear.

"Did you ever fall in love?" I asked her.

"Oh yes, once," she gushed. I saw Sarah's cheeks blush. I could tell she was embarrassed.

"Who was he?" I leaned in, interested in her response.

"His name was Zacharia. I met him in Bangladesh when I was working over there." She took a sip of tea and smiled. "Oh, Joel, he was so dreamy. He was polite and charming and everything I ever wanted to find."

"Was he a doctor too?" I asked her.

"Yes, he was," she said. "He was an amazing doctor. He specialized in treating trauma. The camp we had set up was home to many refugees who had fled their own country due to violence. They went through a lot. He helped them cope with that. He helped me cope with that." She stared into her tea.

"Was he from Bangladesh?" I asked

"No," Sarah said. "He was from Ohio."

"Like me," I told her.

She smiled.

"What happened," I asked her.

"He asked me to marry him, and I said no," she said.

I stared at Sarah, confused.

"Why did you say no?" I asked.

"Because I was afraid if I got married, I would have kids and I would be a terrible mom. I was afraid I would lose my mind and be unable to care for them, like my mom." Another tear fell. "I loved

Zacharia so much I couldn't bear to do that to him. So I did the kindest thing I could think of," she said.

"What is that?" I asked

"I let him go. I let him go be happy with someone who would be a better mother," she said. More tears.

"So he found someone else?" I asked.

"Oh, I'm sure he did. He was quite the catch," she said.

"But maybe he didn't," I told her.

"It doesn't matter now, Joel," she said, smiling as she always did. "That's the past. We can't live there."

She filled my cup back up with tea.

"Do you regret it?" I asked her.

"Every day," she whispered, closing her eyes.

"Maybe you'll still find him someday," I told her.

"Oh, Joel, you're so optimistic. I just love that." She smiled again. "Sometimes, Joel, you don't get a second chance. Sometimes you only get the one. It's important to take it."

"Well, I still believe in second chances," I told her.

"Of course you do." She laughed. "Well, that's why I became a doctor, Joel. I devoted my life to charity to heal the pain I felt inside. I devoted my time to others in place of having children. I gave myself away to others. And now I live with the choices I have made."

I took her hand in mine. "You wouldn't have been like your mom, Sarah. You would have been a great mom," I told her and I meant it.

"I know, Joel. I know now. I made a mistake. I wouldn't have been my mom," she said. "I always imagined having a little girl. I imagined her running around, being wild." Sarah laughed.

"What would you have named her?" I asked.

The sun was just beginning to peek over the horizon. Sarah looked out the window at the rising sun. I turned to see what she was looking at.

"Dawn," she said. "I would have named her Dawn."

CHAPTER 11

THE BOOK OF CHARLES

In the early morning of Jordan's birthday, I went out onto the water and caught two fish at a pond near the cottage. When I came back, I made sure I cooked them in silence perfectly. I didn't want to wake her up. I took the berries I had gathered in days past and chopped them using Eric's knife. I laid the fish perfectly with the fruit accompanying it. I had spent the prior day picking wild wheat with Anthony. Anthony loved to cook. He told me that his family had owned an Italian restaurant in the town he was from. His parents moved here from Italy, but he was born here. He spent his entire childhood in the kitchen learning how to cook. It was his passion, and he had wanted to someday own his own restaurant when he was done serving his country. He told me about how he always thought by this point in his life he would have had a wife, kids, and a restaurant. He told me he hadn't given up on those dreams. He hoped someday the world would be normal and he would get his dream. I liked that about Anthony. He was a dreamer. He had hope. He was one of the most positive people I had ever met.

He had no idea if his family was still alive. He hadn't been able to make it back home to check on them. He told me the same about James and Daniel. Apparently, Daniel still couldn't talk about it. He was the oldest of five children. He was the only boy. Anthony said that Daniel hadn't spoken about his younger sisters since basic training. It was too painful for him. Anthony had helped me pick wheat so that we could make a cake for Jordan's birthday. Anthony told me we could use honey to make it sweet. Luckily, Sarah had some honey saved inside the cottage. I was certain there was honey inside the forest, but neither of us felt comfortable going in. Sarah helped me mix ingredients for the sweet bread that would serve as Jordan's cake. Sarah was a gentle and kind person.

"Parties were my favorite part of the old world," Sarah said to me.

"What about them?" I asked her.

"Oh, I loved everything," she said, smiling. "I loved going to a store and picking out the perfect present. I loved making cakes. The food. The people."

"I've seen them in books," I told her.

"Oh, Joel, I used to try on every dress I had until I found the perfect one. That reminds me. I have something for Jordan." She smiled.

We baked the cake in the woodstove that Thomas had built. Sarah told me he used old metal he found in the riverbed. Thomas was creative. We would need him on our journey.

"Hold on, I have one more thing," she said and excitedly opened a box. She reached in and handed me several small candles. "A gift from the old world," she said, smiling at me. "It's the least I could do for the girl you love." She put her hands in front of her mouth. "Oh, Joel, I'm just so excited. For the first time in a long time, I'm so unbelievably excited about everything. Thank you."

Sarah was golden. She had this amazing spirit inside of her.

"I guess you're kind of becoming like a son to me." She tucked my hair behind my ears.

"My mother would have liked you a lot," I told her.

"I bet I would have liked her, too, Joel. After all, she raised you, and I like you." She turned to walk away and then turned back around. "This world is so lucky to have you."

She smiled as she left the room.

When Jordan awoke, I was waiting for her with her breakfast in bed of fish and fruit in one hand. In the other hand, I carried her cake with her candles lit.

"Good morning," I whispered, inches from her mouth. "Happy birthday, you're officially older than me."

"Wow, thanks, you sure know how to make a girl feel good about herself," Jordan said, yawning.

"Breakfast in bed," I announced. Jordan smiled at me and then gently punched my chest and began eating her breakfast.

"Thanks for this. You know, you didn't have to do all this. This is the best birthday I have ever had." She smiled as she ate.

"Jordan, I have a present for you," I said nervously. At this point, the others had gathered around to watch Jordan's special day.

"What?" she asked me.

"I have a present for you, close your eyes," I pleaded with her.

Jordan closed her eyes and waited patiently for her gift.

"I never knew that I would meet someone like you, Jordan. You are unique and you amaze me with everything you do. You make me laugh, and most of all, you make me excited to live life and to wake up in the morning. I cannot imagine living without you," I said.

Then I stood up and took Jordan's hand into my own and I helped her stand up. I knelt down on the floor of the cottage and said, "I may not be perfect or human, but I will never stop trying to be your prince. As long as I walk this earth, I will protect you and cherish you. You're my favorite person in the world. I want to live each day with you by my side. Jordan, would you do me the honor of being my wife?" I held my hand out to her. Inside my hand was a wooden ring I had made for her. Inside the ring, I had carved our initials.

Jordan seemed shocked as she stared at my hand. She didn't say anything; she just stared. Eric cleared his throat.

"Oh…oh…yes, Joel," she said. "I would be honored to be your wife. I'm sorry it took me a second, it's like I was stuck in a dream."

Jordan smiled as she reached her hand out, and I placed the wooden ring on her hand.

"Are you sure? You paused for a minute. I got nervous," I said to her, taking her chin in my hand.

"Yes, I'm sure. I've known I wanted this since that day in the waterfall," she said, kissing my cheek.

"Me too," I responded, kissing her head.

"How did you know my size?" she said, marveling at the ring.

"When you were asleep and snoring, I sized your finger over and over until I got it right." I laughed.

"I don't snore," Jordan claimed. We all laughed.

We kissed and the others applauded.

My future wife, my soul, my everything. This is the stuff that life is made of. I laughed with Jordan as I swung her around. This is perfection, in a world full of pain to have the most beautiful creation to love.

"I only wish I could send you on a honeymoon after the wedding," Eric said. "Congratulations, kids."

"Well, it kind of is a honeymoon, right? You do get to travel even if it isn't ideal," Thomas said.

We all laughed.

We walked out of the cottage, and everyone was clapping and throwing popcorn at us. The birds swooped down to eat the popcorn. They flew in our faces and swooped to the ground.

"They woke up to celebrate us." Jordan laughed harder than I had ever heard. She was beaming. I wanted to always remember her in this moment, this happy.

"Well, I wish we could have a feast and dance around right now, but we got to get a move on before we lose any more time," Eric said. "I want to be in Nebraska before sunfall."

"It will be a tough one," Sarah said. "On foot…we better move all day even when we need to eat."

Sarah and Thomas had packed relatively light compared to what we thought we would bring. They made sure to go and pick the plants they would need for medicines and bag them before we burned the forest. Sarah packed her microscope in her pack and a few books she knew she would need. Thomas also had books and a few things I had no idea what they were. They lowered the bridge, and we walked across. I watched Sarah and Thomas cry a little and hug, waving goodbye to their home.

"I brought the electricity with me from the moat," Thomas told me. "I could build it again."

"Is it hard to do?" I asked Thomas.

"Not at all. It's actually quite easy…for me," Thomas responded.

I laughed. He was being honest. The rest of us would never figure it out.

We walked to the trench of the river. I jumped in and helped Jordan and Sarah down. We began walking down the desolate, dry river to our destination. As we walked, I held Jordan's hand and rubbed my fingers over her ring. She smiled up at me.

"I love you," she said. "I think we skipped that step. We forgot to tell each other we love each other."

I was shocked as I looked at her and said, "I thought you knew how much I love you."

"Of course, I felt it, but girls want to hear it, too, sometimes, you know," Jordan said.

"Wait, you're a girl?" I joked with her.

She punched me in the arm.

"I love you, Jordan. I love you more than I have ever loved anything in my entire existence. I love you so much that if you told me you wouldn't go on this journey with me, I would stop. That's the power you have over me, but I know you won't tell me to stop, and that makes me love you more. You are my life, my breath, my everything. If you walked away, I would stop breathing. You are the light in the darkness," I told her and then took her hand and kissed it.

Jordan stopped and looked at me with tears in her eyes. She put her soft hands on either side of my cheeks and pulled my face to hers, kissing me deeply, passionately. We stared at each other for a moment more and then knew we needed to catch up to the others. Any other day, Eric would have been hollering at us to stop making out, but today was a special day for us.

"So when are we going to take the plunge?" Jordan asked.

"How about tonight?" I suggested.

"How exciting. We could be getting married on a raft or in a cave or maybe on an island or in a tree. The suspense is killing me." She laughed.

"Or in a dried-up river," I told her.

The fires raged on either side of the trench, but for some reason, we were not breathing smoke.

"Hey, Thomas, why aren't we breathing smoke?" I asked him.

"It's the wind currents," he shouted back to me. "I'm not sure why the currents are this far inland, though. I don't know, Joel, things are really weird now."

We continued down the dusty river, a group of survivors taking on monsters. It seemed like the stuff of legends. I realized in that moment that this was the one thing we all had in common. We survived this. We were strong and smart and creative. Maybe we all met one another for a reason. Maybe we could really change the world.

As the sun started to move across the sky, I noticed our paces picked up. We each handed food around and ate as we walked.

"Let's climb the bank," I told them. "We should find shelter."

The fires had smoldered down a few miles back, and for now, we were safe from that threat. As we climbed out of the riverbank, I saw a pond east. "Let's go see about staying near that pond. We can fill the canteens up."

"What pond?" Eric squinted.

"Trust me." I laughed. I sometimes forgot my vision was better.

We all climbed out of the river bank and made our way to the pond. We walked between two wooded areas, careful not to step into the darkness, and made our way to the sunny pond. That was when I saw it to the west of us. There in the distance stood a large barn with smoke coming out the top of its makeshift chimney.

By this time, the sun was dropping fast, so we started to jog a little.

"Think we're going to make it?" Jordan asked.

"Heck yeah," said Daniel.

The others ran ahead. I stayed at the back with Eric, Sarah, and Thomas.

"Stick together," I shouted. "Nobody gets left behind."

The barn was farther than we thought it was, and I found us all sprinting together in a desperate herd. As we were edging our way to the barn, I saw the first of them in the shadows, watching…waiting. I saw Jordan's terrified face in slow motion as the sun set enough for them to move, and they leapt from the shadows. Thomas shot several rounds as we made our way closer to the barn. Just then, a blinding light lit up our faces, and they stopped chasing us. I looked up to see an elderly man run out of the barn.

"Get back, you disgusting vermin!" He held a shovel in his hands. We all stopped in light a few feet in front of the man. I was shocked to see they stood in the darkness surrounding the barn but not crossing over into the darker areas close to the barn.

"Why aren't they coming closer?" I asked him. "Is it that light?"

"Nope," he said. "The light is solar and artificial. It doesn't hurt them. It's just for me to see who is coming."

"Then what made them stop?" I asked.

He laughed and said, "They aren't just scared of sunlight and water. Follow me, I'll show you."

"Don't you want to make sure we're not infected?" I asked him. "Because we're not."

"Nope, I can smell it a mile away." He patted me on the back. "But you, you smell a bit different," he said as he walked into the barn.

We followed him.

"How do you keep them out there like that, not crossing over into the darkness?" I asked him.

We were all piled in the barn now. It was actually spacious and cozy. He had designated rooms all set up.

"I use a secret that I used for years when I was trying to keep the animals out of my crops. Hot peppers," he said as he started laughing. "I get a bucket of water from the pond and I cut up the hottest peppers I can grow and then I let that fester in the sun for a few days. Then I walk out there and I spray a circle five feet deep. They won't cross it. I can't explain it, except to tell you they're like animals."

We all stood staring at him in shock, as if it could possibly be that easy.

"I'm not pulling your leg. Come here, I'll show you." We followed him around some horse stalls to the very back where he showed us huge crates of peppers. "I was an organic farmer my entire life. I know every trick to keeping animals away from crops. Those are animals right there. It also keeps Herman from running out there," he said, looking up into the loft.

"Who's Herman?" Jordan asked, looking around her.

"Herman, get down here and say hello, don't be rude," Charles said.

We all were fixated on the lofts in the area where Charles was talking, and then we saw it; standing there on the top of the loft was a cat. The cat was black with green eyes. His tale had a white tip. The only animal Jordan and I had ever seen. We stood completely still and in complete awe as we watched Herman jump down to the gate and then to the ground.

Herman purred, rubbing onto Charles's legs.

"This is Herman Roberts. My name is Charles Roberts, by the way. I'm betting you youngins never saw an animal before, have you? Come on, give him a good pettin'. It's good for the soul," he said, showing us how to pet the cat.

Jordan had already picked Herman up and was cradling him like a baby. I could see she really liked him.

"Can we stay here tonight?" I asked.

"Well, I wouldn't have you going down the road and finding another place to stay." He laughed hysterically and slapped his knee. "I'll show you the sleeping quarters."

He showed us each area. Sarah had informed him of tonight's agenda with the wedding, so he gave me and Jordan the entire west loft. When he told us, everyone whooped and whistled. I knew Jordan was extremely embarrassed. I held her hand tight the entire time.

"I have plenty of fresh vegetables and fruits here in this area," Charles said. There were buckets of things we had never seen before.

"We have fish," I said to him.

"Oh, may I cook a feast?" Anthony asked. "Please?"

"Knock yourself out," Charles told him.

"James, can you and Daniel peel these potatoes for me?" Anthony asked them.

They grabbed a few potatoes each and sat down with their pocketknives and began peeling.

"Jordan, come with me. There is something I want to show you, my dear," Sarah told her.

Jordan followed Sarah up into the loft. I assumed she was helping her get ready for the wedding.

"I'll walk her down the aisle and give her away," Eric told me. "I'm more like a father to her than anyone else here."

I nodded in approval.

Sarah offered to perform the ceremony. She had seen many marriage ceremonies over her years. Charles showed us an open area that would serve as a chapel. I didn't know what that word meant, but I assumed it was a marriage place. Charles walked over to a record player and turned a crank over and over.

"This is Etta James," Charles said, shaking his head. "She was the real deal."

I heard nothing as I saw Jordan climbing down from the loft.

"Cover your eyes, it's supposed to be a surprise," she said angrily.

I closed my eyes and then I heard her say, "Okay, you can look now."

I didn't just look; I stared. There standing in front of me was the most beautiful girl in the world wearing a beautiful white dress. Sarah had a white sundress she had packed for Jordan. She had pinned Jordan's hair up so that I could see her face.

"You look beautiful," I told her. I almost forgot to breathe.

Sarah cleared her throat and then began the ceremony.

"We are gathered here today to celebrate the union of Joel and Jordan. These two wish to marry and join their souls for all eternity. Do you, Joel, take Jordan to be your only love, to have and to hold for as long as you both shall live?"

"I do," I stated.

"And do you, Jordan, take Joel to be your only love, to have and to hold for as long as you both shall live?" Sarah asked.

"I do," Jordan said quietly.

"Then I now pronounce you husband and wife. You may now kiss the bride. May each day bring you joy. May each day fill your heart with love," Sarah said.

Everyone began clapping.

"I think Anthony cooked us something. It should be interesting." I made her laugh as she kissed me one more time.

I traced the insides of her arms and ended up stroking her fore-head as I tried to describe her beauty to her. She interrupted me by kissing me every time I spoke. Kissing Jordan was a language of its own. I felt like she knew what I was saying. Anthony had made us quite a feast. He had prepared us fried potatoes with onions. He made us a fruit salad, and we had glasses of wine ready.

"Wow," Jordan said. "This is like a million times better than I thought it would be, and this is the first time I ever had a potato," she said.

We both laughed.

"I'm just happy it isn't fish." I winked at her.

"Anthony, you could probably be a wedding planner in the new world," I said to him. We all laughed. "Charles, thank you for the food. This is the first time Jordan and I have had a potato."

Everyone laughed.

"Wait, I have the perfect song," Charles said. He cranked up the record player again. "This is Brown Eyed Girl by Van Morrison," he said. "My wife just loved this song."

We all danced around to the upbeat song.

"Hold on, let's let those things sing the chorus," Eric said, lifting the needle. We could hear the growling and the snarls of the infected. Eric put the needle back on the record. "I give them a solid 2 out of 10 for effort," he said.

We all laughed.

Charles brought out beet wine for everyone. Eric was picking his brain about the steps to make it. We finished our wine, and then I saw a different look in Jordan.

"Let's go to bed," she whispered. I kissed her.

"Hey, guys, we are getting tired. I think we are going to turn in," I said to the others.

They started whistling and laughing.

Jordan blushed.

"Knock it off, guys," Sarah scolded.

We could still hear the music, and I knew everyone was having a good time. This really seemed like a wedding. She crawled toward me and kissed my chest, and then she kissed my neck and then my lips.

She wrapped her legs around me, and I became lost in her embrace. I felt so close to Jordan I could breathe her into myself and we could become one person. I could hear her breathing in my ear and her heart beating. I held her hand to my chest.

"I love you, Joel," she whispered to me.

"I love you too," I whispered back.

And then we became one soul, one heart, one purpose. Life would never be the same.

Morning came fast, maybe it was because of how comfortable the barn was. I started to wonder if we should all just live here together.

"Congratulations!" Heinrich said, handing us a bag of arrowheads.

"Thank you," Jordan said, embracing Heinrich. "I know how hard these are to find," she said

We used arrowheads for everything.

"Hey, Joel," Eric said, "I have something I've been saving for you for the right occasion."

He opened his hand, and lying in his palm was a necklace. It had a key attached to it.

"Did you make this?" I asked him.

"Of course not, I'm not that talented," he said. "I found it a long time ago floating in the Ohio River."

"Well, it's perfect," I said, hugging him.

"Where is my gift?" Jordan asked.

"Oh, it's right here," he said, pulling out a hair comb.

"Are you trying to tell me something?" she asked.

Eric and I shared a laugh.

"Not at all, just thought you would miss this," he said.

"Actually, I need this. Thanks, Eric," she said.

"Will you come with us, Charles?" I asked him. "We could really use your knowledge of farming. I have never eaten like that."

"Yes, I'm coming with you. They talked me into it last night over Eric's moonshine, but I'm a man of my word, so I'll still come. I have to bring Herman, though. I can't leave him, he's the only family I got."

"Not a problem," I told him. "I think Herman would be a great companion for us all."

"I'm bringing the peppers and my sprayer, but I want to tell you something. It's not as powerful the first few times you spray. It takes time to absorb into the plants you're spraying. It would work better for a permanent farm," Charles explained.

"I understand. We have all made it this far, I'm sure we will be all right." I tried to sound encouraging.

CHAPTER 12

THE BOOK OF DORIS AND NOEL

We walked to our dried-up river path and climbed down into the dusty, rocky earth.

"Climb on my back," I playfully told Jordan.

I wasn't expecting her to leap onto me.

"Did I almost make you fall?" she asked me.

"No, you insult me. I'm much stronger than that," I told her.

It took Heinrich five times to attempt to light the forest before we realized these trees would not burn. We noticed there was much more moisture in the air here. This area was just as hot as all the others but much more humid.

"We can walk a ways and then light," Heinrich said. "Trees can change drastically in an area. If there is one small patch of forest left, it will still work out."

Herman walked on a leash in front of Charles. The others kept making a big deal out of the fact that a cat was walking on a leash, but Jordan and I didn't understand. We barely knew anything about cats.

"Isn't he cute?" Jordan said, gushing.

"I guess," I said, laughing. I didn't want to admit I also thought Herman was cute.

"I can't believe Charles walked away from that barn," Jordan said to me.

"I know, it seemed like the perfect setup," I replied.

"Potatoes are really good. I kind of wish I never had one. Now when I eat fish and berries, I'll wish it was potatoes," Jordan said, laughing.

Every mile looked the same on this path. The trees were all the same type of trees. They were all green. The grass was the same. The dirt was the same. The only thing different was that I was now married to Jordan.

"How does it feel?" Eric slapped me on the back.

"Feels amazing." I smiled at him.

"I remember the feeling," Eric said, looking into the trees.

I waited to see if he would continue. I knew it was painful for Eric to talk about the past and I didn't want to pry.

"It was a Saturday. It was raining. Her dad didn't want us to get married. He felt like I was taking her away. You know what's funny?" he asked me, laughing to himself. "I got a perm before the wedding. Do you know what a perm is?"

I shook my head.

"It's when they take your hair and they twist it up in these little rollers and then your hair is all curly. Just like hers." He pointed to Sarah.

I laughed. I couldn't imagine Eric with curly hair.

"See, you're laughing too. My wife laughed. At the time, it made me mad. I was trying to look good for her, you know?" He smiled at me. "It's those little things I miss the most. The memories. Her smile. Her laugh. Cherish this time, Joel. Cherish Jordan."

He patted me on the back and walked away.

Jordan was walking in front of me, trying to walk the same pace as Herman.

"How do his back legs and front legs know whose turn it is?" I heard her ask Charles. "Wait, are they all legs, or are the front ones his arms?"

I laughed. Jordan was funny even when she wasn't trying to be.

Charles slowed down with Herman in order to talk to me.

"Herman seems to like being out," he said to me.

"I'm glad, I was worried you might get homesick. That was such a nice home you had there, Charles," I said to him.

"What you couldn't see, Joel, is the pain that the barn brought me. Why do you think I had that record?" he said, staring out into the forest as we walked.

I didn't respond.

"I made that barn into a home for my wife and I after the virus hit. It was easier to secure the barn than it was the house." He looked at Herman while he walked. "One day, I forgot to latch the back of the barn. I was still up in the west loft, sleeping. Herman's mother was with my wife in the kitchen area. She had just had Herman's litter. One of those things tried to get into the barn, and my wife tried to close the back gate. I heard her screaming, and by the time I got there, I watched my wife get pulled out. Herman's mom followed her. She was such a good cat, so loyal. I ran down to try and fight for her, but it was too late. She was gone. There were thousands outside the door. I still hate myself for not locking that gate." He stopped and picked up Herman. "I raised Herman and his siblings. He's the last one still living. He's sixteen years old."

Now that I had Jordan, I couldn't imagine the guilt he must feel for blaming himself for his wife's death.

"I'm so sorry, Charles, I had no idea," I said to him.

"It's okay, kid. You didn't know. Anyways, that's why I left the barn behind," he said.

I now understood.

As we walked along, Jordan hummed. Nobody stopped her. It seemed as though we all needed something to get us through this time. The hot rocks blistered our feet. Some of us wore shoes, while others didn't have the luxury of them. I had given one of my pairs of boots to Charles, and the other I gave to Eric. Jordan leapt barefoot from rock to rock on one foot each time. She played a game to pass the time, and I spent my time watching her. I found her unbelievably entertaining to watch.

"Is that you?" I asked her.

"Huh?" Jordan questioned.

"Was that you singing just now?" I asked.

"I haven't sung at all today," she told me. "I was humming earlier but not singing."

I knew I could hear it, the faint sound of a woman's voice singing.

"Hey, do any of you hear that?" I asked them as I heard the sound again. I was faced with nine people shaking their heads.

"I hear a woman. I think we should follow the voice," I told them.

"Yeah, but we will lose so much time," Daniel said. "Are you certain you hear it?"

"Absolutely positive," I told him.

"Okay," Daniel said. "Let's go."

We climbed up the slope of the riverbed and walked along the edge as I racked my brain as to which direction the sounds were coming from. Up ahead, there was yet another expansive meadow, and I decided that this would be the place I would be staying if I lived here. We walked out onto the meadow and kept walking. We had just gone up a hill, and as we made our way to the top, we could see a woman standing at the bottom of the hill. She was singing and seemed to be writing something in a book.

"Hey!" I called down to her. I waved.

"Oh." She jumped back and began to run from us.

"That was about as smooth as when we met," Jordan said, laughing.

"Wait," I called after her. "We aren't infected. We're just trying to find people," I told her.

I saw her run toward a lake and jump inside a boat and paddle a little off shore.

"Stay back," she said.

I ran to the edge of the pond before the others. Jordan was right on my heels. I could tell this girl was only a few years older than me.

"Don't worry," I told her. "We won't hurt you. Are you alone?" I asked her.

"Walk into the water, all of you," she said.

"Are you kidding me?" Daniel said. "We have to get in the water for this girl."

"Just get in the water," I told him. "Trust me, it will feel good after the hot day, anyways."

I walked in the water, and the others followed. Jordan dove into the pond.

"This feels good," Jordan said.

"All right, I believe you," said the young woman. "No, I'm not alone. I live on this lake with my grandma," she said. "My name is Noel. My grandma's name is Doris. We have lived here our whole lives."

Eric stepped forward. "How far does that river go?" he asked.

"I don't know. We traveled down pretty far once, but the current was so strong it almost flipped our boats. Maybe it's changed, but it's too risky to try again alone with my grandma," she said.

Eric pulled the map out of his pack and began to read. "What state is this?" he asked her.

"This is South Dakota," she said to him.

Just then, another female came up in a larger boat behind Noel.

"You must be Doris," I told her. "Very nice to meet you, I am Joel."

"I see you met Noel." She smiled at us.

"Come out here, let me get a look at you," Doris said.

Doris had to be in her eighties. For an older woman, she was quite agile.

"I have more boats, you know," she said to us. "A collection, really… Where you headed?"

"We are on a journey to help people. We have been burning the forests that hold us prisoner to the infected. I started this journey on my own, and now we are ten. Would you like to accompany us on our journey, or I guess I should ask if we can accompany you?" I said as I watched Noel talking with Doris.

They discussed for a few moments, and I watched them arguing. I could hear their voices and I knew Doris would win this fight.

"Noel wants me to ask if we can stay on the water for the journey," Doris told us. "She's afraid."

"Yes, that is fine," I told them. "That is an ideal situation, being that water is still our safest route."

We all swam out to Noel and Doris and climbed onto their boats. We split up to distribute weight. I climbed on with Doris,

Jordan, Heinrich, Sarah, and Thomas. Eric climbed onto Noel's boat with Daniel, James, Anthony, and Charles. Herman crossed the water, sitting on Charles's head. He was not a fan of the water.

"Noel can be a worrywart. Give her time," Doris said to me. She looked at my face and then tilted her head.

"What's wrong?" I asked her.

"Nothing is wrong, you just look out of place," she said with a slight frown. "I'm sorry, that was rude."

"No, it's okay," I said. "I get that a lot."

"It's because he isn't fully human," Jordan interjected.

I had decided that Jordan loved to tell people this.

"Is that so?" Doris said, studying my face. "Well, what are you then?" she asked.

I told Doris my whole story as we drifted out into the lake in hopes it connected to a river.

"Interesting," she responded.

"You doing okay, Grandma?" Noel called from the other boat.

"Yes, dear, I'm fine," Doris responded. Then she shook her head and looked straight into my eyes. "I love that girl, Joel, don't get me wrong. I do…but she will be the death of me with her constant anxiety and worry."

I laughed.

"Are you a religious man?" she asked.

"Maybe. I think I am. I'm not sure what religion, though. Why?" I said in response.

"I just wasn't sure what was behind your purpose," she said to me.

"At night, I hear people screaming for help. I feel like I need to do this," I said to her.

"Sounds religious to me," she said as she looked me up and down.

"How did you get here?" I asked her.

"Well, about twenty years ago, we were trying to flee our town. I was riding with Noel's mom and dad. Noel's mother was my daughter. At that time, everyone was trying to escape. I tried to talk them out of it, but they wouldn't listen. Noel was two. Well, we came to a spot not far from here, and there was a tree in the road. I urged them to turn around, but they wouldn't listen to me. They thought I was old, a burden. I was only sixty-two at that point. My son-in-law got out of the car to move the tree. It was dusk. One of those things leapt out and took him in a second. My daughter got out of the car." A tear fell from her eye. "I tried to pull her back in. She was gone a second later. Noel was asleep. I took her out of her car seat. The car had one of those seats where you could access the trunk from the back seat. I took Noel and climbed into the trunk with her. We lay there all night. The next morning, I found the lake and a boat and I made it work," she said, looking at me.

"Wow," was all I could muster.

"You haven't asked me who I am," Doris said, smiling at me.

"I'm sorry, Doris, you're right. Tell me who you are," I said to her apologetically.

"Why, I'm the storyteller," she said.

She reached into a box on the boat and pulled out a thick book.

"What is that?" I asked her.

"It's our history," she said. "All of it, even the parts they left out."

"Can I look?" I asked her.

"Sure," Doris said excitedly.

She switched seats with me so I could look through. The book was handwritten. It included drawings of animals with descriptions, expeditions, wars, things I had never read about. I was enthralled looking through it.

"You're an artist," I said, looking up at Doris.

She laughed. "No, I'm not. Noel is the artist."

"Will you write about this?" I asked her.

"Oh yes, Joel," she said as she pulled out a notebook. "I've already started."

Doris led us to a boatyard filled with around fifteen boats all tied together.

"I rounded these up over the years," she told us. "The first two days here, Noel and I slept on a rowboat in the open sun. It was blistering. I had nothing but the shirt on my back to keep her sheltered.

I prayed hard. I didn't ask for a miracle, I asked for something that would let us save ourselves. That day, I found that boat right there."

Doris pointed at a houseboat. The paint had completely peeled off, and the boat was half sunk.

"Not only did that boat have a shelter for us, it also contained supplies. There were cans of food from the old world. Fishing poles." She smiled at the boat. "That was my gift from God. He sent that for me to save us. The other boats I gathered over time. I would set out, and when I would see a boat floating or docked, I would grab it and tie it to ours and bring it back."

"How did you navigate the boat?" I asked her.

"See that long pole?" Doris said, pointing to a pole sticking out of the water. "We used that. This water is shallow, Joel. It's only five feet at its deepest. It used to be about eight feet. I feel like it's disappearing."

By this time, the sun was starting to move toward its setting point. Even if you couldn't see the sun setting, you could hear it. The birds were flying in the sky and chirping.

Doris looked up at the sky. "I'll never get used to the birds coming out at night," she said. "I understand it. I definitely do, but I'll never get used to it."

"Let's camp here on a few of these boats for the night," I told the others. "As long as that's okay with Doris and Noel."

Eric and Heinrich started to push boats away from the shore and anchor them. They used the long pole Doris had used to navigate. This area was beautiful. The forest stood back away from the water. In the day, it would be easy to dock and get some supplies.

We chose two houseboats to sleep on. They were anchored and ready. One floated well, one seemed like a slight gamble.

"Doris, is this boat safe?" I said as I stepped onto it.

"Just because it's old and unlevel doesn't mean it's useless," she said, winking at me. "It's a strong one. We'll be fine."

We sat on the boats and shared food. I stayed on the boat with Doris, Jordan, Thomas, Charles, and Sarah. And of course, Herman.

"Are you on the boat with the old people on purpose, Joel?" Charles said to me, laughing.

"I am not old." Doris shot him a look.

I actually did do this on purpose, but I wasn't going to tell them that.

"No, it just worked out that way," I lied. "Jordan is here and she's only nineteen, and Herman is only sixteen," I said.

They all laughed.

Jordan lay at the front of the boat, petting Herman. She had shared her fish with him, and now he was her best friend.

"He rattles when he cuddles," Jordan said, confused.

Everyone except Jordan and me erupted in laughter.

"He's purring, honey," Sarah said.

"What is purring?" I asked them.

"I actually don't know. I never tried to study it that deeply. It's just something cats do," Charles said.

"I can help with this," Thomas said, putting down his book. "Cats purr to show emotion. Their brain signals to their voice box muscles to vibrate. Those muscles are called the laryngeal muscles. What makes the noise is the air that Herman is exhaling and inhaling."

"Wow, I can't believe I didn't know any of that," Charles said.

"Interesting," said Doris. "My ex-husband sounded like that when he slept. I think it was the whiskey causing it, not the laryngeal muscles."

We laughed.

"Fetch my notebook, Joel," Doris said. "I need to write this down."

I decided to step onto the other boat and check on the others. I hadn't talked to them all day other than Heinrich. It was strange. I actually started to miss Eric.

"Hey, kid," Eric said to me as I stepped near his sleeping spot. "How are you doing?"

"I'm all right," I responded.

"Missed me, didn't you, kid," Eric said and he sat up and rubbed my head.

"Wow, the boys are all asleep," I said to Eric. There sleeping on the boat were Heinrich, James, Daniel, and Anthony.

"Yeah, they took turns rowing all day. I think it made them crash," Eric said.

"You didn't row, did you?" I said to him.

"In my condition, of course not." Eric chuckled.

"Hello Joel," a soft voice said to me from inside the house of the boat.

"Hey, Noel, how are you? I haven't gotten the chance to talk to you much today," I said to her.

"Can you come here for a moment? I want to show you something," she said.

I went to the house of the boat where Noel was sitting on a bed. She reached into a bag next to her and pulled out a book.

"Hold on a second," she said as she reached in her pocket and pulled an object out and struck it and lit a candle.

"Whoa, how did you do that?" I asked her.

"Oh, it was my dad's. It's a match that keeps lighting over and over. It was in his backpack when he…when he died. My grandma took their packs with us when we fled," Noel explained.

I watched as she opened the book, thumbing through the pages.

"This is my sketch notebook," she said. "I just… I wanted to show you something, but I don't want you to think I'm like a weirdo," she said, looking at the page.

She held the page to her chest for a moment.

"I drew this a year ago," she said as she laid the notebook in my hands.

On the paper was a drawing of a man in the air. He had large wings that were extended across the page. His hands were raised to the sky. In the sky, the sun shined down through the clouds. Below the man, there were sheep walking in a giant herd.

At the bottom of the page, it read, "*Angelus Misericordiae.*"

Angel of Mercy.

I looked at the man's face. It was mine.

CHAPTER 13

The Book of Secrets

I sat staring at the drawing of myself floating over the land with sheep underneath me. I had no idea what it meant. I handed the book back to Noel. She seemed embarrassed by the drawing. I looked toward the other boat. Everyone was asleep.

"Do you see things like this often?" I asked Noel.

I stared at her as she sat on the edge of the bed in the houseboat.

She was again clutching her sketchbook to her chest. She looked from side to side. She seemed nervous. I could understand Noel's fear. It's hard having something inside of you that makes you different. It's even worse if the wrong people find out about it.

She nodded her head. I saw hesitation in her nod. She didn't want to tell me. I knew that.

"When did it start?" I asked her.

She turned away from me when I asked.

She didn't answer. I could tell Noel had secrets. I tried to think of a way that she would open up.

"I don't think you're weird, Noel. In fact, you're the second person to call me the angel of mercy on this journey," I told her. I needed her to trust me.

She looked intrigued.

"Who was the other person?" she asked, almost whispering.

"Father Siloam. A priest who lived where we found Heinrich," I told her. "He told me my name, my father's name, and even called me the key."

"Oh," she said. "That makes sense, though. He's a priest. I've never even been to church."

"That doesn't mean anything," I told her. "I've never been to church either, Noel, and I've been called the angel of mercy twice."

I stared at her.

She was staring at me but seemed to be looking through me.

"Can you keep a secret?" she asked.

She looked down at her book and then toward the boat her grandma was on. Noel fidgeted with the pages of her book. I could tell what she was about to tell me was important.

"Of course I can. I kept that I'm not a human from everyone in my town my whole life," I told her. "Except for Lois. I told Lois."

"Right, the seamstress," she said, not paying attention.

She thumbed through her book.

She didn't realize how her last statement had made the hair on my arms stand up.

"I'm sorry, did I say something wrong?" she asked. "I do that a lot, that's why I don't talk. Well, that's one reason that I don't talk much. I have so much inside I don't know what's important to share and what's not."

"No, it's okay," I told her. "You can tell me anything."

"Sometimes I see things, and then then they come true. That's why I drew that picture. I started to draw the things I see so that I can remember," she said. "Sometimes I also see things that already happened." She looked at her book again. "It's not often that I get to know that what I've drawn is real."

"What do you mean?" I asked her.

"Well, I only see my grandma normally, so anybody else I draw isn't actually real. That's why it surprised me so much when you showed up. I guess in a way that you were the first real vision I've had other than the vision of my parents," she said. "Or at least confirmed vision." She looked down at her book. "This book is filled with strangers," she whispered.

"You have a gift," I told her.

"You can't tell my grandma," Noel said to me, looking toward the other boat. "She will think I'm crazy."

"I won't tell her. Even though I don't think she would think you're crazy," I told her.

"You don't know her," Noel said. "She's very religious. She told me once that we can't play God, or we go to hell." She held her book against her chest.

"Isn't this pretty close to hell?" I asked Noel, pointing to the snarls and growls in the forest.

"I guess so," Noel said. "It's just she's all I have. I've always wanted to make her proud. She likes that I draw for her book. Sometimes she asks what I'm working on, and I don't tell her... I can't tell her."

"I can understand that. It's the same reason I never told people back home that I wasn't fully human. I just pretended that I was. I would even try to slow myself down so nobody would notice," I told her.

"It was hard for you," Noel said. "Lonely too," she added.

She looked at my face and made eye contact.

"Sometimes you wondered if your dad was still alive if it would have been easier for you," she said.

I sat staring at her, stunned. She looked away.

"Noel, where did that come from?" I asked. I looked intently at her, waiting for a response.

She started to tear up.

"I'm sorry, I was wrong," she said, looking down.

"No, you were right," I told her. "I just want to know how you think. I was lonely growing up and I did wonder about my dad."

"I'm sorry, Joel. That was too much. It's weird how my brain works. I looked at your eyes, and they told me that." She looked away. "That's why I don't look at people. If I do, it's like having twenty people in my head."

"It's okay," I told her, taking her hand.

"I don't know what I should say and what I shouldn't. Like, just now, you already knew what I told you. It wasn't necessary, but I just blurted it out to you. I don't have any control over it," she said. A tear fell from her eye. "I want to control it."

"You're young. Father Siloam saw things, too, but he is like one hundred. Maybe he used to be like you," I told her.

"When did it start?" I asked again.

I had already asked once, but I felt this time that Noel might open up.

"It started when I was little…actually as far back as I can remember I've seen things." She spoke in a low voice so nobody else could hear her.

"What things did you see?" I asked her.

"Well, I only asked my grandma what happened to my parents once. She didn't even tell me, but when she looked at me, I saw it." Noel shuddered. "I never asked again."

"What else did you see?" I asked her.

"I used to ask her questions on purpose so that I could see memories. I would ask her what my mother's favorite color was, and while she was talking, I could see images of my mother being excited about a green sweater she got for her birthday." Noel smiled. A tear fell down her face. "That's how it started. It started as a comfort."

"And now?" I asked her.

"Now it's just part of my life," she said. "I'm the one who knew where to find all those boats. My grandma thinks she found them, but really I would tell her where we should look that day."

"Interesting," I told her. "What about the others I brought here? Have you seen things about them?"

She shook her head.

"For some reason, my visions are only focused on you," she said. "Maybe they're focused on things that I think are important."

"You think I'm important?" I asked her.

"I know you are," she responded.

"I know you're important too," I told her.

She looked down again.

"So you saw the boat's location and you knew where to find it?" I asked.

"No, Joel." She shook her head. "That's not all I saw. Sometimes when I would see the boat, I saw what happened to the family." She started to cry. "That's why I want to control it. I wanted to find the boats. I didn't want to see their pain."

"I'm so sorry," I told her. "Can I tell you a secret?"

I hoped that I could trust her with this.

"Sure," she said, leaning closer.

"I can't sleep sometimes because I can hear people screaming for help," I told her. "I've heard it all my life."

Her eyes filled with tears, and her lip quivered.

"I understand," she said. "I can see them. I can't sleep either."

I reached out and took Noel's hand.

"We are connected in this somehow," I told her.

"I guess so," Noel said. "Maybe we are both the same type of broken."

I looked at Noel, timid, clenching her book to her chest. I realized she was scared. I felt sorry for her. I realized she had something powerful inside of her.

"So Doris thinks she's been taking care of you, and it's been the other way around," I said to her.

She nodded her head.

"Yeah. I let her think that. She needs a purpose, Joel. She's getting older. I feel like if she knew I didn't need her, she might die. I can't lose anyone else," she said.

"I know that loss," I told her.

"You know what I think, Joel?" she asked, looking at the stars.

"What's that?" I asked her.

"You know how my grandma said she prayed when I was little and asked God for something that would let us save ourselves?" she said, looking at me.

"Yeah, I remember that story. your grandma said the gift was that boat," I said.

She shook her head.

"I don't think that was the gift," she said.

"Then what was?" I asked her.

"I think the gift went to me," she said.

"Did you know I was coming?" I asked her.

"No, I don't see everything," she said. "I had no idea you were coming up that hill. I never saw that."

"Did you know I was there?" she asked me.

"Yes, I heard you singing," I told her. "My hearing isn't human."

"Oh. I see," she said.

"Is that why you're so quiet?" I asked her.

"What do you mean?" Noel turned her head, confused.

"I mean because of your gift, your visions. Is that the only reason you're so quiet?" I asked her.

"Maybe." She thought for a moment. "It could also be my grandma's fault," she said, looking toward the other boat.

"Your grandma's fault how?" I asked her.

"Well, when I was little, my grandma used to tell me if I made a noise, the monsters would come and eat me," she said. "And if I tried to touch the water, she would tell me the same."

"Why did she do that?" I asked her.

"I was two, Joel. She was trying to keep me alive," Noel said. "I forgive her for lying to me. She was just doing it out of love."

I nodded my head in agreement.

"Besides, I lie to her every day," she said.

"You're not lying, you're just holding back the truth," I said. "I think that's different."

"It might be, but it feels like a lie," she said.

"I won't tell the others about your gift," I told Noel.

"Thank you, Joel," she said, looking at the water. "It can be overwhelming."

I stood up and started to walk to the doorway of the houseboat.

"Well, I'm going to go check on the others," I said. "It was so nice to talk to you, Noel." I shook her hand.

She stared at my necklace for a moment and then looked at my face.

"What is it?" I asked her.

"Where did you get that?" she asked.

She scooted away and put her knees to her chest.

"From Eric, when Jordan and I got married," I told her.

She seemed confused.

"Noel, why did you ask?"

She didn't answer.

"Noel, please tell me what you saw. Remember, you can trust me," I told her. "Why did you ask me where it came from?"

Noel looked straight at me and said something that sent chills through my bones.

"Because it used to be your father's."

CHAPTER 14

THE BOOK OF SELFLESSNESS

The next day, we docked on the side of the water the way we had planned. Heinrich had said we could continue to burn. As the river level dropped, the trees became drier. I heard nobody in the forest. The only thing I could hear was the infected. Doris told me she had never seen a single person on these waters. I climbed off the boat with Jordan. The others stayed behind. I did carry with me a tool that would make lighting the fire much easier, Noel's match kit. As we waded to the shore, Jordan hummed.

"You kids good?" Eric called out to us.

"We're fine," I shouted back.

"Where should we light?" Jordan asked me, walking toward the forest.

"Don't go too far, Jordan," I told her, pulling her arm back. "Stay near the water."

She sulked a little as she walked back.

"Hey, I love you. I need to keep you safe," I said to her.

I walked to the edge of the forest in the dimmest light. Those things were in there, but my scent wouldn't be strong enough to trigger their senses. I made sure I was quiet. I leaned down to touch a few branches. They were definitely dry enough.

I could hear Jordan humming behind me.

"Joel, I see echinacea," she said.

"I'll grab it before we go," I responded.

"I can grab it," she said. "I'm bored. It's right there in the light." She pointed.

"Okay." I sighed. "Grab it and then go back and sit by the water," I told her.

I heard her humming as she went to pick the echinacea. I grabbed some dry bits of the forest floor that I would light. This place was dry enough to catch quickly. I realized in that moment that the humming had stopped.

"Jordan!" I yelled as I turned.

She was gone. The echinacea was still there, covered in darkness. I ran into the darkness of the forest.

"Joel!" I heard her scream. "Joel, help me, please," she cried.

Just feet from me, I could see them attacking her. She reached for me.

I ran faster than I had ever run and grabbed the two on top of her and slammed them to the ground. Their heads crushed on impact. I turned around to face three more. Just then, I realized they were all around me. I had to get Jordan and get out of this forest.

I ran to her and was hit from the side. I struggled, throwing the beasts off me.

"Jordan, no! Jordan!" I screamed, punched, bit, and threw.

I jumped up, knocking one into a tree, and made it to Jordan. I threw them off one by one, throwing, tearing, growling. I threw Jordan over my shoulder and ran to the water. I was faster than them, stronger. I told myself this over and over. I made it to the light and to the lake, and just as I was about to leap in, I stopped. I sat Jordan on the side of the lake. Her tiny body was covered in blood. Bite marks shrouded her arms, her legs, and her neck.

"Joel, I'm going to die," she said to me, tears in her eyes.

"No, Jordan, I won't let you. I'll take you back to Sarah, we will find a cure." I knew I was lying.

"Joel, please," she told me. "I will die. I want to be brave like your parents. I want to die with pride."

I held onto Jordan and rocked her. We cried together until we knew we had to return to the others.

The sun was starting to move through the sky, and we knew that we didn't have much time. We walked in silence, hand in hand. I had used my shirt to make bandages for Jordan. I was surprised she wasn't more injured than she was; then again, Jordan was a fighter. She was a warrior with a heart of gold. Fire spit through her veins, and her mind was sharp. She was kind but strong, a natural leader.

I stopped my mind from continuing and realized that she was all of these things. Was. They took this from her. I sobbed silently all the way back to the shore where the boat was anchored. I couldn't hold it in anymore and I cried like a young child. Someone should cry for her. She was so many things, she could have been so many things.

I saw the boat in the distance, and Eric gave a wave and a thumbs-up, checking that everything was good. I looked back at him and shook my head. I gave him a thumbs-down.

"It won't light," Eric asked, frowning.

"It will light, it's dry," I told him.

I looked at Jordan. Eric could see now the blood pouring through her bandages. Her pale face. My tear-stained face.

"Jordan has been bit," I told the others.

They all sat up staring in disbelief. Doris and Noel held each other and cried. Thomas hugged Sarah and rubbed her back. Eric turned away from us and drank from his canteen. This was a tragedy.

"I want to be brave," Jordan told everyone. She was shaking, and tears were coming from her eyes. "I will go to the water."

I shook my head no to her, but she reached up and stopped me.

"I want you to have faith and I want you to save people. I want you to know I will always be with you here," she said, pointing at my heart.

She leaned up and kissed me deeply one last time. She turned and ran to the river. I watched as she blew a kiss to me and dove in.

I thought of my mother who had gone to the forest to pick daisies. Jordan had gone to the forest to pick echinacea. I decided I hated flowers. Flowers served one purpose in this world. They made women that I loved drawn to them so that they die. It wasn't just the flowers. I blamed the sun for shifting. I cursed the trees. Nature had tricked them both into thinking they were safe.

"No!" I screamed.

I fell to the ground, beating the earth under my fists. Why would this world give me this girl and take her from me so cruelly? Why should I save anyone? It didn't make any sense anymore, not without her. I looked at Eric, who now had left the boat and was holding onto me.

"You have to be strong, Joel," Eric said. "She would want that."

I laid my head on the ground and I gritted my teeth together. I was frozen in pain, paralyzed. I was ready to run into the dark forest when I heard laughing. Anger filled my veins, and I clenched my fists. I dug my hands into the soil and crushed it with rage. Who could possibly laugh at Jordan's death, at my pain? Who would be this cruel? I stood up ready to kill the person responsible for the laughter.

That was when I saw it—Jordan standing in the water. She was there standing in the fading sunlight with her head tilted back, looking at the sky. She was laughing.

"Can't you see how perfect it is, Joel," she said to me.

I walked to her in awe, through the water. Eric waded after me.

"Can't you see, Joel?" she asked again. "Can't you all see?" she asked the others who stood on the boats with their mouths wide open.

I realized what she meant when I saw her standing there.

"She's perfect, Joel," Jordan said, clenching her stomach.

CHAPTER 15

THE BOOK OF SASHA

"We are safe," I told Jordan, stroking her cheek. She was so beautiful it hurt to look at her sometimes. I could see the deep worry. She was no longer that prancing child I had met in the waterfall. I traced my hands along her scars. Her wounds had healed but not like mine. Her wounds healed like a human's would. A human who was immune to the virus but still very human. Sarah had examined her this morning. She told us that it was likely Jordan wasn't immune to the virus, but the baby caused her to be for its own protection. The baby saved her life. Sarah came over and sat with Jordan. She had been taking her blood pressure and vitals every hour.

"You look pale, dear," she said. "Eric, do you have any berries?"

Eric brought a cup full of berries over.

"You're tough, kid," he said gently, putting his hand on her shoulder.

Jordan placed her hand on top of his.

I watched the members of our group. We were a family. A complete family, I thought to myself. We decided to let the river float us for a while while we figured out our move. I had been able to return to the shore and light the trees. The fire took quick, and we could still see the trees burning as if they were following us. I could hear the screaming infected from a distance. They weren't following us. They seemed to be running the other direction. I wondered what was in the other direction. Maybe the forest was more dense than I realized. Eventually, they would be forced into the light.

We had used the time we had been floating to fish. I spent my time with Jordan lying on me, resting. I was so thankful to have her, to hold her. When she had dove into that water, I thought for sure I would never see her again. I stroked her dark hair and tucked it behind her ear. My baby saved her, I thought to myself. I placed my hand on Jordan's stomach.

"Not a monster," I whispered. "You're not a monster, and neither am I."

This river in this area moved faster than it had.

Thomas and Eric sat examining a map and talking. Daniel fished with Heinrich. Sarah was mixing herbs together in a bowl and explaining while Noel drew them for Doris. Anthony was busy making lunch. James and Charles chopped vegetables. Herman rubbed Anthony's legs, begging for fish. Jordan slept. Jordan slept the whole day.

"She needs her rest," Sarah said, carrying the herbs over.

She mixed some water into them.

"Jordan, honey, sit up. I need you to drink this. It will help you heal," she said.

I helped Jordan sit up, and she choked down the mixture. I could tell by Jordan's face it didn't taste good.

"What's in it?" I asked Sarah.

"Turmeric, aloe, flax seed, and some chamomile," Sarah said. "It may make her a little tired. The rest is good for her body."

Anthony finished lunch and brought Jordan and me our share. I had to force Jordan to eat. I didn't tell her but I gave her my fish too. We had been on the boat for way too long by this time. I think we all had started to get a little tired of just floating around.

"Eric, think we could dock and stretch our legs?" I asked him.

There was still plenty of sunlight.

Eric looked around the boat. "Yeah, we can. We just need to make sure nobody goes anywhere near the forest."

The fires were behind us enough that we knew we would have a good hour to stretch.

We docked and everyone climbed off. I carried Jordan and placed her on her feet. Although I did understand that Sarah wanted

Jordan to rest, I didn't think it was good for anyone to lie there. I thought it would make you feel worse and weaker.

When it was just herself, Jordan was confident and risky. But now that there was another life to protect, I watched her become timid and scared. I watched Jordan becoming a mother, loving someone more than herself or me. Someone helpless. She no longer leapt and twirled; she took careful steps. She even let me help her sometimes.

"Would you like me to carry you?" I asked her.

"No, I don't. I can walk by myself. I need to make sure my body stays strong. Just stay close in case I need to lean," she said.

The others walked up and down the river faster than we did, stretching their legs. Thomas and Sarah did calisthenics. Jordan and I walked at a snail's pace.

"Is your leg still hurting?" I asked her.

"It's not as bad. It's healing," she said, half-smiling at me.

It hurt her to even smile. When those things grabbed her and slammed her on the ground, she had hit her knee on the forest floor.

Before we knew it, the hour was up. It seemed like it had just been a few minutes. We made our way back onto the houseboats. We had tied them together so that they floated in one unit. This didn't always work. Sometimes the boats would spin around in circles. Earlier today, when they started spinning, Jordan had thrown up. She had already changed in just a short period of time. Before she carried my child, she would have been the person screaming in joy about the boats spinning.

As we boarded the boat, we decided on the same sleeping arrangements we had been using. Eric knew what I was up to. I had taken the boat with the older people in the group. On my boat, I kept Jordan, Sarah, Thomas, Doris, and Charles, as well as Herman.

We were all exhausted.

I lay down with Jordan lying across my lap. I leaned against the side of the boat and let myself drift off to sleep as the sun settled into the horizon. Just as it happened every night, I heard the screams and cries of people who begged for help.

My eyes shot open as I heard an unfamiliar noise. A man's voice. Close but not close enough for human ears.

"Eric." I crawled over to him on the other boat. "Eric, there is a man coming."

Eric sat up.

"What is he saying?" Eric asked me.

"I can't tell. I just hear that it's a man." I listened again. "It's men, three of them."

"What's the plan?" Eric asked.

"I don't have one," I said. "Either they're good people and we don't need a plan or they're bad people and I have no idea what to do to help us. In the water. In the dark."

I looked at him nervously.

"Hold on," Eric said. "I have a plan."

He crawled away and woke up Daniel, James, and Anthony. He also woke Heinrich.

"I'm taking the boys into the water to hide in case you need us. We will hide behind the boats. Just act like we don't exist. Heinrich will stay here to help you if anything goes down. I've got this, Joel." He pointed at the soldiers. "We've got this."

I crawled back onto the other boat and woke the others up.

"Listen. I hear men coming on a boat. I need you to be real quiet. We have a plan but just be super quiet," I said to them. They all looked scared. Jordan went and grabbed Herman and sat with him.

"Ahoy, matey," a voice came from the distance.

We said nothing.

"I said ahoy, matey," the man said again.

I heard it. I hadn't heard that noise in a while, but I knew exactly what it was. I heard someone loading a gun.

"Jeremy, just shoot the boat," I heard a man say. "I see them people on there tryin' to hide. We ain't doin' this to make friends, anyways."

"Bad, they're bad," I said loudly.

I needed Eric to know.

Just then, a gunshot hit the house, pinging off.

"Wanna come out and play kids?" one of the men said.

Their boat ran into ours. A man on the boat shined a lantern onto Jordan and Herman.

"Oh, lookey, a girl," the man said. He smiled a toothless, evil smile and licked his lips.

"Jeremy, there is another girl over there," the third man said, pointing at Noel.

He had already climbed onto our boat and made it to the other one. She shuddered and held her knees. Jeremy had tied their boat onto ours, and we floated as one unit of three boats.

"Listen," Jeremy said. "We run these waters. We been following you for days and days." He spit in the water. "We are taking your supplies and burning your boats."

"What about us?" I said to him.

"What about you?" he said. "Why would I care what happens to you? I guess either I'll shoot you or they'll eat you." He pointed at the shore. "We'll keep the girls, though." He smiled at Jordan.

All along the shoreline, I could see the glowing eyes and snarling teeth of the infected, waiting for something to happen. I shuddered when I realized those things were following these men. I wondered how many people had escaped their burning boats to get to shore only to realize they would die a different death.

Just then, I saw Daniel behind Jeremy. He leapt up and grabbed his throat from behind and pinned him down to the boat. James already had another of the men against the houseboat and was tying his hands behind his back.

"Trevor, shoot them!" Jeremy yelled. Trevor took his gun and held it to Daniel's head.

Anthony came from behind, and he and Trevor started wrestling with the gun on the boat. I had no idea where Eric was. As the two men wrestled around on our boat, I led the others onto Jeremy and his men's boat. Heinrich was the last on the boat. He was carrying Jordan and Herman.

"Grab the supplies," Sarah shouted to us.

We all grabbed what we could.

"There, got him!" Anthony said, standing up. He had tied Jeremy to the side of one of our boats and taken his gun.

Daniel and James dragged the other two over and tied them to the boat as well. The three soldiers climbed onto our new boat with us. The only person missing was Eric.

I looked around for Eric, trying to sense him. Just then, the river picked up speed. We started to spin, connected with the other two boats. A hand flopped onto the side of the boat, a knife inside it. I peeked over the side of the boat and saw it was Eric.

"Hold on," he said. I almost got it.

He took the knife and cut the ropes attaching the boat we were on to the two boats we previously inhabited. Now we were all together on Jeremy and his crew's boat. They were floating away from us on ours, spinning out of control.

"Eric!" I yelled. "Eric, waterfall!" I screamed at him.

I heard it before anyone else.

Eric pulled himself up onto the boat.

"Turn the wheel clockwise!" he yelled.

"What wheel?" I shouted.

"In the house," he yelled.

Inside the house, part of the boat there was a wheel. I followed Eric's advice and turned it clockwise. We started to turn toward our side, slowing momentum.

"Find the anchor!" he yelled.

Daniel ran to the back of the boat and threw in the anchor.

The boat abruptly stopped.

We had just a moment to catch our breath before we saw the other houseboats fall over the waterfall, still spinning, and heard the screams of the human monsters who tried to end our lives.

"We have an extra gun now," Anthony said.

"Let's dock tomorrow and get some river rocks for Thomas's gun," I told the others. "We need all the weapons we can get. Apparently, human monsters lurk around every corner."

"I'm sorry, Joel, we should have gathered some today," Thomas said.

"It's not your fault. I think we all started to get too comfortable," Eric said, ringing out his clothes.

"On a positive note, this is a fantastic boat," Doris said, admiring it.

"It belonged to this family." Noel brought us a picture from the cabin.

In the picture, a smiling family had their arms around one another—a mother, a father, and two children. I shuddered thinking about what had happened to them.

"Let's get some rest," I told the others. "Let's at least try."

We lay down all together. I heard Jordan snoring and Herman purring.

Safe. I thought. Safe for another day.

I closed my eyes. I drifted off. I heard less voices. I wasn't sure if it was because I was tired or because three more bad men were gone.

The next morning, we brought the boat to the shore to gather river rocks and other supplies. Eric, Heinrich, and Daniel walked down the side of the rocks leading to the bottom of the waterfall to figure out what our course of action would be. I could still see the smoke in the distance from the fires we had set, but if it was still blazing, then it should have been here by now. We would have to burn again.

"Think anyone is in there?" Jordan asked me.

"No, I don't. Normally if there is a person in there, I can sense it. I may not be able to tell if there is a person or if there are people. I can't determine the number. Like when I sensed you were in there, I didn't know if I would find one person or twenty," I told her.

"I understand," she said, rubbing her knee.

Sarah and Thomas collected rocks. Noel would carry the buckets back with Anthony and James. Charles chopped up fish and fed Herman, who was on his leash.

"Bad news, Joel," Heinrich said as he came back up.

"What? Did they survive the fall?" I asked, shocked.

"Nope, they definitely did not survive," Heinrich responded. "That's not the issue. The issue is that where that waterfall ends, so does the river that it was supposed to connect to."

"So what do we do?" I looked at Eric.

"We walk it," he said to me. "I guess we walk it and try to get to the next body of water. I don't know what else to do at this point. We can't just stop."

"Come see," Heinrich said to me.

I followed him down the rock slope to the point where we could see the waterfall splashing into the bottom lagoon. At the west shore, there were tiny pieces of the boat, which had been shattered on impact. I saw pieces of torn clothing from the edge of the water spread all the way into the forest.

"They got dragged in," I said to him.

"Yes, they did." He pointed toward the land beyond the waterfall. "It's super rocky."

"What do you think happened?" I asked him.

"If I had to guess, I would guess there was an earthquake. You see those mountains over there." He pointed to the north. "Eric said those don't belong there."

Just then, Eric walked up behind us. "See what I was saying? We will have to walk it."

"Okay then. Let's do this," I said.

Let's camp on the boat one more night. We can spend today gathering supplies we need. It will give Jordan one more day to rest as well. Then tomorrow, as soon as the sun comes up, we can start our journey."

"Okay, I think that sounds like the best course of action." Eric nodded.

Heinrich nodded in approval.

"Okay, let's go talk with the others," Eric said and started to walk back up the rocks.

We waited until we were all ready to board the boat and settle down for the evening when I spoke to the others.

"The bottom of the waterfall is where the river used to begin. It no longer exists. We will have to walk down the rocks and continue on foot. We will stop only when we reach a body of water or an alternative safe space if a body of water is not available." I paused to read everyone's face. "Does anyone have any questions?" I asked.

"Joel," Noel said meekly, "I can't do this."

I walked over to her and leaned toward her. I took her hand in mine. "Noel, do you remember that drawing of me that you made? It's right. That is exactly what I will do. I will lead you to safety. I will protect you all in the process. I promise."

Noel nodded her head.

"Who will carry my book? It's heavy. I can't carry it on land," Doris said, worried. "It has our history. It's important."

She looked around.

"I'll carry it," said James. "I would be happy to as long as you let me read it sometime." He smiled at her.

"Absolutely," she said, patting him on the back.

"Okay then, let's have some dinner, get some sleep, then tomorrow bright and early, we will be on our way," I told everyone.

The morning came quickly. I always knew when the morning was coming because the birds stopped chirping at the same time.

I woke up, kissed Jordan, and then began packing for the journey on foot. As I was packing, I realized I hadn't seen Eric drink in a while. It seemed that he was drinking less and less as time went on. In fact, I hadn't seen him drink at all since the incident with Jeremey and his men. I decided I wouldn't share that observation with Eric.

Thomas and Sarah took Jordan's vitals and then began to meticulously pack their equipment, their plants, and their other supplies. Anthony was in charge of food. He wrapped the cooked fish in paper that Doris had given him. He packed the berries in jars. Noel filled all the canteens and let Jordan screw the lids on so that she felt she was helping in some way. Jordan was in better spirits today than she was yesterday.

Heinrich went to shore with a piece of cloth and a hunk of charcoal. He wrote something on the cloth and then tied it onto a tree that overhangs the water. When he came back, I asked what he had written.

"I wrote a warning about the waterfall," he said. "I wouldn't want someone to accidentally go over."

After we were all packed and ready to go, we pulled the boat to the side and tied it to a tree. It would be a safe place for anyone who came to this spot.

We all started walking down the rocks that lined the sides of the waterfall. Jordan rode on my back. Herman walked in front of us on a leash while Charles sat down and scooted down the rocks. Everyone had their own way of getting down safely. Once we reached the bottom, Noel looked at the scattered clothes trailing into the forest and gasped.

"It's okay," Doris told her. "We aren't like them." She took her hand.

The walk was almost completely rocks. It was like the earth had been scooped up with a shovel and turned over.

We walked in a line, two by two. Most of us spoke in pairs. Jordan walked in front of me with Charles and asked him about one hundred questions about cats. I walked with Daniel.

"Do you miss your family?" Daniel asked me.

I realized I had never told him about my family.

"My family has passed on, but I do miss my mother. I never met my father. He passed before me," I said to him.

"Did you have any siblings?" he asked.

"No, I was an only child," I responded. "How about your family, do you miss them?"

I knew he did based on what Anthony had told me, but I felt this was a moment where Daniel might feel comfortable opening up.

Daniel paused. He looked up at the sky.

"I do miss them. Actually, this is the first time I've been able to speak about it in years."

He seemed to be searching for the words.

"I'm the oldest of five children. I have four younger sisters. When my youngest sister was born, my dad left. I wanted to join the military so my mom would be taken care of. I promised to send her all my checks to take care of my sisters."

He kicked a rock as we continued to walk.

"When the phones went down, I couldn't call anymore. The mail was gone, I couldn't write. There was no internet. I made a promise I didn't keep. That hurts. That hurts the most. I told my mom it would be okay, and it's not."

"Maybe it turned out okay," I said to him.

"What do you mean?" Daniel responded.

"Maybe they made it," I said.

"Why do you think that?" he asked.

"You don't have any proof they didn't make it. You're afraid you've lost them. Do you know what's stronger than fear?" I asked him.

Daniel shook his head.

"Hope," I said.

Daniel stopped in his tracks, and I knew he was reflecting, so I kept walking forward to check on the others.

Eric was at the very front of the group talking to Thomas and Heinrich when I approached them.

"What's going on?" I asked.

"We need to cut through that forest," Heinrich said. "The path is ending, and we need to pick a place to enter."

Eric pointed to the west. "You see that place at the top of the canopy of trees that is very open?" he asked me.

"Yes, I see it," I responded.

"Well, I think there might be water there," he said.

I looked at what Eric was saying and I did feel that this was probably the safest course. I looked all around us for a different route even though Eric might be right. He might also be wrong, and moving into the forest is a dangerous feat. I decided we had no choice.

"Okay, Eric, lead the way," I said to him.

We walked the last stretch of rocky terrain before coming to the opening of the forest. I could see the sun shining a large path for us to enter.

"You want point, Joel?" Eric asked.

"No, let me fall back," I responded.

I wanted to make sure I could see everything.

We walked into the forest, and I made sure that the shifting trees didn't cause any shadows. Jordan walked directly in front of me.

We walked this way for about an hour in silence. I had reminded the others that the infected were also sound-based. Up ahead, I could see a pond. Eric was right.

Eric fell back to speak to me about this.

"Let's stay here tonight. Any ideas?" he said.

I looked above the small mountain and I could see a cave.

"See that cave above the pond?" I asked him.

"Yes. Want to go check it out?" he asked.

I nodded my head, and Eric and I motioned for the others to stay put while we did. The others stood near the pond in a group.

Eric and I had just started to climb the rock wall up to the cave when we heard a scream. It was Jordan.

I turned around, and Jordan was on the ground holding her knee. Sarah had come to Jordan's side and was kneeling next to her, helping.

I saw the next few minutes in slow motion. The first thing that happened was the blowing of the trees. At that moment, the soil shifted for a moment. I heard a crack, and a large tree fell over the others. This tree was caught by other trees and encased them all in darkness.

I leapt from the rock wall to the forest floor and heard the snarls. I had just leapt down when I saw the first one jump. The sun shifted at that moment and it retreated.

"Run to the light," I yelled as they all shuffled to a lighted area.

Then the trees blew, and the sun shifted to another area. Everyone ran. Doris fell. I ran to her and picked her up. I carried her into the water and told her to stay.

"Run into the water!" I yelled at them.

Eric had already jumped into the pond and was calling the others.

They were all sprinting into the water when I saw it. One of the creatures was leaping through the darkness and was headed straight for Noel, who was in the back of the others. I sprinted in vain, as I knew I wasn't fast enough to stop it. I realized in that moment I would break my promise. I wasn't that person in Noel's drawing. I wasn't able to protect them. I wasn't going to be fast enough to save her.

The monster was just about to make contact when I saw something from the other side of the forest make contact first. It grabbed the monster's head and slammed it into the earth. I saw it get up and take two more down as Noel and the others ran into the water. I watched it limp away into a patch of light where it fell.

I walked toward the creature.

"What is it?" Jordan asked.

"It looks like a wolf," Charles called out. "Be careful."

"Best just leave it, Joel," Sarah said.

I ignored them as I walked toward it. I crouched next to the creature and realized it was hurt. I felt someone behind me and turned around fast. It was Eric.

"It's a wolf hybrid, Joel," Eric said.

"What's that?" I asked.

"A wolf and a dog mixed," he said.

I reached out my hand to touch it.

"Joel, don't," Eric sai sternly.

"Eric, he saved us." I looked at him.

"She," Eric responded.

"What?" I questioned.

"She saved us. It's a girl." He pointed.

I placed my hand on her head, and she whimpered.

"It's okay, girl. You're okay. You saved us. You're so brave." I stroked her head.

She had bites oozing with blood covering her arms and the back of her neck.

"Joel, be careful," Jordan called.

"Listen, I want to thank you," I said to her. "I know you may not realize this but I made a promise to protect these people, and you helped me keep that promise."

She whimpered as I held her head.

"Let her have peace," Thomas said to me.

I started to stand up, and then something caught my eye. I watched the oozing scars on her arms start to close. Her torso wounds started to heal. Right there in front of my eyes, she healed completely. Then she stood up, looked me straight in the eyes, and licked my face.

"Whoa, Joel," Eric said.

I looked back at Eric.

"What does it mean?" I asked.

"Well, I think it means two things. Number one, you now have a pet dog-wolf. Number two, you found someone just like you," he said, looking down at me.

"What's going on?" Anthony yelled.

"She's like me." I laughed. "She's just like me."

I sat with her and petted her. She was huge. When we sat, she was larger than I was. Her fur was black and her eyes were blue. Her paws were bigger than my hands.

We made our way up to the cave above the pond. We would be safe there. The only way into the cave was to enter the pond and climb the tree.

Inside the cave, I petted our new friend. Herman sat in the corner, growling. His hair was still drying from the pond.

"What are we going to call her?" Jordan asked me, stroking her dark fur.

"Sasha. Her name is Sasha," I told them.

Sasha turned around in a circle three times before lying down. She laid her head right next to Jordan's stomach. After lying with Jordan awhile, she got up and went around visiting with each member of our group. She smelled each person as if she was learning their scent. She even tried to visit with Herman. He wasn't accepting.

"What a good girl," I said to her as I stroked her back.

Her tail wagged.

That night, I realized that I couldn't do this alone. I needed Sasha. Maybe, just maybe, she needed me too.

CHAPTER 16

THE BOOK OF FORGIVENESS

The cave was unable to be reached by land. Someone would have to enter the water to access. We knew we would be safe from the infected there for the night. Anthony lit a fire by the entrance. He used sticks that had been placed at the back of the cave. Charles said the sticks were probably from someone or some animal who had previously made their home in this cave. We were thankful for them. We were thankful for the warmth of the fire after having to submerge ourselves in water. The cave was large and extended back at an angle. We laid the items from our packs by the fire to dry.

"You warm enough?" I asked Jordan. "Not that I have anything to offer you that would help," I added.

Just then, Sasha walked over and lay between Jordan and me. Jordan leaned over and wrapped her arm around her.

"This will do," she said, smiling. "I always wanted a dog."

"Oh yeah?" I asked. "I thought Herman was the cutest?"

I pointed to Herman, who was sitting on Charles's lap, recovering from the stress he had just encountered.

"Herman is the cutest cat, and Sasha is the cutest dog," she said as she petted Sasha's head.

"And what am I?" I asked her.

"The cutest husband." She kissed me and then lay down, cuddling Sasha. "Her eyes are the same color blue as yours. It's like you're related," Jordan said, staring at Sasha's face.

We were all settling in, getting ready to go to sleep. The cave was damp and cold. The fire offered very little warmth the farther you slept to the back wall.

"You know what's funny?" Anthony said to the group. "When I was little, my parents used to take us camping, and I actually looked forward to it."

We all laughed. I was amazed any of us could possibly have a sense of humor after the evening we just had.

"I remember camping," Heinrich said. "We cooked hot dogs on the fire."

"And s'mores," Daniel added.

"Oh, I love s'mores," Sarah said. "Thomas and I used to make those."

"We had sleeping bags," said Anthony. "What happened to all the sleeping bags in the old world? We should have kept those."

"Before you ask what a s'more is, Joel, it's a dessert that is made using a bunch of things you couldn't imagine and would be too hard to describe to you." Eric laughed.

"Oh, Eric, we can try to explain. Joel likes to learn things," Sarah responded.

"I understand that. Go ahead and try. You won't be able to describe a s'more to someone who has never had one, never eaten candy, never had sugar…trust me. I tried to think of a description in my head while you were all talking and I couldn't," Eric said.

"Joel, they're made with a type of cookie, chocolate, and a marshmallow that's roasted on a fire," she said.

"I thought it was a cracker," Daniel said.

"No, it's a cookie," Eric argued.

"But…it's called a graham cracker. It literally says cracker in its name," Daniel responded.

"I think it's a sweet cracker," Anthony said.

The others agreed with him.

"What's a marshmallow?" I asked.

"Here we go," Eric said, laughing.

"A marshmallow is a fluffy thing…" Anthony tried to help.

"Like fluffy bread?" I asked.

"No," the others said in unison.

Jordan was laughing.

"What is so funny?" I asked.

"You want to know everything," she said, laughing.

"You don't want to know?" I asked her.

"We will never have one, anyways," she said.

For a second, I had forgotten that. We would never have one. We would never have camping trips with our family. We would never have all of these amazing foods the others remember. Jordan and I would never have that, and we wouldn't have the memories either. We had only ever known this world. We had only ever known fish and berries and tragedy. I took Jordan's hand in mine. She was the only one who understood.

"Hey, Joel," Anthony said, "if I ever find a way to create a s'more, I'll make one for you."

He smiled.

"Thanks, Anthony," I said.

"So can we all agree you can't explain everything?" Eric said.

"Well, we can always try," Sarah said.

"This conversation made me forget how cold it is in here for a moment," Thomas said.

"Herman and I are a little warm here. Want to switch us and be closer to the fire?" Charles asked him.

They switched places, which brought Herman closer to Sasha. Herman growled and sat on the other side of Charles, farthest from our new friend.

Jordan laughed. She yawned and then laid her head in Sasha's fur and fell asleep.

"How are we getting out of here tomorrow?" Eric asked me.

"What do you mean?" I asked.

"Like, are we leaping into the pond or are we going to make an assembly line to get the others down?" he asked. "Doris is a wonderful person, but I don't think she can get down that tree."

"Watch me," I heard Doris shout from across the cave.

We both laughed.

"We will figure it out tomorrow," I told him. "Sasha and I will head out first and find the path with the most light."

"Jordan shouldn't be climbing or jumping out," Eric said. "We will find a way to carry her down."

"Yes, I agree," I told him.

"It's like having a family." Eric smiled at me. "It really is."

"Yeah, I guess you're right. It is like a family," I said.

I noticed Eric had been drinking water. I hadn't seen Eric drink since the incident with Jeremy and his group. I didn't want to ask him about it. I figured he would talk about it if he wanted to.

"She's a good dog," Eric said, sitting next to me.

He took a drink from his canteen.

He saw me look at it.

"It's water," he said. He half-smiled.

"I noticed," I said to him.

I reached down and petted Sasha.

"You know, Joel, guilt is a powerful feeling," he said quietly.

We were the only ones still awake.

"What do you mean?" I asked him.

"Well, you know I told you about the guilt I felt about my wife and children. You remember that, right?" he asked.

"Yes, I remember," I told him.

I would never forget.

"Well, I've been carrying around guilt pretty much my whole life," he said.

I didn't say anything; instead, I waited for him to continue. He leaned back on the wall of the cave as he thought.

"When I was young, my father drank himself to death." He looked at the canteen. "My mom...well, she didn't take that very well, which is strange because he wasn't a good husband. He was terrible to her. He was always running around on her and he could be violent. Well, after he died, she started drinking too. I never understood that, Joel. I never understood how she would do the exact thing that killed him." He looked at me. "Until I chose to do that too."

I looked at Eric; I could tell he was trying to work through something in his mind.

"When my mom started drinking, I let it happen. I was old enough and I could have tried to stop her…but I didn't," he said.

"Why not?" I asked him.

"I think I let it go because I felt sorry for her, and the drinking seemed to make her forget about her pain. So I would keep getting more and more for her. I enabled her. Most days she just lay on the couch, completely comatose. When she did get up, she would do insane things, like try to drive to the store after she had been drinking all day. I just kept helping her numb away the pain." He closed his eyes. "Then she drank herself to death too."

I sat next to Eric in silence. I didn't know how to respond to what he was telling me.

"So I carried around that guilt until I found the service," he said. "That's the path I chose."

"That's why you became a Marine?" I questioned.

"Yes, it is. I joined so that I could somehow redeem myself. I had to try and redeem myself…for me. Does that make sense?" he asked. "I felt so guilty for my mom. I could have saved her and I didn't."

"Yes, it does," I told him. "It makes a lot of sense."

"I was good in the Marines, Joel…we were a perfect fit. I was fearless. I took on the most dangerous part of every mission…and I climbed up in the ranks."

He looked at Anthony, James, and Daniel.

"When we found them, I saw myself in them. I saw whom I used to be." He took another drink of his water. "It made me think back to who I was before this world turned me into something else."

"I understand," I told him. I put my hand on his shoulder.

"I started to feel like I was part of something again," he said.

I looked at Eric. He had been through more than me, much more. I cherished him. I wasn't sure if he knew that.

"My life was perfect before this virus." A tear fell from his eye. "I had lost my parents but I had created a life where I could save others. I had a wonderful wife and amazing children. I had the ability to raise them differently than how I was. And I let them down."

He shook his head.

"Eric, you didn't know," I said to him.

He looked at the canteen.

"And it was that guilt, Joel, it was that guilt that drove me to drink. I would have drunk myself to death too. You know, Joel, I didn't really want to go on this journey with you in the beginning. I didn't want that. I wanted to float along and drink until I died, numbing myself to this world, but I'm a man of faith, Joel. I believed you found me for a reason."

Eric looked at me with tears in his eyes.

"What made you stop?" I asked him.

"The mission where we saved everyone from Jeremy and his men," he said to me. "I remembered who I could be."

I watched him looking around the cave.

"I liked who I was during that mission, Joel," he said. "I haven't liked who I was in a very long time."

I patted Eric on the shoulder.

"I had to forgive myself. I had to forgive myself for my mother… and for my wife and my kids. It doesn't mean I don't carry guilt. It will always be there. Always," he said, looking at me. "But punishing myself for the rest of my life won't bring them back. It won't."

I leaned over and put my arm around him.

"When you go back east, I'm going with you," he said. "I need this, Joel. I know I'm older, but I won't slow you down."

"I would like that," I said to him. "If you slow me down, I'll carry you." I laughed.

"Not a chance," he said as he rubbed my head.

"I'm proud of you," I said to him.

"Why?" Eric asked.

"Because I don't know anyone who has had as much happen in their lives as you have and you're the best person I know," I said.

"Joel, I like to think that if my sons had grown up, they would be half as good as you," he said, tears in his eyes.

"I think they would be better," I said.

He smiled.

"Eric," I said.

"Yeah, kid?" he responded.

"I like to think that you're the dad I never got to have," I told him.

He leaned over and smacked my back.

I could tell he liked that.

CHAPTER 17

THE BOOK OF SEBA

We left the cave early the next morning and headed west. I felt more comfortable with Sasha by my side. Even on all fours, Sasha was taller than my waist. Sarah told me that because her wounds healed completely, Sasha must have been conceived similarly to me. She told us that animals who were bitten eventually died; they didn't convert. It was believed that this wasn't their burden to carry. We were the ones who had destroyed this world. They were victims in it. The walk in the forest was short. Just beyond the forest was a desert. We seemed to find one surprise after another. The map had become pointless on this journey. Nothing was the same anymore.

"Everyone has their water, right?" Eric asked, looking at the group.

We all checked and made sure. Nobody wanted to go out into the desert without their water. We made sure we caught fish in the pond before we left, and Anthony had cooked them. Sasha stood next to Jordan. Herman glared sideway at Sasha and clung to Charles's legs. He still hadn't warmed up to her.

The last thing I did before the journey was to walk back to the forest and light it on fire. The forest immediately went up in flames.

We started our journey across the sand. I hoped I wasn't leading my group into a bad situation. I thought about what I had told Daniel about hope. That it's greater than fear. I had never thought about that before, but I believed what I told him was correct.

"Hey, Joel, can I talk to you?" Anthony asked.

"Sure," I said.

"When we get to where we are going. Can I be the chef?" Anthony asked.

I laughed to myself and then I realized he was serious.

"Yes, Anthony, you can be the chef," I said.

He smiled and walked away.

I walked up to Jordan and took her left hand in mine. At that exact moment, Sasha walked up under her right hand.

"Oh, Joel, I think someone is jealous," Jordan said, smiling.

"No, she's not jealous, she's protective," I said to Jordan, kissing her nose.

"My goodness, it's hot," Heinrich said, tying his shirt on his head.

"It is hot," I told the others. "Make sure you drink your water. Let us know if you need a break."

I stopped for a moment and poured Sasha some water into a bowl we carried. She gratefully lapped it up and then licked my hand. Charles did the same for Herman, but Herman refused to drink it. So far on the walk, we had all been mostly silent. I wondered if the others were starting to question this journey like I was. It seemed the desert was a never-ending walk.

"Where are we stopping tonight?" Eric hollered at me.

"I guess we need to find something safe. Maybe a cave. It probably won't be on water," I responded.

As we continued to walk, a sandstorm was building. I ripped my sleeve off my shirt and tied it around Jordan's face. I couldn't imagine how hot she must feel, carrying herself and the baby through this desert.

Up ahead, we could see rocks jutting from the cracked dry ground.

"They formed from the earthquakes, I'd reckon," Eric said.

"Think we should build a fort behind them and hunker down through the sandstorm?" Daniel asked.

It was like Daniel had taken the thought right out of my brain.

"Let's sit beneath the rocks on the west side. It seems the wind is coming from the east. They should protect us," Thomas told us.

Sarah and Thomas went behind the rocks and held onto each other's shoulders and leaned in to each other. James led Doris to sit down, and she shielded her face with a sweater. Noel held Jordan's hand, and they sat behind the rocks next to Thomas. Sasha lay between them. The others huddled behind.

"Joel, how long do you think this will last?" James called to me.

The sandstorm was so loud that even though we were feet apart, he was yelling at me.

"I don't know," I replied. "Thomas, any ideas?"

Thomas thought for a moment. "Sandstorms can last anywhere from a few hours to a few months," he said.

"Wow, Thomas, thanks for the morale booster," Eric responded. "There shouldn't even be a desert here. It could be over in minutes," he added.

Sasha buried her head into the bottom of the rock. I petted her head.

We had barely sat by the rocks when the storm picked up. Sand thrashed against our already weather-beaten faces. I held Jordan's head into the middle of my chest. Charles had made his body into a tent for Herman, who growled through the whole storm. The storm lasted maybe twenty minutes but felt like hours. As the winds died down, I used my hands to cup the sides of my head to see if moving would help us.

That was when I saw her. She was walking toward us through the sandstorm as if it wasn't happening.

She walked with purpose. Her head was wrapped in brightly colored cloth that matched her long dress. Her staff hit the ground harmoniously with her right foot with each stride. She saw us but wasn't nervous. I could hear her steady breathing even from afar.

"Hey, guys, we have a visitor," I said to alert the others.

As they each peeked over the rocks, the confusion settled in.

"Welcome," she called out twenty feet in front of us.

Just then, the sandstorm suddenly stopped.

She looked around as she smiled. "Nature agrees with your purpose, whatever that might be."

I looked around at the others, who seemed just as confused as I was.

"You!" she said, pointing her staff at me. "Your eyes tell a story, come closer."

"I'm coming with you," Jordan said. If I felt this woman was a danger, I wouldn't have let her, but I felt that she was safe.

I held Jordan's hand as we reluctantly walked toward this brightly clothed woman. Sasha stayed close to us while we approached. As we edged closer, I could see that her features were regal. Her dark skin was smooth even in this desolate wasteland. She looked like royalty. Sasha ran from us and lay down at the feet of this woman.

"Hello, I am Seba," she said, extending her hand to me and then to Jordan.

She looked in my eyes and then turned her head to the side. Then she crouched down and took Sasha's face in her hand and stared in her eyes as well.

"Two of a kind, I see," she said, smiling at us.

I told Seba about my immunity and our mission. I explained how Jordan had been attacked and survived and how Sasha had saved us. I told her about Sasha's immunity as well. I walked Seba back to the rocks where the others were staring with wide eyes.

Seba introduced herself to the others and invited us back to her home. As we walked, she told us about where she was from and who she was.

"I grew up in California. I was raised by my mother and father just south of Pasadena. My father moved here from Africa in his twenties. He was a Christian in Africa. Islamic terrorist groups were angry about any sort of religious deviation from what they believed in. They took him and others in the night. He escaped, and a local church helped him and my mother move to the United States. He was one of the lucky few who were able to escape. My father became a minister. He wanted me to be a minister as well, but I decided I wanted to learn about every religion before I made a determination about who I was. I decided I was all of them, so I became a religious studies professor at Stanford University. I left before things got bad. I told my colleagues that I sensed a change in the air. I felt I was being told to leave. They laughed at me. They called me crazy. That was ten years before the lights went out. I now realize if I had stayed, I wouldn't be alive. At the time, I wondered if it was my own subconscious telling me to leave or maybe God. I wasn't who I was meant to be, I knew that. I had come to a point in my life where I felt I needed to self-exile and reconnect to nature. Just like many people in the old world, I had started to worship materialistic items and I stopped standing for what I knew to be true. I started walking and I settled here."

Seba pointed to a cave in the middle of the desert. "It wasn't always a desert. It changed over time."

"Wow, that's amazon," I told her.

"Home sweet home. I've been here for thirty years. Those things don't come here much. Nothing does. Nothing grows either. It was here that I figured out my purpose in life. I figured out who I was. It's a strange thing, making a decision to live life with only the basics. I have found, though, that when you have to go find your own food and water, you don't have room in your head to worry about much else."

"How do you eat? How do you get water?" I asked.

"There is a lake about five miles north. It's small. It has fish. It's fresh. I go there three days a week. I leave in the early morning light. I'll show you if you would like," Seba told us.

"Is California gone?" Heinrich asked.

Seba looked at him as if in pain.

"It's all gone. This is the last state before the ocean. Earthquakes swallowed everything and everyone. I've met people as they wandered through. I've been lucky that these people weren't malicious. I've met people walking west and I've met people walking east. This is the last state before the ocean on the west. Ohio is the last state before the ocean on the east. Half of Ohio is even gone and everything south of that," she explained.

We entered the cave with Seba leading us. We were surprised you could actually stand in the cave. The place was tidy. There were holes in the cave that let plenty of light in. Rocks were placed around as chairs. We all sat to rest while Seba prepared food for us.

"Fish stew," she said, smiling, "that's what we eat now."

We swallowed the soup without chewing. I can't remember the last time I tasted and enjoyed food. Probably the night of my wedding.

"Who wants to walk to the lake in the morning?" Seba asked.

"I'll go," I told her. "I think Jordan should stay with Daniel, Doris, and Sarah. If anything happens, they can care for her."

"I want to go," Jordan said to me, frowning.

"That's a ten-mile round trip. In the heat. That's not good for the baby. I'm sorry, Jordan, it's just not safe," I told her.

She settled down in the corner and laid her head on Sarah's shoulder.

"Okay, I'll stay...for the baby," she said.

"For now, let's all settle in for the night and try to get some sleep," Heinrich said.

We all spread out inside the cave and settled into the hard ground. I let Jordan lie on my chest while I cradled her.

"I can hear her heart beating," I said to Jordan.

"Does it sound normal?" she asked.

"Yes, it does. It sounds perfect," I said, kissing her on the forehead.

I had just closed my eyes and began to drift off when I heard the digging. I remembered what Jordan had said to me about being able to hear the digging in the cave behind the waterfall. The difference between the cave Jordan was in and this cave was that this one wasn't solid rock. I could tell this cave was just hard dirt and sand. I looked around the cave, and the only source of light was a lit candle that Eric was sitting next to as he laid out a game of solitaire.

"Pssst, Eric... Eric," I whispered.

"What?" Eric whispered.

"Come here. Quietly," I said to Eric, waving him toward me.

I was at the farthest wall of the cave and I wasn't sure if I was the only one who could hear the digging. I didn't want to wake Jordan and scare her.

"What is it?" Eric asked, crawling over to me.

"Do you hear that?" I asked him. "Sounds like digging."

Eric placed his ear to the rocks, and then he placed his hand on the rocks.

"I can hear it when my ear is against it and I can feel vibrations. Those things are close," Eric said with nervous eyes.

"Wake Heinrich," I said to Eric. "We need to know how much time we have. We may just need to leave when the sun rises and not come back."

Heinrich came over and placed his ear against the wall and then his head. At this point, everyone had woken up, and they all sat away from the wall. As the things got closer, dust started to fall from the cave ceiling.

"How far do you reckon they are away?" Eric asked Heinrich.

"I'm not certain. I would say maybe a half a day's time until they reach us," Heinrich responded.

"But you think we will make it until morning?" Seba asked.

"Yes, I'm certain we have until daybreak," Heinrich answered.

"Let's plan on walking out of here tomorrow," I said to the others. "Let's sleep in shifts. We need rest."

"I'm coming with you," Seba said. "I guess this is nature's way of telling me it's time to leave."

We decided that we would use the buddy system to do shifts. Jordan was my buddy. Heinrich paired with Daniel. Anthony paired with Noel. Doris paired with James. Thomas paired with Sarah. Seba paired with Eric. Charles paired with Herman, but they both slept through the entire ordeal. Sasha sat next to me, on high alert.

Both shifts had about a total of four hours of sleep by daybreak. Those not sleeping helped pack and prepare for the journey west. By the time the sun permeated the cave, the monsters had managed to get so close that everyone could hear them without putting their ears to the wall.

I woke Jordan and tucked her dark hair behind her ears. I kissed her forehead and then I kissed her stomach.

"Good morning, girls," I said. "I heard Jordan's stomach growl."

"You're hungry," I said to her.

"No, I'm not. I'm okay. I'll wait," Jordan said, her stomach growling again.

"Does anyone have anything Jordan could eat?" I asked the group.

Charles reached into his sack and pulled out a turnip. "It won't taste great raw, but it will fill you up good. It's the only one I got, so we won't have turnips when we settle down somewhere."

"That's perfectly fine," Eric said. "If you got any parsnips in there, why don't you do us a favor and just get rid of those too."

Charles laughed.

"Thanks, Charles." I said, shaking his hand.

We headed east to the lake Seba had told us about. The plan was to get to the lake, fill the canteens, catch fish, and then continue west. The five miles to the lake was just about the hottest walk any of us had ever been on. I was thankful Seba had encouraged us to leave at first light, and I understand why she chose this time. Any closer to noon with that desert sun could have given us heatstroke. The lake was just as Seba had described—small, very small. It did have fish in it, though. It was fresh water. I was thankful for that. Unfortunately, the water was stagnant. We would have to boil the water before we could drink it. We set up a fire using a small amount of dry brush. Noel's match worked well to light the pile of brush.

"I'm going to catch some fish." I told the others. "Seba, want to help?" I asked. I really wanted to know how she knew we were in the desert. It would have been too far from her cave to see us, and she wouldn't have been out walking in a sandstorm.

"Sure," Seba said with a smirk on her face.

I could tell that Seba knew why I had asked her. She waded into the water with me, and I began to swirl my hands in the water slowly, feeling the vibration of life circling us. I snagged a decent-sized crappie and threw it to Eric on shore. He grabbed it and, in one motion, slammed it down and cleaned it.

"Impressive," Seba said with that same smirk. "It's almost as if you're not human."

I laughed.

"How did you know we were in the desert?" I asked her.

"The same way I knew I needed to leave California ten years before the virus hit," she said. "I just felt I was being told. I felt I needed to walk that direction. I feel that nature guided me."

"That's it?" I asked.

She didn't respond.

"I was talking to Thomas on the way here, and he has some very interesting theories about the baby that he hasn't shared with you," she said, changing the subject.

I felt that Seba knew more than she was saying. "Oh, okay. Well, I guess you can send him to help me then," I told her, sensing she wasn't open to sharing.

"It looks like you're all set here," she said, wading back to shore. "I'll send Thomas."

I hadn't thought in detail about what had happened to Jordan. She had healed; she was immune. I wondered what the baby had to do with that. Was I venomous? Did I make her immune? Or did the baby somehow do that?

Thomas waded out to me. It took him awhile. He seemed not to like the water much.

"You know I can't swim well," Thomas said to me with a frown.

"It's okay, I won't let you drown," I said to him with a smile on my face. "Seba said that you had some theories."

As I said the last word, I reached down and grabbed a large catfish with such force that I frightened Thomas, who stumbled backward into the water. I reached down and pulled him up. Thomas sputtered and caught his breath.

"You startled me good that time. I'm still not used to your quickness," he said. "So you want to know what I think?" Thomas said, staring at the sky. "Well, I'll be honest. I thought Jordan was a goner that night. I really did. When I saw her come out of the water, I was in shock. When she held her stomach and said that the baby was perfect and a girl, I was in more shock. First of all, Jordan was so early at that point that the baby wouldn't have a determinable sex. Second was that the baby is yours, you're not a human. You're only half human. Your DNA wasn't human enough to make a vaccine, but it was human enough to conceive a child with a full human woman."

He rubbed his chin. "That's the part I can't figure out. I was talking to Sarah about this. You know, Sarah used to work in a women's shelter. She's seen just about everything you can imagine."

Thomas tried to grab a fish and almost fell back in.

"Jordan is only about twelve weeks right now," he said, looking me straight in my eyes. "Except she's not. Sarah took her blood, Her HCG levels placed her at around twenty-four weeks. Now normally that would make us think twins—normally—but Jordan is certain there is only one baby. It's a girl. When she dove into the water, she saw the girl. She described what she would look like in detail. I believe her. I think this baby is growing faster than a full human baby. I don't know how long this pregnancy will last. She may go sooner rather than later."

"So what's your theory about the baby?" I asked.

"I think this baby may hold the key to that vaccine we tried with your blood. I think she may be the key," he said, looking into my eyes. "I believe the baby made Jordan immune. Not forever but while she's carrying her."

"So you don't think I'm venomous? That I caused this?" I asked.

"No, I don't. If you were venomous, then you would have infected Jordan. You wouldn't have made her immune," he said.

"And you think that this immunity Jordan has is only temporary?" I asked.

"Yes, I do. It will wear off after birth," he said to me, his face in a slight frown. "But the baby is immune, and she's more human than you are. I think this could work for a vaccine."

"Would we be able to save the already infected?" I asked.

I looked at Thomas, knowing I was not going to get the answer I wanted.

"No, I don't believe we could. I think about this like the flu. If someone has the flu and we give them a flu shot, will it take it away? No, it won't. Those who are already bitten will succumb."

"I don't want the baby to be tested on. I don't want her to be like a pin cushion for this. She's innocent," I said, shaking my head.

"Don't worry. We will use the placenta and the umbilical cord. She will be safe," Thomas said, placing his hand on my shoulder.

I threw two more fish on the shore.

"That'll do it!" Eric shouted.

Thomas and I waded back to shore.

"You know, you really are a miracle," Thomas said to me. "I didn't even believe in those before I met you."

CHAPTER 18

THE BOOK OF ABIGAIL

We were now in Wyoming. There was grass here, but it was extremely dry. Eric told us he could smell the ocean. There were seagulls sleeping on the patches of dry grass.

"If only my geography teacher could see this," Eric said, shaking his head.

"Yeah, we should map this at some point," Heinrich said.

"I can map it," Noel said meekly.

Noel didn't talk much. This trip seemed like a lot for her. She spent a lot of time sketching in her book. I saw that she drew the trees and plants as we were walking, probably for Doris. Unlike Noel, Doris never stopped talking. She reminded me of an older version of Jordan.

"You should draw the map," Heinrich said to Noel. "You will have to go back east with Joel, though, when he heads back to burn."

He looked at Noel as if that would be a deal breaker.

"Well, maybe," Noel said, flashing a false smile.

I wondered if she already had a map drawn in her book.

Doris patted Noel on the back. "It's going to be the most precise map we've ever seen."

"Well, at this point, there is no other map, so even if you drew a circle, it would be more accurate than what's currently available," Eric said sarcastically.

"Stop. Stop!" Jordan yelled.

She suddenly leaned over and placed her hands on her knees.

"I need to sit. I think I pulled a muscle."

Jordan sat down on the dry earth and held her thigh.

Sarah ran over and kneeled next to Jordan. Everyone else turned away out of respect for Jordan's privacy. I leaned down and let Jordan lie against me. I held her hand. Her palms were cold and sweaty.

"You need sugar," Sarah said. "I can tell by looking at you. Thomas, grab my bag."

Sarah grabbed a bag of white powder out of the bag and placed a spoonful of it in Jordan's mouth.

"There, that should be better," Sarah said to Jordan.

"What is that?" Jordan asked.

"It's sugar," Sarah said.

You aren't getting a proper diet for a pregnant mother. We need to find fruit. You need to eat more natural sugar." Sarah turned toward Charles. "Think berries would grow here?" she asked him.

Charles leaned down to the ground. He felt the dirt. He picked up a little and tasted it.

"Maybe," he said. "I'll tell you what might grow here. Oranges."

"In Wyoming?" Eric asked. "Weird. Really weird."

"I know it's weird, but this dirt is tropical. You see those plants over there? Those plants are native to Florida. It's like someone took the country and shook it up like a snow globe," Charles said.

"What's a snow globe?" Jordan asked, trying to catch her breath.

"I'll draw you a picture of it," Noel said. "I don't know what it is either, but if they explain, I can draw it."

"Okay, we good to move?" I asked Sarah and Jordan.

"As long as Jordan feels up to it," Sarah said.

"Yeah, I'm fine now. Let's move," Jordan said, slowly standing up.

Sasha put her head under Jordan's arm and helped me lift her off the ground.

Jordan was the strongest woman I had ever known. This journey was hard on all of us, but Jordan was carrying a child.

We walked for several more hours before we reached the coast. The waves crashed fiercely onto a rock-filled beach...in Wyoming.

"Let's camp here for the night," I told the others. "We still have half a day to come up with safe lodging. Any ideas?"

Just then, something caught my eye to the left. I looked over, and there standing on the beach was a small child. The others followed my gaze.

"Hey!" I shouted. "Hey, come here."

The little boy ran.

We all took off after him. I was in front.

"Wait, I won't hurt you, I promise," I shouted.

Sasha ran right next to me, keeping pace.

The little boy ran around a bend, and as I rounded the bend chasing him, I stopped to a dead halt. There standing in front of me was a line of women. They were women of all ages. Some of them had children hiding behind them. They were standing, holding sharpened sticks, coconuts, and one of them even had a handful of sand.

"Stay back," one woman yelled. "You people have taken enough from us," she screamed.

I put my hands up.

"We aren't bad people. We have met some very bad people, we aren't them." I tried to convince her.

"Stay back!" she shouted, poking the stick toward me.

"Look, my wife is pregnant. Would I be here with my pregnant wife if I wanted to harm you?" I asked.

"We've had bad men and women come here," she said, squinting. "Just because she's a woman and your wife doesn't mean you're safe."

We stood staring at each other, unsure how to fix these people's understanding of who we are. I could see pain in each and every one of these women's faces.

"Help me up," an elderly woman said.

She had been sitting on the sand behind a younger woman. I saw three women help the woman to her feet. She looked to be about one hundred years old, if not older.

"Take me to him," she said.

"Which one, Grandma," one of the women said.

As I looked at this woman, I could see the shade of blue in her eyes. I watched her looking around without focusing on anything. She was blind.

"Take me to the one who spoke," she said.

They walked her over to me. She took small steps. She had a woman holding her on either side and one behind. She walked up to me and stood directly in front of me, holding her hands up to my face.

"May I?" she asked.

"Yes," I responded, not knowing what she was going to do.

She reached up and touched my head, my hair, my ears, my face, and the sides of my neck. Then she reached down and felt my necklace in her hands.

"The key," she said. "I knew you were coming. I saw you."

"Grandma, what do you mean you saw him?" a woman asked.

"In my dream. I saw a man with a key," she said. "These people are safe. They are with him, therefore they can be trusted," she said, taking my hand in hers. "You are good."

She placed her hand on my chest.

"I've seen your heart." She started to cry. "I've waited a long time for you."

"I'm Joel, I came from the east. These people came with me from different places. We want to fix this world."

The women lowered their sticks and stared.

"How?" one asked inquisitively.

"By burning the forests that separate the towns. We burned from the east to the west. Now after the baby is born, I'll head back to the east and keep burning. I want to bring everyone to one location. I want to rebuild. I want to create a new world. A new world with a vaccine."

"And where will this vaccine come from?" another woman asked.

Sarah and Thomas stepped forward. "It will come from our lab, using a sample that is part human and part infected."

They seemed confused.

"I am a part-infected, part-human hybrid," I said to the women. "Jordan is carrying my baby who we believe is also part infected. She is more human than I am, though, and we believe her DNA may be the key to creating a vaccine so that we are no longer susceptible to the virus."

One of the women stepped forward with the boy we saw earlier hugging onto her leg. I presumed she was the leader by where she stood when they believed we were a threat.

"We have a shipyard filled with boats. At night, we let the line out so we can drift but not get carried out to sea. It's only women and children. We do have a school on one boat. We have three teachers. We need help, though. We need builders. We need a doctor. We need people," she said. "It's been really hard."

Another woman stepped forward.

"Most of our husbands became infected and went into the water. Some of our husbands were killed defending us from bad people," she said.

"They took my sister," a teenage girl stated. "They took her when they went east."

I looked at Eric, and he shook his head. These people had been through so much pain.

The female leader reached out her hand.

"I'm Abigail. This is my son, Grayson."

The little boy reached out his hand and shook mine. Abigail did the same and shook all of ours.

"Theresa, can you take Grayson and feed him lunch?" Abigail asked another of the women.

The woman took Grayson under her arm.

"You can all go with Theresa, she can show you where you'll be staying," Abigail told the others.

Eric, Heinrich, and I stayed behind to talk to Abigail.

"I guess we were a little crazy when you got here," she said. "You have no idea the types of people who came through here."

"I think we might have some idea," Eric said.

"We went through two groups of human monsters on our journey," I told her.

"Just two, huh?" she said. "In the last twenty years, I think we have had at least fifteen groups of bad people come through. My grandma and Grayson are the only family members I have left. When we came here, I was only six years old. I arrived with my parents and my grandparents. I had three brothers. They're all gone other than Grandma."

"What about Grayson's father?" I asked.

Abigail didn't respond. I didn't push any further.

"What's winter like here?" Eric asked

"Hot, super hot," Abigail said. "It's always hot. Also, don't swim in this ocean. There are tons of sharks. If you walked in, they would eat you."

Eric walked to the edge. He pulled a fish out of his pack and threw it into the water. We watched as something grabbed it as soon as it hit.

"Unreal," Eric said. "Totally unreal."

"Where do you get water?" I asked.

"There is a fresh water source nearby with a waterfall," Abigail said.

"I'm going to walk to the shipyard to see what we need to do to make this place more secure," Heinrich said. "I'll take Eric."

"Okay, I'll be right there soon. Can you also check on Jordan?" I asked him.

"Sure, no problem," Heinrich said.

"You seem to know what you're doing," Abigail said to Heinrich.

"I'm an engineer. I used to build houses in the trees. This will be my first time building a home for the ocean," he replied, smiling at her.

I watched Eric and Heinrich walk toward the beach.

"So my grandma said you're good. She said she's seen your heart. I've never heard her talk like that," Abigail said to me.

"Well, I spent most of my life feeling like I'm half a monster," I said.

Abigail looked at the sky, and I could tell she was thinking about something.

"When I was twenty-two, a group came to camp. A mix of men and women. We trusted them, because they had women with them." She paused.

I saw her rub her hands together. She was fidgeting.

"They tricked us. They weren't good, they were bad. The women that were with them were also bad. They took two girls from camp. I was one of them," Abigail said.

She looked down at her body. I had seen that before. That was the same thing Jordan had done when she spoke about her uncle.

"My grandma and some others fought them. They tried. That's why she struggles to walk. The second night after we were taken, one of the men took me away from the group. He attacked me. I fought him the whole time." She shuddered and closed her eyes. "I was able to get him off me long enough to run away. It was so dark that night. As I ran, I knew I was being chased by two different types of monsters. Human and not."

I looked at her, not knowing what to say. I waited for her to finish. I knew this wasn't the end of her story by the look on her face.

"I ran to the first water I could see and jumped in. It was a pond in the middle of the forest. I found a log floating and held on. I was so scared. The next morning, I ran as fast as I could home. I can't believe I was able to find it," she said.

She closed her eyes.

"Nine months later, Grayson was born," she said, looking at me. "Joel, you aren't half a monster, and neither is Grayson. It doesn't matter where you came from. We all have a choice between being good and being bad. You've chosen to be good regardless of your genetics, the same as Grayson. In a way, I think you guys are even better because you overcame that other part of you. You're even more good," she said, smiling at me.

"Thank you," I told her. "I never thought of it like that. I'm so sorry you went through all that."

"Come on, let's go back," she said. "By the way, keep that story between us. I'm not ready to have that conversation with the others."

"Absolutely," I told her. "I would never."

"I know," she said. "You have a good heart."

We walked back to the others. I couldn't wait to check on Jordan. When I got back to camp, the others were hard at work. Heinrich was sitting with Noel. He was talking, and she was drawing. Eric was fishing. I walked over to where Jordan was sitting and stroked her hair. Sasha lay at her feet. I petted Sasha. So loyal.

I looked at Jordan and smiled. She smiled back. I looked down at her protruding stomach. Sixteen weeks today yet not sixteen weeks. I remembered what Thomas had said. *Any day*, I thought to myself. I tried to remember what my mom had told me. She never spoke of her pregnancy with me or the birth. Maybe she never thought I needed to know. Maybe she thought I wouldn't be able to have a baby. Whatever the reason, I knew her intentions were good.

We could see the boats in a line tied together. Women were cooking and hanging clothing. Children sat on a pontoon boat being read a story.

Abigail walked up to us.

"See that last boat? It's empty. You can all sleep there," she said.

"What's wrong with it?" Eric laughed.

"Nothing, it belonged to my parents. They've passed on," she said to him.

She smiled at Heinrich as she walked away.

"Wait, Ms. Abigail, I have a question." Heinrich chased after her.

"Just Abigail," she replied.

"What?" Heinrich said.

"It's just Abigail, no need to be formal." She smiled again.

I could tell Abigail might like Heinrich. Heinrich was so mannerly he didn't show whether or not he felt the same. The two walked away as they talked. Occasionally, Abigail would point out to the water, and Heinrich would take notes.

As night approached, we moved into the boat designated for us. The boat was spacious. It had a roof over half of it with open sides. Jordan and I chose to sleep on the open part of the boat. Eric slept near us as well as Daniel.

"Being on this boat reminds me of being on Eric's boat," I said, tucking Jordan's hair behind her ear.

"Except Eric isn't drunk," Jordan said.

We both laughed. I placed my hand on Jordan's stomach.

"How much longer?" I asked.

"I don't know," Jordan said. "She's growing fast."

"How do you know it's a girl?" I asked, leaning toward Jordan.

"When I dove into that water, I had this vision," Jordan said. "I saw this little girl with long black hair. She was standing on a beach. In the dream, she turned around and called me mom." Jordan started to cry. "It was so real, Joel."

"Black hair, huh?" I asked Jordan, smiling. "Did you see her eyes?" I asked.

"Blue," Jordan said. "Blue like your eyes." She laid her head down on my chest.

"I'm scared, Joel," Jordan said.

"Why?" I asked.

"Because I've never loved anyone like I love her... I'm afraid something will take her away," Jordan said, tearing up again.

"Nothing will take her," I said. "Everything is going to be okay. We will all live happily ever after, like that story you read about the princess. I promise."

I kissed Jordan's head and then I kissed her growing belly.

In the early morning, the sun was shining bright in the sky as everyone got to work on their assigned projects for the day. Some of the women were assigned to help Charles with the garden. The children in camp also had a job working with Charles; they were sorting seeds into piles of similar ones. In the rush to leave the barn, Charles had dumped all his seeds into the same bag. You would think this task would be monotonous, but the children seemed to be enjoying it. They took handfuls of seeds and carefully placed them where they belong.

"Good morning, Charles," I said.

I walked up to him and shook his hand.

"Good morning, Joel," he said. "Glorious day today, isn't it?"

"It's beautiful out," I replied.

"It's even better because I get to garden." He beamed. "Come here, I want to show you something."

Charles showed me where he started digging up the ground.

"When I first started digging, I got nervous," Charles said. "I thought this ground would be nothing but sand. But, Joel, about two feet down is that good old Wyoming soil."

He showed me the dark soil below the sand.

"I'm going to dig a two-foot sunken garden about twenty by thirty feet and start there. When that starts to grow, we can clear out a portion of the forest and plant an even bigger garden. We can transplant some of the growing plants there while we plant new seeds."

"Sounds like you've got it all planned out," I said to him.

"Charles, what kind of seed is this?" Grayson asked, holding a seed up.

"Well, that's a pumpkin seed," Charles said, smiling. Grayson wrote the word *Pumpkin* on a rock and ran back and placed it in front of a pile. He continued to do this with each seed until he had each pile labeled.

"Hard worker that one," Charles said, nodding at Grayson. "Maybe I'll make him my apprentice."

Sasha had started digging next to Charles's hole in an attempt to help. Every time Sasha would start to dig, Herman would climb into the hole, forcing Sasha to start digging a new hole. Charles and I watched them and laughed.

"Herman will come around," Charles said. "He's just never had to share me."

We both laughed.

Heinrich was already busy in the air cutting back the canopy of the forest. He had brought several pulleys with him. He attached a rope to the pulley and was hoisted into the air on a platform he made out of logs. Several women held the rope.

"Want a break?" I asked them, taking the rope.

"Heinrich," I called up to him.

"Hey, Joel," he said. "I'm cutting back the trees so that we get more light in camp and no chance of shadows."

"I'm almost done," he said.

He made a few more cuts with the machete. I pulled him down.

"Noel finished drawing the plans this morning," he said, smiling. "You should go check them out."

I walked with Heinrich to the boatyard. Sitting on one of the docked boats was Noel, who was just finishing the final touches on the plans.

"Want to see?" she asked, handing me the design she had created.

In the picture, there was a base for the floating town that was made out of logs that had been halved and tied tightly together.

"The base is flexible, so the water won't break it," Heinrich said. "Each family will have a house on the base. The houses will be elevated to keep water out."

"What's that?" I pointed at a taller structure in the center of the boat.

"It's a kitchen." Heinrich smiled. "For Anthony and Theresa."

"There will be a place for us to store all of our vegetables and fish," Noel said excitedly.

"Ideally we can catch fish and keep them in a submerged tank inside the kitchen. The tank will be covered in wood so that no predator can see them," Heinrich said.

"Then when we need to cook, we can just pull the fish out fresh," Noel said.

"How will the city be safe in the night?" I asked them.

Heinrich pulled out a second paper with an elaborate drawing.

"I made this one," he said. "This is a system we will build under the water. It works with a series of cranks to send our city out to the ocean and then to be able to turn the crank to bring it back in. Thomas is working on setting up electricity, and it would be ideal to use that, but we all know we can't only depend on electricity, so the crank would be used if the electricity went down. If we are out in the ocean, we are safe from anyone who might wish to harm us. They won't be able to reach the track the base will move in and out on because it's under shark-infested water, and they won't come out to get us in this water," Heinrich said.

"This is amazing," I told Heinrich and Noel.

"Thanks. It's all coming together," Heinrich said.

I patted him on the back and went to check on Jordan, who had been lying in bed all day on one of the boats.

"Hey." I kissed her head. "How are you feeling?"

"Amazing," she said. "Absolutely wonderful," she said sarcastically. She smiled at me.

I tucked her hair behind her ears.

"Why do you always do that?" she asked.

"Do what?" I questioned.

"Tuck my hair behind my ears," she said, smiling at me.

"I guess I just want to see your whole face. I love you," I said to her.

"Want me to shave my head?" she asked.

She laughed. I laughed too.

"Only if you want to." I kissed her head again. I kissed her belly. "I'm going to check on the others. I'll be back."

I went to find Seba. I hadn't seen her today. It didn't take me long to find her. She and Doris had taken over one of the classes the small children were attending on a boat. I could see Seba telling a story and Doris writing. I walked up to them and sat cross-legged with the children. When Seba asked the group a question, I raised my hand with the children. She laughed. After their class was over, I sat with both of them.

"So you are teaching again," I said to Seba.

"I took a class over so that the younger women can help Charles. I'll tell you, they didn't need much convincing to run off to tend a farm. Teaching is a very difficult job." She fanned herself.

"And, Doris, I presume you're adding to your book?" I asked her.

"I'm working on something new," Doris said, smiling at me.

"You're not going to tell me what it is, are you, Doris?" I smiled back.

"Not a chance," she said.

She turned around to continue writing and shielded the book from me.

"Okay, Doris, I can take a hint." I laughed at her.

"Have you seen Eric?" I asked them.

"He was down the beach with Daniel and James," Seba said. "You should go down there and visit if you want a good laugh."

I started to walk down the beach. Thomas was sitting on the rocks with all of his equipment out.

"Working on electricity?" I asked him.

"Yes. Right now, I'm just making sure I have all the components I'll need. I really can't make it until the platform for the floating city is created," he said.

"Oh, okay," I told him. "I'll leave you to it."

"Oh, Joel," Thomas said, "Sarah wanted me to tell you that Jordan is at a two."

"Okay, thanks, Thomas." I started to walk away. I had no idea what he meant, but I was guessing her pain on a scale of one to ten was at a two, which seemed like an improvement from before.

I walked about a half a mile and I could see Eric standing on the beach, carrying something that looked like a netted cage. Daniel and James were both picking something off the beach and running to Eric and throwing it in the cage. Daniel screamed as he ran back and forth. I saw James flip his hand, and something flew off it into the water. I laughed to myself as I walked. I could tell what Seba had found so amusing.

"Hey, what's going on?" I yelled.

"Just teaching these Kentucky boys how to catch some crabs," Eric yelled back.

I could see now. The crabs were running from the rocks to the ocean, and James and Daniel were trying to catch them in the middle.

"I'm not going to have any fingers left," James said to me, holding up his sore hand.

"I hope everyone enjoys their dinner," Daniel said as he grabbed a big one and ran over, tossing it toward Eric. It missed the cage, and Eric picked it up easily.

Eric looked at its face and said, "You look delicious." Eric asked, "How is Jordan?"

"She's good. Thomas told me that Sarah checked on her, and she's at a two," I responded.

"At a two? Then why are you here?" he asked.

"I guess if her pain level is only a two…that's an improvement. She's probably resting," I said.

"Joel, being at a two isn't referring to pain level. That means she's dilated to two centimeters," he said, looking at me.

I still had no idea what he was talking about.

"Joel, she's in labor!" Eric shouted.

I turned around and ran back as fast as I could.

I ran onto the boat to the bed where Jordan was resting. Sarah turned around to look at me. She lowered her glasses.

"It took you long enough," she said.

"I got confused with the message. It's a long story. I'm sorry." I went to Jordan and took her hand.

"Are you in pain?" I asked her.

"It's not bad yet," Jordan said to me.

I sat by Jordan until she drifted into sleep. I turned when I heard a knock at the door.

"Joel," Eric said.

He had a concerned look on his face.

"Eric, what's wrong?" I asked him.

"A storm is coming, Joel. I see it in the sky. It's a bad one. A really bad one," he told me.

He looked at Jordan.

"Everything will be okay," I told him.

"How do you know that?" he asked me.

"It has to be," I said. "I promised."

CHAPTER 19

THE BOOK OF PURITY

Jordan was resting peacefully. I pulled the blanket over her to keep her warm. I went to the side of the room and made sure her water glass was filled and that she had a snack for when she woke up. I kissed her head and went to check on the others.

Eric was making sure the boats were ready for the storm. He was walking around them, inspecting each one. I watched him walk up to one and kick it. Then he stood over the side, looking at the point where it connected to the rudder.

"How bad is it?" I asked him.

"How bad is what?" he asked.

"How bad is the storm?" I asked him, pointing at the sky. "It's dark."

I didn't want to talk about it in front of Jordan. She had enough to worry about.

"I would say it's a hurricane," he said, looking at the sky. "You see all those colors in the distance," he said, pointing at the horizon. "Those colors are bad, Joel. They're hurricane bad."

"Have you ever been through one of those?" I asked him.

"Yep, dozens," he said. "Never any good ones, though."

I thought for a moment about what he had just said.

"What's the worst one you've been through?" I stared at him.

"You don't even want to hear about it, Joel, trust me," he said, kicking another boat.

The boats were arranged in rows of five. Most of the boats had some type of structure on them that provided shelter. Heinrich was walking on each boat and shaking the structures. He would then take a rope and tie loose ends together to make them more secure. The boats were all old, most rusty, but they still floated. They definitely wouldn't last forever.

I decided to help Abigail and the others prepare the boats. I found her tying boats together.

"Hey, I got this," Abigail said. "Go be with Jordan."

"It's okay," I responded. "Jordan is resting."

"If we tie them tight, then they won't knock into each other so hard," she said.

I helped her tie knots between the boats. Together we were making good time.

"I remember when I had Grayson," she said, laughing.

"Was it an easy labor?" I asked her.

"I wouldn't go that far. I will say it was worth it." She smiled toward her son, who was sitting on a nearby boat, drawing.

Heinrich walked by, and I watched Abigail stare at him before she went back to work.

"Do you like him?" I smiled at her.

"Like who?" she asked.

"Heinrich," I said to her.

"No, of course not," she said. She rolled her eyes.

I had seen Jordan roll her eyes a thousand times. I could see straight through it.

"You do," I said, laughing.

"No, I don't," she said, pulling a knot tight.

I looked at her until she looked up.

"What if I did?' she asked. "He wouldn't go after someone like me."

"What do you mean someone like you?" I asked her, confused.

"I have a child, Joel." She continued to tie knots.

"And?" I responded.

"Heinrich is better than that, he's pure," she said, looking toward him.

I took her hand off the knot and held it.

"You're pure too," I told her.

"Joel, I appreciate that but I'm not pure. Grayson is proof of that," she said, taking her hand from mine.

"That doesn't make you less pure, Abigail. If anything, it makes you more pure," I said to her.

"How so?" she asked, staring at me.

"What happened to you was terrible, Abigail, awful. I can't imagine what you went through. You were kidnapped and had to escape. You were assaulted, Abigail. Then instead of becoming angry or giving up, you had Grayson. You didn't just have him, you loved him and you raised him to be a good person." I took her hand in mine again.

"Thank you," she said. "But that doesn't mean he would think the same. Anyways, nobody can know how Grayson was conceived."

"Is that because you're embarrassed?" I asked. "Because you shouldn't be."

"No, Joel, that's not why." She stood up and wiped her hands on her pants. "Do you see that woman over there?" she asked me.

She pointed toward a woman who was separating berries into containers.

"The woman with the berries?" I asked.

"Yes, her," Abigail said, walking to another boat.

I followed her.

"That's Grace. Her daughter was taken along with me," Abigail said. "Her daughter was younger than me. I was twenty-one when we were taken. Her daughter, Claire, was only sixteen."

"That's terrible," I told her.

I watched Grace. There was a sadness surrounding her.

"Grace's husband died trying to stop us from being taken," Abigail said to me. "He fought so hard." She closed her eyes. "Grace lost everything in one day."

"So how does that make you not able to tell your story?" I questioned.

"Joel, if I told people how I conceived Grayson, it would destroy Grace. She would worry her daughter was going through the same thing I went through, and in all honesty, she might be...but Grace can't handle that." Abigail tied another knot.

"So who do they think Grayson's dad is?" I asked her.

She wiped her forehead and laughed.

"We used to have men here, Joel. Most were married," she said. "I guess people think it was one of them… Anyways, I'm sure Heinrich has been warned of my reputation."

"That's not fair, Abigail," I told her. "It's not fair to you."

"Nothing is fair, I've learned that," she said.

She moved to the next boat. I was right behind her.

"You're selfless, Abigail," I told her.

"I don't think that makes me selfless," Abigail said, looking at me.

"Who were you before that happened?" I asked her. "Who did you want to be?"

She thought about that for a moment.

"I guess I always wanted to be a doctor, like my dad." She smiled, thinking about it. "But that's not possible now, Joel."

"Why not?" I asked her.

"Because there are no schools. There might never be," she told me, continuing on with her knot tying.

"What was your mom like?" I asked her.

"My mom was a nurse," Abigail said. "She met my father at the hospital where they both worked."

"That sounds romantic," I told her.

"Not quite," Abigail said. "My mother thought my father was full of himself. She hated him."

"What made her change her mind?" I asked.

"Well, my dad got tired of working at the hospital, so he opened a small office and treated everyone, even people who couldn't pay. He needed a nurse. My mother was the only one who applied. She liked his mission of helping people."

"Romantic," I said.

"I guess so," she said. She tied a knot.

"What happened to them?" I asked her.

It was the inevitable question we all asked when someone talked about people who no longer existed.

"They came here initially. They helped set it up. They helped find these boats."

She pointed around.

"Then they became infected from people they tried to help," she said.

I could see she was crying.

"I'm sorry, I didn't mean to upset you," I told her.

"It's not your fault. I would be sad even if you didn't ask," she told me.

She walked toward the edge of one of the boats. I could tell she was trying to gather the words.

"They went into the water, right over there." She pointed to the beach.

I thought about her having to watch them do this. These waters were shark-infested. It wasn't like my parents going into the river in Ohio.

I saw her shudder.

"I'm so sorry," I told her. "My parents are gone too. They also went into the water."

"They were brave, like my parents," she said, wiping a tear.

"They would want you to be who you want to be," I told her. "They would be proud of you."

"I guess, maybe you're right," she said. "It's just hard. I planned out my whole life. I wanted to wait to become a doctor, wait for the one I love, then have a whole house full of children."

"Things rarely work out the way we plan them," I told her.

"Not this far off," she said.

"But...you could still have all of that," I told her. "You can still be a doctor and find your love and have a house full of children."

"You think so?" she questioned.

"Now that we know more, you could become a doctor and avoid infection," I told her.

"I don't know, Joel. Without school, I would feel like I am pretending," she said.

"There doesn't have to be schools. Sarah could train you," I told her. "You could still be a doctor. Sarah is kind. She would enjoy it."

"I'll think about it, Joel," she said.

"Does your grandma know the truth?" I asked her. "About Grayson?"

"Of course she does." Abigail laughed. "She knows everything about everybody."

"I don't know, Joel. You see me differently than everyone else. You think I'm better than I am." She shook her head.

"Think about everything you do here in this camp," I told her. "You've protected them, you've kept everyone safe, you've made sure everyone is fed, and you've made sure the kids learn every day."

"That's just my duty." She smiled at me, tying the knot.

"You know who else talks about duty?" I smiled back.

"Who?" she asked. She looked intrigued.

"Heinrich," I told her. "Look, Heinrich is reserved. He grew up around only family members. He doesn't know how to talk to a woman. I bet if you went over there and talked to him, then he would start to open up."

Abigail looked toward Heinrich and then looked back at me.

"Okay, I'll go talk to him," she said. "But if this goes badly, it's your fault."

She stood up and walked across the boats toward Heinrich.

I thought about the conversation I had with Noel about not telling people things. I thought about how that didn't make them a lie. What Abigail didn't know was that Heinrich stared at her too. I had seen him many times. He always looked away when she looked at him. I had actually seen him look at her at least ten times while I was talking to her.

I walked back to where Jordan was resting to check on her. As I walked by Heinrich and Abigail, I could see that he was showing her how to tie a different type of knot. When she didn't get it the first time, he took her hands and showed her how by using his hands to guide hers. I smiled to myself as I walked in the houseboat.

"Hey, beautiful," I said, leaning down and kissing Jordan's head. She was awake, lying on her side. I wiped sweat off her head.

"I saw you talking to Abigail," she said. She lowered her eyebrows, and I laughed.

"You're not jealous, are you?" I said to her.

"I don't know, maybe, Joel. I'm just lying here having a baby, being all gigantic," she said.

"Don't be jealous," I told her. "Look."

I opened the fabric that covered the window, pointing to Heinrich and Abigail talking.

"Oh," Jordan said. "That makes sense. I'm sorry." She lifted her arm up, and I went and held her.

"I love you, Jordan," I told her.

"I love you too," she said.

I kissed her head again and went to find Eric to see what we would need to do to secure the boat Jordan was on.

"Hey, Joel," she said as I was walking out of the door.

"Yeah." I turned around.

She pointed outside to Heinrich and Abigail. "They end up together."

I laughed. "How do you know that?"

"I saw it," she said, yawning.

She closed her eyes.

"Where?" I asked.

"Where, what?" Jordan replied.

"Where did you see that?" I asked again.

"In Noel's book," Jordan said.

"What was in the drawing?"

I walked toward Jordan, who was just starting to fall asleep.

"Heinrich…and Abigail…," she yawned, "and their kids."

CHAPTER 20

THE BOOK OF PROMISE

"Man, we are in for a doozy," Eric said, staring at the sky.

We were trying to get the house part of the boat covered on all sides and safe for Jordan to deliver the baby. On the other boats, the women tied the boats tighter together so that if the storm hit us hard, they wouldn't ram into each other hard enough to throw anyone off. The sky was dark, and the rain had just started to fall.

We all settled into the house part of the boat at nightfall and waited. We waited for the baby and we waited for the storm. Jordan lay on the bed of the houseboat. I lay half on the floor and half on the bed with my hand on her stomach. Sasha lay at her feet. Jordan was asleep, but Sarah told me that the pain might be stretched out over a long period of time, or it could be sudden. She told me that each woman is different in how they deliver. I hoped that Jordan was going to have a quick delivery that didn't hurt her, but I knew that was an unrealistic expectation.

Sarah was next to me on the floor, medical bag in hand. I had just drifted off to sleep when I heard the first signs of the storm.

Craaackkkk. Lightning and thunder. We all jumped.

"It's close," Eric said. "When you hear the boom immediately, it means the lightning is very close." He popped up.

It was as if someone flipped a switch, and the winds started. The boat was blowing back and forth in the water. The other boats took turns colliding with one another. Women lay on the boat with their children underneath them. The waves crashed into the sides, making a pounding sound that was almost deafening.

A huge gust of wind caused the roof to blow off our boat.

"Joel!" Sarah called. "Joel, the lantern."

The flame in the lantern was starting to succumb to the rain.

"We need to keep it lit so the doc can see!" Eric called to the others.

Eric grabbed a tarp and handed it to Daniel and Anthony. They each stretched the tarp out over Jordan. Thomas grabbed the lantern and held it above Sarah. James grabbed the other corner of the tarp, and each of the men braced themselves against the poles that formerly held the roof.

Every time a boat would collide with ours, the men shifted, and at one point, I thought Eric was going to fall into the water. Heinrich jumped up and took Eric's place holding the tarp, and Eric sat next to me on the boat, helping me hand supplies to Sarah as she needed them. Noel sat with Doris and Seba. She sat between each of them, holding onto them. They huddled together, bracing against one another so they wouldn't fall. Charles held Herman in the corner, and Sasha sat next to them. She would periodically lick Jordan's foot.

We spent hours in these positions, waiting for the storm to stop and the baby to come. Jordan was working on breathing with Sarah. Thomas was now holding the lantern, making sure to keep it lit.

Jordan sat up and winced as she held her stomach. I put my hand on her head and moved her hair out of her face. Her breathing was heavy.

"It hurts," she said. "It hurts." Tears fell from her dark eyes.

Sarah ran over, moving me aside. "We have to get her pants off," she yelled.

I helped her get Jordan's pants off as I apologized to Jordan for putting her in this situation. I felt terrible for her. I had imagined every possible scenario except for a hurricane. I grabbed a blanket and put it over Jordan to try and keep her warm. The damp blanket did little to help.

Just then, Jordan let out a scream like nothing I had ever heard. She started breathing heavy and let out another scream.

"Jordan, you can do this. You're so strong." I stroked her face.

"It hurts." She held her stomach and looked at me. I wanted to take the pain away. I wanted to take this onto myself, instead, but I couldn't.

The boat was splashing about now. Besides the storm, you could only hear Jordan screaming and Herman growling.

The rain and wind pelted us as boats crashed into one another. I was worried the boats were going to fall apart. I worried about Jordan, about the baby, about the violent ocean, about the sharks…

"Breathe, Jordan," I said. "Breathe."

Jordan struggled.

"Jordan, I have some pain medication I'm going to give you that will help you through," Sarah said, taking out a syringe and injecting it into her arm.

We used the small window of time that Jordan wasn't in pain to tie the tarp onto the poles so everyone could sit safely under it.

Jordan's shrill scream ended that moment.

"Sarah, please, can you give her more pain medicine?" I begged.

"I can't give her any more. We have to make sure the baby isn't asleep when she's born." Sarah looked at Jordan with concern. "I'm going to check to see if she's more dilated. She's at a nine. That's why her pain is so intense. She's almost there."

The storm was still raging. Boats were clanking. The ocean tossed and turned violently.

"Jordan, I can see the sun. It's just waking up. It's coming," I said and kissed her wet and sweaty forehead. This wasn't how I imagined things for Jordan. I couldn't imagine what she was going through.

Jordan let out another scream and sat up; she bared her teeth and screamed again.

"What's happening?" I asked.

"She's ready," Sarah said. "Push, Jordan. Listen to your body. You'll feel better when you push her out."

"Joel, I can't," she whimpered. "Joel, it hurts." She struggled to breathe. She pressed her face against my arm.

The sun started to rise up in the ocean.

Jordan let out one more cry and a piercing scream.

"That's it, Jordan, that's it," Sarah said. "There you go…almost there…you did it, Jordan, you did it!"

Jordan sobbed quietly, and another cry took over. A loud cry, a strong cry, the cry of our daughter.

Just then, the storm stopped as abruptly as it started. The seas calmed.

"Well, that was weird," Eric said, standing up, looking around.

"Jordan," I said with tears in my eyes, "Jordan, you did it. You're a mommy."

Sarah put the baby on Jordan's chest as she finished cleaning Jordan up.

The men lowered the tarp, letting the sun into the boathouse. I stood up and shook each of their hands. I checked on Doris, Seba, and Noel. Sasha was licking Jordan, she licked the baby, and then she tried to lick Herman. He ran.

The sun continued to rise as Abigail made her way to our boat to check on Jordan.

"Oh, she is just beautiful," Abigail said. "What will we call her?"

I looked at the sun and then at Jordan. She nodded.

"We will call her Dawn," I said, staring into the most beautiful blue eyes.

"Oh, Joel," Sarah said. Tears streamed down her face. "You didn't have to."

"It fits," I said, smiling at Sarah. "I have one request, though."

"What's that?" Sarah asked, smiling.

I took Sarah's hand and placed it on Dawn's back.

"Can she call you Grandma?" I asked her.

"Oh yes. Oh, Joel, yes, I would really love that." Happy tears rolled down her face.

The sun was the brightest I remembered seeing it.

Thomas and Sarah collected what they needed to test a vaccine. The boats were pulled in.

As soon as we docked, Charles was tilling the earth, planting seeds with Herman. Heinrich got right to work cutting down trees to start building. I could see that Daniel was helping him. Anthony was learning how to cook crabs with Theresa. James and Eric were fixing some fishing equipment.

I sat with Jordan on the bed of the boat, stroking our baby's head. Sasha was lying across Jordan's feet.

"She is so beautiful," Jordan said, kissing her head.

"She looks like you," I told Jordan. "That's what I wanted."

"Yes, like me," Jordan responded. "With your eyes."

"I'll be right back. You guys rest. I want to see if anyone needs help," I told her.

"Okay, but come right back." Jordan smiled at me.

"I'm so proud of you," I told her.

"Why?" Jordan asked.

"Why?" I laughed. "Jordan, you just had our baby on a boat in the middle of a hurricane."

"Oh, that." She laughed. "It was nothing. Piece of cake." She winked at me.

I walked out of the boathouse and onto the sand. Heinrich had a team assembled, and they were cutting trees down and chopping them in half. After the trees were cut in half, another group would tie them together.

"Hey, Heinrich, need any help?" I asked.

"No, I think we are good," Heinrich said. "You see the rounded side of each of the halved logs? Those will float down so that the top of the base of our city is flat."

"Will we need air like we needed with the rafts?" I asked him.

"I thought that same thing. I talked to Eric, and he told me that since this is saltwater and the salinity is high here, we will float fine," Heinrich said.

"I hadn't thought about that," I said. "I learn something new every day."

Charles had the garden all dug up and had been planting seeds all day. Grayson followed closely behind him as he explained the process of gardening.

"Hey, guys, how is it going?" I asked them.

"It's going well," Charles said. "Grayson here has a natural green thumb." Grayson smiled. "Did you know Grayson is only four?"

"Almost five," Grayson clarified.

"He can already read and write," Charles said. He rubbed Grayson on his head.

I went to visit with Doris, who was sitting on the deck of a boat with a brown package in front of her. She was staring at the sun.

"Hello, Doris," I said to her, smiling.

"Well, hello, Joel," she said. "I figured you would be making your rounds this morning."

"What do you have there, Doris? Did someone give you a present?" I looked down at the brown paper package wrapped in front of her.

"Actually, Joel, this is for you," she said to me. She slid the package across the table to me and smiled. "Open it."

I slowly pulled open the paper on the package and removed the contents. Inside I found a book. It was bound and handmade. I started to look through it.

"Oh, a journal. Thank you."

Doris laughed. "It's upside down, Joel, flip it over."

I turned the book over, and the cover read "The Book of Joel." I opened the book and started to read chapter 1. It spoke of my decision to leave home, to help others. It spoke of me hearing people screaming for help.

"You don't have to read it now," she said.

I flipped through and realized it stopped partway through.

"Oh, it's blank after this," I said, holding the book open where the words ended and the blank pages began.

She closed the book and took my hand. "That's because your story isn't over yet. I'll need that back after you've had time to read it."

I stood up and gave her a hug. "Doris, this is so sweet of you."

"Oh, Joel, I didn't do it to be sweet. I told you before I'm the storyteller. Your story needs to be told."

Over the course of the following months, things were starting to fall into place. Heinrich had the base of the city complete and had completely finished fifteen houses. He was putting the finishing touches on the kitchen. Thomas had built the track and the mechanism for the crank using Heinrich's blueprints. He was still working on the electricity. I knew he would eventually figure it out. Charles's garden was now starting to produce. His hot peppers were the first to grow. He taught Grayson how to mix the peppers with water, let them fester in the sun, and then spray them around the camp. Grayson loved every minute of working with Charles, and I could tell that Abigail appreciated having her son model himself after a man like Charles.

Dawn was growing fast. Sarah said she was growing at double the rate of a baby her age. She felt this was probably due to her being not fully human.

The days had taken on a comfortable schedule. Nights were filled helping Jordan take care of the baby. She said she felt lucky I didn't need much sleep so I could stay up and hold Dawn. Jordan said she was probably the most well-rested new mother who ever existed. Dawn was quiet. She stared a lot. Sometimes at night, she and I would stare at each other for hours.

Everyone was in high spirits. Today would be the day we would test the crank and put the city out to sea. I went to help Heinrich as he stocked the fish into the submerged fish tank.

"You really did an amazing job," I told him

"Thanks," he said.

"Why fifteen?" I asked him.

"What?" he replied.

"Why fifteen houses? It seems excessive for this many people and extra work for yourself," I said to him.

"Well, I decided to make extra in case we have visitors at some point," he said.

I realized that this was actually a smart move. When we came here, Abigail had let us stay on a boat they had kept for this same reason.

Anthony and Theresa were busy organizing the kitchen. They had baskets filled with vegetables against the walls. Eric caught fish as Heinrich placed them into the submerged tank.

"What's for dinner, Anthony?" I asked

"You'll see." He smiled as he pointed to the fish tank. I laughed.

"All right," Heinrich said. "Let's get everyone loaded up and test this out."

Everyone came onto the boat carrying their items from the old boats. We kept the old boats just in case we had to leave at some point. The crank mechanism was attached to the base that moved out to water so that nobody on land could access it.

After we boarded, Heinrich started to turn the crank, and our new city slowly moved out to sea, stopping a safe distance from shore. Eric walked around and lit lanterns that were hanging from poles surrounding the base. It wasn't dark yet, but it was exciting to see them lit.

Anthony and Theresa made a feast for us as we celebrated our new safe home. We had all worked so hard on this. The sun danced across the sky as we sat laughing and enjoying each other's company.

I had just settled next to Dawn and Jordan to relax. That was when I heard it—a familiar sound.

"Someone is coming," I told Jordan. "I have to warn the others."

I caught Abigail first. "Someone is coming. I hear them," I told her.

"From where?" she said, worried.

"From where we came from. Around the bend," I said.

"How much time do we have?" she asked.

"Minutes," I responded.

Abigail turned to face the others. "There is someone coming around the bend in a few minutes. Joel heard them. We are safe here. If they have guns, then we will go into our houses and lie flat until they leave. Does everyone understand?" The others stayed where they were as we watched the bend and waited.

We stood on alert.

"They have a wagon," I whispered to Abigail. "What does that mean?" I asked her.

"I'm not sure. I haven't seen that before," she said.

We could now see them approaching the bend through the trees. There was a group, a large group, and they were pulling a wagon.

The birds started to chirp. I realized two things at that moment—either these people were bad and nature would fight our battle for us, or they were good and were now in a lot of danger.

As the first person rounded the corner, we waited. Then the second. The wagon. As they turned the last corner of the bend, the people saw us and started to walk faster. I realized there must be about seventy people in the group. They started to jog as a desperate herd.

In the wagon was an elderly man. On either side of him, people were pulling the wagon along. I squinted in the fading light. It took mere seconds for me to recognize him.

"Father Siloam!" I shouted.

"Mom!" Heinrich was right behind me.

I turned to Abigail as I ran. "They're good people. We have to dock."

"Joel, if we do that, we are putting everyone in danger," Abigail said, concerned.

"I won't let anyone get hurt, Abigail, I promise," I said to her.

"Okay, we have to be quick," she said. She turned to address everyone as Heinrich frantically turned the crank. "We are docking to let them on. They're the family members of these people. It will be okay. I promise." She turned to me, and the look on her face told me that she, too, kept her promises.

"Mom!" Daniel shouted. "My mom and sisters are out there." He ran to the edge of the boat.

As Heinrich cranked, I stood, ready to jump into action with Sasha by my side. She eyed the forest, and I knew what she heard because I heard it too—the snarls and growling, the jumping in anticipation of the sunset.

"Charles, I saw you spraying today. Please tell me it's safe," I said.

"Joel, today was the first spray. It's not safe," he said nervously. Grayson sat hiding under his arm. Abigail ran and whispered something into Charles's ear and gave Grayson a kiss.

She lined up next to me. Daniel stood next to her.

I looked at Daniel, Abigail, and Heinrich. "When we get off here, I want you guys to get everyone on the boat. Sasha and I will protect you."

As the crank stopped, we were at the shore and we all leapt off. People ran desperately toward us. Daniel, Heinrich, and Abigail ran for the people. Sasha and I ran past them to the edge of the forest as the sun dropped and the first one leapt.

Sasha leapt through the air and grabbed its throat, slamming it down on the ground. I ran to the back of the line where I could see them breaking through the edge of the forest. I grabbed two of them and flung them into the trees. I turned around to see that Sasha had gotten two more.

I walked backward while the last of the people ran by me until Sasha and I were back-to-back. Three leapt toward us. Sasha grabbed one, and one of them landed on top of me. The other hit Sasha from the side as a hoard of them ran from the forest. I looked over to see the last of the people board the boat.

"Crank it!" I screamed. "Crank it now," I said, trying to pull them away from the entrance of the base.

I grabbed two of them and dragged them back from jumping on the base. Sasha pulled another of them back. Sasha and I guarded the edge of the water as the base moved farther away.

Heinrich turned the crank as I saw my friends, standing, staring at us. Crying. I could hear Sasha fighting and whimpering. She was injured. *We are not immortal,* I told myself

I heard Heinrich yell for Eric. The crank was stuck. The base wasn't moving out anymore. They weren't far enough. They weren't safe.

I held onto the infected, keeping them close to me as they tore into my body. I knew what I had to do. I thought of Noel's drawing. I would have to trade my life for the people I loved. I let the infected overtake me as I held them. They stopped focusing on the base and started to focus on me. I lay on my back and watched as Eric got the crank working. I saw him look at me. Our eyes met. I saw a tear fall.

"I'm sorry, Sasha," I called to her.

It was too late. Sasha didn't make a sound. She had lain down her life as well. So loyal.

I closed my eyes as they started to tear me apart.

"I'm a good shepherd," I whispered.

As I drifted away, I saw my parents. My mom and dad were standing in a field of daisies, my mother's favorite flower. They were holding hands. They both smiled at me as I got closer. As I reached out to touch them, my mother shook her head. I looked at my father, and he did the same. My mom put her hand up to me with her palm facing me. She was telling me to stop coming toward them. I felt it. My dad was wearing the same necklace I was. I watched as he grabbed the necklace and nodded at me. At that moment, I realized they were telling me it wasn't time. I wasn't done. I started to float away from them. I felt like I was sucked out of the vision and back into my body.

I gasped as I came back.

A voice rose up above all of the snarls and the growls.

"Joel, you promised!" I heard Jordan wail. "You promised it would be okay."

My eyes shot open. I looked at the base. It was too far for the infected, but it was also too far for me. Sasha, though, she might make it. I decided if I would die, I would die trying to follow through with my promise.

I threw four of them off me into the others fighting for their meal. I ran and hit the one on Sasha from the side. I took off running for the base, which was now far enough off shore that they couldn't get on it. Sasha jumped up and ran just behind me.

"We're going to jump, girl," I said to her, looking into her eyes. "We are going to jump and we are going to make it." I didn't promise her.

I knew if we missed, the sharks would take us in seconds.

We hit the edge of the water and took a leap. It was the farthest leap I'd ever taken. As we soared through the air, I could see the faces of the people I loved in slow motion. I could see their pain and their fear. I wanted to make that jump. But bad things happen to good people every day. Sometimes hope isn't enough.

Sasha made the jump; I didn't. I landed in the water right by the edge near the crank. The seconds I was underwater felt like minutes. I desperately flailed my arms to get to the surface. I felt the movement of the sharks around me. I was surrounded. I broke the surface and gasped for air.

Heinrich pulled me up just as a shark came out of the water. I watched it leap from the water, miss me, and then land on its side.

Sasha and I lay on the base of the city and caught our breath. I watched Sasha as she began to heal.

Jordan walked over with tears streaming down her face and put her hand on me. "I thought you were gone forever," she said to me. I placed my hand on the side of her face. I tucked her hair behind her ear.

Father Siloam walked over and kneeled next to me.

"You burned. We came," he said.

"How was your journey?" I asked him.

"Long. Bumpy." He laughed. "A little scary at the end."

Sasha apparently healed faster than me and had already popped up. She was lying on her back, letting Grayson rub her belly.

"Come on, kid," Eric said to me, helping me up. "You're like a ninja, you know. You and your dog. It looked like a movie. You don't know what that is. Hopefully Thomas gets that electricity running and I can show you one. Also, don't ever do anything like that again, okay?" I could tell he had been crying.

After I had caught my breath and healed, I went to visit with our new friends. The boat was now full. We would have to expand if we wanted to accept any more visitors. People were shaking hands, taking tours. Living arrangements were being changed to make room for so many new friends. Daniel sat with his family, taking turns hugging each one.

"Who is hungry?" Anthony asked everyone. "I'm working on dinner now. We have plenty to share."

I admired him for being positive. His family didn't come.

I was walking to the house to lie down for a bit when a woman stopped me. She had a teenage girl with her. It was Grace.

"I had hoped my daughter, Claire, was part of that group," Grace said.

"I'm sorry," I said to her.

"No, you don't understand. She was taken from here. Some men took her away from me. I spoke to some of those people, and they saw her alive. About two months ago," Grace said, wiping a tear from her eye.

I looked into this poor woman's eyes.

Sarah came up and interrupted us. "Joel, it worked," she said, smiling. She ran back into the lab. Sarah waited for me at the door. I put my finger up to her to ask her for a few minutes.

I thought about this woman and her loss. I thought about Jordan and Dawn and how much I loved them. I thought about the pain that must live inside this woman every single day her daughter was missing.

I thought about duty and how Heinrich had told me our duty was never done. It was a promise we made to the world. I realized that my duty was to rescue anyone I could. That was my promise to the world. I realized that Heinrich was right about duty. He had told me that our duty was more about others and less about us. He didn't want to be a builder. I got it. I wanted to go lie down with Jordan and Dawn and never leave their sides, but that wasn't what I was designed for.

"I'll go east and look for her the day after tomorrow. Point out the people who saw her," I said to her.

As I went to speak to the people who saw Claire, I turned around to Grace and said the one thing that I knew would drive me to find her.

"I'll find her. I promise."

THE BOOK OF HOPE AND GOOD LIES

"She's amazing," I told Jordan, kissing Dawn's head. "You're amazing." I kissed Jordan's head.

"You'll be right back, right?" Jordan said, smiling at me.

"Yes. I have to go talk to Daniel. He told me it was important. I'll be back as soon as I can." I ran back and gave them both one more kiss.

I walked out on the base of our floating city and looked around. Most of the people had gone into their homes for the night. Sitting on the edge of the base at the far end was Daniel.

I made my way over and sat down next to him.

"Hey, you wanted to talk to me," I said.

"Yeah, I did, I mean I do need to talk to you." He had been crying. I could tell from his eyes.

"What's wrong? Is your mother okay? Your sisters?" I asked him, putting my hand on his shoulder.

"They're fine, I'm not crying for me," he said, looking down. "I'm crying for James."

"Why, what's wrong with James?" I asked him.

"My mother and sisters told me that James and Anthony's families didn't make it. Remember, Joel, we are all from the same town. It's small. We went to grade school together, high school, then we enlisted together." Daniel shook his head.

"Does he know?" I asked.

"No, that's the problem, Joel. See, when Anthony's parents didn't show up when mine did, Anthony knew. He actually went to

my mother and asked if they made it. My mother told him. James…
he didn't do that, Joel. He keeps talking about how he wants to go
back and get his mom. He hasn't put things together yet. I don't
know what to do," he said. "I was hoping you could give me advice."

"Maybe he will figure it out on his own like Anthony," I said to
Daniel. "Maybe he already has, he just hasn't vocalized that to you.
Maybe he just needs some time to cope."

"So you think I should just wait then?" he asked.

"Yes, just wait a while and let's see if he figures it out himself," I
said to Daniel, placing my hand on his shoulder. "Do you want me
to tell him? Maybe it would be better since I lost my mom too."

"Thanks, Joel." He wiped his tears. "Maybe it would be better."
He turned and went back to his house with his family.

I sat there thinking about the advice I had given and wondered
if it was the best way.

"What a beautiful night," a voice behind me said. "The salty air,
the nocturnal birds, the plague forcing us all to sleep on a giant raft."

I turned around to see Doris standing behind me.

"May I?" she said, asking to sit.

"Sure." I wiped off a spot for her next to me.

"What's on your mind?" Doris asked me. "Something is trou-
bling you."

She stared at my face.

"What if I knew something that someone needs to know, but it
would hurt them to hear it, possibly even destroy them," I said to her.

"Hmmm… I would say it depends on what it is, Joel," she said.
"Have you ever heard of good lies?" she asked.

"Is it where you lie but it's for a good reason?" I asked her.

"Yes, but it's also more. Sometimes we have to lie to protect
people," she said.

"What do you mean?" I asked her.

"Take Noel, for example. I know about the visions, Joel. I know
about the book. She doesn't want me to know about it yet, so I pre-
tend I don't. It's a good lie, Joel." She looked out into the dark ocean.

"Noel's only afraid you will think she's crazy," I told Doris.

"That's not the only thing she's afraid of, Joel," she said.

"What else is there?" I asked.

"She sees more than she says. Why do you think she's always clutching that book to her chest?" Doris looked at me.

"What do you think she's hiding?" I asked her.

"Everything, Joel, she's hiding everything. She has to. She has to let everyone else live their lives. Do you know how heavy that burden must be?" she asked.

I hadn't thought about Noel's gift as a burden, but I could understand that now.

"We don't need to know every little thing before it happens. That would take the fun out of life." She laughed. "And even if she's seen my death and drawn it in there, I don't want to know. Otherwise, I'll live the rest of my days terrified, looking over my shoulder."

I breathed in deeply.

"It's James," I told her.

"What about James?" she asked.

"Daniel told me that James's mother didn't make it," I told her.

"Oh, I see," she said.

"Anthony figured out his parents didn't make it when Daniel's mom and sisters showed up, but James still hasn't connected the pieces," I said. "And I don't know if I should tell him or let him figure it out himself."

I put my head down.

"Listen, Joel, you don't have to tell him today. Let yourself figure out the right time," she said. "You will eventually have to tell him, though. How he chooses to handle that is up to him."

"I just don't want to hurt him," I said.

"You don't think he's strong enough," Doris said to me.

I didn't say anything.

"He may not be strong enough yet, Joel," she responded. "This world hasn't hardened him up quite like the rest of us."

"I guess you're right. I'll let it go for a while. Maybe he will figure it out himself," I told Doris.

She stood up and started walking toward her home.

"Joel," she said as she was walking away. "Maybe he's already figured it out and he just doesn't want to accept it."

I thought about what she had said for a minute. She was right. He might just be in denial. I got up and went back to Jordan and Dawn.

The next morning, the sun was shining brightly on our floating city. We were able to turn the crank and dock early.

I was meeting with the group that would head east with me to find Claire. I was taking Daniel, Anthony, James, and Eric on the mission. Heinrich and Sasha would watch over things here while we were gone.

"Baby keep you up last night?" Eric said, slapping me on the back, laughing.

"No, I think I kept her up." I laughed. "You know I don't sleep."

Daniel, James, and Anthony came together. Their uniforms had been patched together and looked new.

"New digs?" I questioned.

"My mom sewed them," Daniel said.

"She did a good job," Eric said, looking them over. "Think she could make me some?"

"I'm sure she could," Daniel said, smiling at Eric.

"We will be leaving tomorrow at first light," I told the others. "We need to make sure we have enough rations for three days. We will most likely be heading back through that desert."

"I'll make sure I get fish from the kitchen and dry it," Anthony said. "Also, Charles has some vegetables for us to take that would last in our packs."

"I can make sure we have the canteens filled," Daniel said. "Also, I need to get a first aid pack from Sarah."

"Hey, Joel," James said. He seemed unfocused. "You think once we find this girl we can go back east and get my mom?"

He looked at me, waiting for an answer. I debated telling him right at that moment, but I didn't feel it was the right time. I thought about good lies and decided to tell one.

"Yeah, James, we can talk about it after," I told him, patting him on the back.

Daniel looked away.

"James, why don't you make sure we have a good description of Claire," I said.

I pointed at Grace and told him she was the mother. He headed over to speak with her.

"When are you going to tell him?" Daniel asked me.

"Do you want me to tell him?" Anthony offered.

I thought about it for a moment as I looked toward James.

"No, I'll tell him. I'll do it when the time is right," I told them, patting them both on the back.

I realized then that the truth would rob James of hope. He had lived this long hoping to see his mom. Could I really take his hope away? I decided I would tell him when we got back from this journey. I would have to.

I walked away to find Jordan and the baby. I wanted to spend every second with them before we left. As I walked to our home on the floating base, I passed by Noel, who was drawing. She was staring at James.

"Hey, Noel," I said to her.

"When are you going to tell him?" she asked.

I sighed.

"When we get back from this journey," I told her.

She looked at James and then back at me.

"You better," she warned.

E N D

ABOUT THE AUTHOR

Ashley Stone is a former high school chemistry teacher who lives in New Jersey with her husband and five children. Although she has lived in New Jersey for the last thirteen years, she grew up on a farm in Indiana. It was on that farm with only three television channels and no cable that she developed her love of reading and writing. It was her imagination that kept her from ever being bored.

CPSIA information can be obtained
at www.ICGtesting.com
Printed in the USA
BVHW031803211221
624618BV00013B/90